SCARS

*A story of Love
and Redemption*

MELISSA STEVENS

WESTBOW
P R E S S®
A DIVISION OF THOMAS NELSON
& ZONDERVAN

WestBow Press books may be ordered through booksellers or by contacting:

WestBow Press
A Division of Thomas Nelson & Zondervan
1663 Liberty Drive
Bloomington, IN 47403
www.westbowpress.com
844-714-3454

All Scripture quotations are taken from The Holy Bible, New International Version®, NIV® Copyright © 1973, 1978, 1984, 2011 by Biblica, Inc.® Used by permission. All rights reserved worldwide.

ISBN: 978-1-6642-4204-3 (sc)
ISBN: 978-1-6642-4205-0 (e)

Library of Congress Control Number: 2021915658

Print information available on the last page.

WestBow Press rev. date: 08/04/2021

CONTENTS

1

"Do you know how you got all your scars?"

We were sitting cross-legged on the wide front porch at my aunt's house when Cameron asked me that question. It was summer, just a few days before my sixteenth birthday, and a few weeks before his fifteenth birthday. I didn't care that Cam, as I called him, was a little over a year younger than me. He got me in ways that no one else in my life ever had. And he was only the second person who cared about me because he chose to. I knew that my family cared about me, even daddy in some strange way, but Cam and the teacher I had in fifth grade were the two people I was sure cared even though they had no obligation to.

Almost absent-mindedly, my right index finger went to the jagged, almost oval-shaped scar directly on the front of my right shin. Cam's eyes didn't miss the movement, as he extended his left hand and gently placed his index finger next to mine, together we traced the silvery scar. I had only met Cam a couple of months earlier, but somehow he knew me better than any other person on earth, maybe even better than I knew myself. A smile curved my lips every time I thought of him. Even now in the gentle touch of his finger and mine a sweet shiver traveled up and down the length of my spine. I always felt that shiver when Cam touched me. No matter how many times he held my hand or touched my face with his long fingers that still looked boyish, I still felt that shiver. I wasn't really sure what it meant, but I know I liked it. Very much. I suddenly remembered that Cam was waiting patiently for an answer to his question, with a little laugh I replied, "Oh, Cam, I've told you about every single scar on my body already. I love that you asked again."

His hand retreated, leaving my finger feeling exposed all of a sudden. But his touch was only gone for a moment as he reached to cup my downturned chin in those fingers I loved so much. With purpose he tugged my face to a position where he could look me in the eyes. I guess I was too young and lacked the experience to understand the pull his presence had on me, like a magnet attracted to metal. He pulled me into his gaze. I was never comfortable looking anyone in the eye until Cam.

He was almost whispering, and the wind threatened to carry his words away before I could capture them, "Andi." I had always hated that nickname my parents gave me, also until Cam. "I know all about the freeze tag in the dark, rusty metal bar that combined to scar your shin, and I know all about the scar on the bottom of your right foot where you stepped on a nail that went through your shoe and into your foot. I can imagine how much it hurt to have to pull the nail out before you could even remove your shoe to check the damage. I also remember the scar on your left elbow from your first bicycle wreck. But those are not the scars I'm talking about."

I rarely felt uncomfortable with Cam, but suddenly it felt like he was stumbling into a part of me that I had protected behind walls too high to scale. I tried to tear my eyes away from his face, but I just couldn't. I swallowed, hard. "I don't know what you are trying to ask me Cam?"

He was the one to break the gaze between our eyes. He looked away, but only for a moment, then he was looking at me again. Inside his eyes I saw something I had not seen before, I realized that this moment was going to matter, maybe not right away, but someday this moment would be a reflection I would seek often. He looked away again, and his hand that had still been holding my chin dropped to his lap.

"I don't know why my brother has to cause so much trouble for my parents,"

His statement caught me off guard, like our conversation was veering in a totally different direction.

Before I could respond he continued, "If anyone thinks that using drugs only affects the person using them they are so wrong." Cam's gaze shifted again, toward his own two hands.

I noticed then that he was rubbing furiously at his thumb nail. I had a silly thought that he might rub it completely off. As I watched him, I suddenly remembered several occasions during the past two months when he had done the exact same thing. I didn't know how to respond. I felt awkward. For the first time ever with Cam, I didn't know what to say. I glanced down at my own hands, cuticles rough and red from the almost constant biting. I had been a nail biter for as long as I could remember, it was like something with no beginning and no end, just me biting my nails, and Cam rubbing furiously at his.

"I hear my mom crying every night when she thinks everyone else has gone to sleep. She cries so hard sometimes that I think she might use up all of her tears. But then, she always starts to pray. I hear her asking God to take care of Clayton and to bring back the lost sheep someday. After she prays peace settles over the house. I know God hears her prayers, and I know He hears mine too, but that doesn't mean that the hurt of having Clayton choose drugs over his family is not leaving a scar."

I looked away then, I wasn't so sure about God. I had not been to church a lot growing up, but I had been several times with Cam and his mom. It always seemed odd to me that his dad never came along. Maybe he wasn't so sure about God either.

I was still a little confused about what Cam expected from me in this conversation so I just sat there, mute, looking over his shoulder. I could see all my cousins in my Granny and Grampa Harrington's yard. They were running around, squirting each other with squirt guns; they were laughing and I just wanted to be able to really laugh too. I hadn't really laughed in a long time.

"Do you have any scars that can't be seen with human eyes?" Cam asked in my silence, he sounded desperate, almost as if he wanted the answer to be yes so he wouldn't be by himself. And I knew that I did have such scars, but I wasn't sure I wanted to share them...not even with Cam.

"Yeah, I guess I do. I was nine years old when the scars began." I heard myself saying those words and I couldn't believe it. I wanted to clamp my lips shut and not say another word, but it was almost as if I had no power to do so.

"My Granny Morgan died that year. It was a stormy day, May, I think. I was laying on the porch swing, swaying in the brisk wind." I closed my eyes and was transported right back to that swing. "That wasn't the day she died though, it was a few days after. She was already buried in the ground. I remember how the wind was getting stronger and stronger as the tears I cried flowed faster and faster. They ran down the sides of my face, some of them pooled up inside of my ears, while the rest flowed into my hair." I shivered as a chill ran through me. Cam slid closer and put his arm around me. It felt nice, safe. I heard myself continue talking, even though I didn't really want to, "It was sad to lose my granny, but the part that left the deeper scars had begun a few months earlier, being able to grieve almost felt like a relief. At least I could cry, no one had to know that most of my tears were for a different reason. Daddy never did cry, as if not admitting he grieved by crying he could hold it away, but that was a scar he needed to accept."

I made myself look at Cam, but not in the eyes, just a peripheral look really, I needed to ask him if he thought the stuff in my head made sense. "Cam, do you think there are some scars that we need to embrace?"

He looked almost as confused as I had been during this conversation. I could tell he was giving his answer some thought. Finally he replied, "Andi, you're amazing. I never thought of it that way before, but it makes sense, I mean, how else can God use me to help anyone else if I have never survived anything myself. Survived, but with scars, not crippling ones, but the kind that gives me a real story."

I suddenly felt uncomfortable when Cam mentioned God again. I so much wanted to believe whatever it was he and his mom believed, but I guess I was afraid. Every time my mom tried to take me to church when I was younger it just made my dad get meaner than usual, so I just didn't know if God was worth it. Maybe that was another scar I didn't even realize I had. I suppose Cam could sense the tension in my body, he tightened his embrace slightly, then whispered, "That's enough scar talk for today." Then he leaned forward and kissed me on the head. Even through my hair, I could feel the warmth of his breath, there was that shiver again. Then we just sat there for a while.

I'm not sure how long we sat there in silence before my ten year old cousin, David ran up chanting, "Cam and Andi sittin in a tree, k-i-s-s-i-n-g. First comes love, then comes marriage, then comes Andi with a baby carriage!" Then he laughed hysterically, as did his brother, Clay, who was four years older, he had ran over to where we sat as well. I must admit I blushed a little. In reality Cam and I had not shared a kiss, except the one he had just left on my head. I had kissed other boys on the lips, but Cam was different. Somehow it seemed important not to rush things with him. And somehow I wished I could undo the other kisses I had given away. I especially wished I could get back the ones that were not given, but taken. That was another story for another day.

I heard Clay saying, "Are you two going to sit on this porch all day? We want to play softball and we need a couple more people."

Softball sounded safer to me than talking about scars and God so I jumped up, grabbing Cam's hand as I did to tug him up as well. "Softball sounds like fun." I said with much more excitement than I really felt.

Since our conversation had pretty much ended Cam agreed, "Yeah, sounds like fun. We'll be there in a minute."

That was all my cousins needed to hear as they turned to run back to the "playing field".

Before I could run after them Cam stepped right in front of me, I was trying to look anywhere except at him, but he was intent on looking me in the eye. Finally I lifted my eyes up toward his as he said, "Please tell me that you won't let the scars consume you."

"Cam, what are you talking about? You're acting so differently today, is something wrong?"

"Just promise me Andi, even if I am not around anymore will you please not let the scars consume you? Will you try to trust God, please?" Cam's voice sounded huskier than I had ever heard it before. I was pretty sure he was trying not to cry.

I wanted to comfort him, and I didn't know what else to say, so I finally said, "I promise Cam. Now let's go play ball." I slipped past him then and ran as fast as I could toward the others. The wind rushing across my face as I ran made my eyes water. At least that was what I would say if anyone asked me if I was crying.

2

A couple of days after that talk with Cam I celebrated my sixteenth birthday. It should have been the best day of my life to that point, but my parents forced me to spend it with them. Which would not have been so bad, except that they decided a short road trip was in order. We would visit our old house. I was not enthusiastic about the trip, even more so I hated that I would not get to slip off and see Cam. I tried to convince my mom that it should be my choice. It was my birthday, after all. But sometimes things were so tense around the house that we all had to do whatever daddy wanted if we expected to have any peace. This was one time mama was not willing to chance him finding out that she had been letting me see Cam.

I laid my head on the groove created by the open window as I sat in the backseat, riding back to the place I really did not want to revisit. Not yet anyway. The wind whipped my hair furiously, I knew it would be tangled and messy, but I didn't care since I wasn't going to see Cam anytime soon. Beside me, my much younger brother and sister were blissfully unaware of my lack of desire to be on this trip. Derrick, who was almost five, was tickling two year old Casey's bare feet. For the moment she found it amusing, thankfully, because to be so young she had a temper that almost scared me sometimes. Somehow, David, my eighteen year old brother, had gotten out of this trip.

It was not really a long drive, just two hours, but it seemed longer because I didn't want to be going there. It was just past noon when daddy stopped the car in front of the old building that had once housed a general store owned by his dad and then his oldest brother. It was just an empty building now. The property didn't belong to anyone in the family any more. After Uncle Carl died everything had been sold so the money could be divided amongst daddy and his siblings. David and I had played among the rocks and trees in the pastures for hours on end when we were little. We built forts and even chopped down small trees and built a little log cabin in the shadow of the dolphin shaped rock that had been dubbed "Flipper" at some point. The story was told that the owner of a Florida football team heard about Flipper once and came all the way to tiny little Clearmont to see it for himself. Supposedly he offered to buy it from my grandfather so he could have it moved all the way to Florida to a new home at the back of the end zone, maybe it was true, maybe it wasn't, but it was a cool story.

I was still sitting in the car, pouting, I guess, as mama and daddy went toward the concrete steps that led up to the empty building. Derrick was running ahead as usual, while Casey was perched on mama's hip. I wondered why they were going up there, it was trespassing. I opened the door and almost pointed out that fact to them, but mama hollered for me to join them before I could say anything. Reluctantly I slid out of the car, my feet thudding onto the dusty gravel parking area, which was really just a wide spot in the dirt road. Without looking before crossing, I took a step toward them. There was not much traffic in Clearmont, so looking seemed like a waste of time. That's why I was startled when I heard the blaring horn from the pick-up truck that was barreling toward me. I stretched out my stride and hurried out of the way as my heart almost jumped out of my chest. I heard a few not so nice words carried on the wind as the truck proceeded on until it went out of sight around a curve.

Daddy was standing on the concrete porch staring at me as I finally made my way up the steep steps. The whole place seemed so much smaller now than it had when I was a child, but the memories that were about to come loomed larger than I could imagine.

I stopped in my tracks, hoping daddy and the others would just go on with the adventure without me.

So there we stood, daddy and me, staring at one another. I felt tears sting the back of my eyes, and I blinked them away. I knew how angry daddy always got when I cried. I would have to save those tears for another time. Maybe that burning pain in my throat was like a wad of scars like the ones Cam had talked about. I might never gain control again if I let them go.

"Girl, I don't know where you got your head these days, but you better pay attention or you won't make it to your seventeenth birthday. You act like you are scared to death of this place. You're not too old for me to give you a whipping!"

I finally stepped further onto the porch. Then the memories flooded my mind. I could see myself as clear as crystal square dancing for the old cronies who came to sit and drink coffee and spit streams of brown tobacco juice, sometimes into the brass spittoon, but often missing it altogether. I liked to joke sometimes that it was my first job, a dancer, because those old men gave me quarters for entertaining them. I was around eight years old then and as innocent as an eight year old should be, but that would change in less than a year later. I walked past the front of the building then, not pausing to peer through the windows as my family was doing. No telling what part of myself I might see beyond their dirty, age discolored panes.

As I stepped off the porch in front of the store my foot landed on the edge of the narrow concrete walkway that led a hundred yards or so up a slight slope to the house where my daddy grew up. A few steps up that path on the right sat one of the chicken houses where I used to have the task of feeding the chickens and gathering eggs each day. I hated the odor inside that place, especially on hot summer days. It was a little sad now to see the half door hanging by one hinge, leaving a gaping hole that looked surprisingly dark for the brightness in the early afternoon sky. As I moved slowly up the path I tried very hard not to look to my left, because there was where a scar had started to form in the life of that little girl who used to dance for quarters. It was a small, old boxy house. I remembered that it was one large room inside sectioned off only by curtains. The lone resident had seemed harmless for a while, but that was just because he was waiting for his opportunity. David and I went inside the house sometimes on Saturdays because the man, Wayne, had a color television and World Wide Wrestling came on Saturdays at noon, usually followed by a baseball game. It was always dark in that house. He had even hung thick blankets over the windows, which he said were Army surplus. No light penetrated them. The funny thing was I never felt afraid in that house as long as David was there. But then the day came when he wasn't. I had been told not to go into the house without him, but the months of going inside had given me a false sense of safety. Wayne had also given me a nickname that no one else ever called me and that made him seem like someone I could trust. Every day when he saw me at the chicken house getting the eggs he would call out, "Hey there, Doodle Bug, how are you today?" In fact, I was supposed to be feeding the chickens that day....

"Hey Doodle Bug. Why don't you come on over here and see me?" Wayne beckoned. He was sitting on the built in seat on his tiny porch, his walking cane was propped beside him. He had been injured in an accident when he was a young man that had caused one of his legs to be quite a bit shorter than the other. He was sitting there with his shorter leg crossed over the longer one, I could tell because the shoe he wore on that foot had a real thick sole. He called it his elevator shoe. I waved at him, but kept tossing out the corn for the chickens. He called again, "Hey, Doodle Bug, I got some new books today. I know how much you like books. Come on over here and I will let you see them."

Wayne was right about me liking books. One of my favorite days every month was the third Thursday because the county book mobile would come by our little school and we could check out three books apiece. Every month I got three books I had never read before. I was very careful to take them back on time because I knew I could not get more if I didn't.

I tried hard to focus on my task and forget about the books Wayne mentioned, but I was also curious and wanted to see what kind of books he had. Quickly I tossed out the last of the corn and skipped the short distance to his house. I was standing at the edge of the porch, anxiously I said, "I would like to see your books, Mr. Wayne, where are they?"

"They're just inside the house there, come on in and I'll show you."

"But it's so dark in there...I can't read in the dark." I said, for the first time I felt strange talking to Wayne and I did not understand why.

"Oh, I have an oil lamp already lit inside." He assured me. Then he glanced

at the sky, which did hold a few clouds, "I think it might rain and I don't want my books to get ruined."

"I don't think I can come inside without David." I started to walk away, but Wayne was persistent.

"I don't know when you will have another chance to see my books, but go on and get if you are going to."

And I started to....but then I went right up on his porch and said, "If I hurry I guess it will be ok."

Considering his disability he was up on his feet quickly, cane in hand and ushering me inside the yawning black cavern. It took a moment for my eyes to adjust as I stepped inside, until the faint glow from the oil lamp caught up with me, Wayne was so close behind me that I felt him against my back. That made me take a quick few steps away, I felt like something was not right, so I turned around and started to go back toward the doorway, but he had pushed it shut behind him. How does a little girl know when there is a shift somewhere that changes things? I'm not sure, but that is how I felt. I thought I might throw up. "Mr. Wayne, I need to go, daddy will be mad at me."

"Your daddy won't be home for an hour or so, I see him coming in from work every day. Besides, wouldn't he want you to look at some books? He gestured then, with his walking stick, to where the one stuffed chair he owned sat about four feet away from the color television set. There were two straight backed wooden chairs on either side, which is where David and I usually sat. In the corner to the left of the chairs was his bed, on it there was a box, and on a table by the bed the oil lamp's light danced as the flames flickered with life. "Go look in that box."

By now I didn't even want to see his books, I just wanted to get out of that house. I almost felt like I couldn't breathe the air was suddenly stagnate and stale. But he had not moved away from the closed door and I was afraid, so I decided I would just look real quick so I could leave. I didn't even want to turn my back on him so I walked half sideways toward the bed. Though the room was tiny it felt like I walked a mile to get there.

I was drawn in by the cute story and the colorful art work of a children's book. Sadly my eyes would see things inside that house that no child should be subjected to. I would struggle for many years to free myself of the things that happened that day. In fact I would never be able to get free in my own strength.

I tried not to see the next book, and the next, but the images were so vivid. I was trying to figure out how to get out of Wayne's boxy little house because *suddenly I felt like those walls were closing in on me. When I saw a chance to scurry past the old man I did. I never looked back. And I never went inside that house again. I did everything I could to make sure David didn't either... everything except tell anyone what had taken place inside those dark walls. I felt much too ashamed to speak those things out loud. That was the beginning of a wound that would need to heal.*

Suddenly Derrick slammed into me as he propelled his little body up the path toward daddy's old house. He grabbed my hand as he passed by and almost made me fall down. He was so full of little boy joy that I felt it in his tiny grip. I wondered, not for the first time, why I couldn't just have some joy myself. The memories in that little box house could only hurt me if I let them. Somehow that thought seemed like a victory to me because I had always thought of it as the memories controlling me, consuming me. That simple conversation Cam had begun a couple of days ago was suddenly changing my perspective, I almost felt like I could control them instead.

The remainder of my birthday trip to Clearmont was spent exploring the old farm place. I found out that daddy had gotten special permission from the new owner so we could. That felt kind of awkward because it was really a nice thing to do, and daddy wasn't usually nice. I know that sounds awful, but it was true.

Mama had brought her little 110 camera and she took pictures of me and Derrick and Casey, we were perched on Flipper's nose, which was probably not safe, considering that Casey was a squirming two year old, and Flipper's nose was at least twenty feet off the ground. But, I would be so grateful to have those pictures someday. After a picnic meal we headed back to the car. I was still wishing I could see Cam before the day ended, but I was sure that wouldn't happen. I needed to talk to him about the box house and how I just realized why I was claustrophobic, but I couldn't do that over the phone.

3

"I 'll be leaving tomorrow and won't be back until the day before school starts" Cam told me as we walked hand in hand through the town park. It was a hot summer afternoon, some weeks after both our birthdays. I had decided not to tell Cam everything about the memories that haunted me from Clearmont, though I did tell him that our conversation about scars had helped me somehow.

"It's your vacation, right?" I sighed.

"Yeah, we are going to our camper at the lake." He didn't sound any happier about the upcoming trip than I was.

"Sounds like fun." I tried to interject enthusiasm, when in reality I was feeling lost already and Cam wasn't even gone yet. We had been together almost every day for two months and three weeks and I had begun to think that I had never really lived until Cam came along. In nine days school would start back. I would be a junior at a brand new school. I had taken exams early at my old school since my family was moving, that had been four months previous, so I had not been to the high school yet. I spent my days with Cam and had no desire to meet anyone else, so I only knew him and a few cousins who would be at my school. I was not good at meeting people or making friends so I was not looking forward to being the new girl.

"I love to fish and to water ski, I'm sure there will be some fun in that, but I will miss you." Cam said caressing my hand with his thumb.

"You could have left that unsaid Cam, I'm missing you already."

"I'm sorry, but at least you have your job." He was referring to the job I had gotten the first week after I moved to Oakdale. I was a cashier at local department store, not exactly an exciting job, but I was in desperate need of a car. I would have to buy it with my own money. So far I had saved almost eight hundred dollars.

"Maybe I can ask for extra hours since my days will be wide open."

"So, do you think your dad has changed his mind about you and me?" Cam asked me, trading one unwanted subject for another. Ever since my dad found out who Cam was, or namely who Cam's dad was he had forbidden me to see him. Thank goodness, my mom could see that Cam was good for me, so she allowed me to see him at "unintentional" places. That's how we ended up at the park together that day.

"No. And he probably won't anytime soon. What are the odds that our dads have a history, considering that Daddy only came to Oakdale on rare occasions when he was young? I guess it was all about competing, I've tried to tell him that your dad is a cool guy now, but I guess daddy holds a grudge."

"I feel bad about sneaking behind his back. I'm not sure God is pleased with it. It's so hard to know." One thing I could say about Cam was that he was consistent when it came to God. He was always bringing Him up.

"Well, I don't know about God, but I sure hope my dad doesn't find out. There's no telling how he would react."

"I guess we should quit looking for things to worry about and just go to the pool. It's so hot!" Cam suggested.

Even though I had lost quite a bit of weight a year and a half earlier when I struggled with an eating disorder, I was still quite self-conscious, so the prospect of being in a nothing but a bathing suit at the pool was daunting. But to be fair, I had to admit that Cam had forsaken all of his friends to be with me for long enough. I had agreed to go, the only problem was I couldn't swim and I was terrified of water. I decided I better mention that little fact to him, which I did as we walked up the steps toward the front entrance to the pool. He assured me that I would be fine. I could just lay in the sun if I wanted to.

The pool was so crowded when we got inside the gate. There were squeals and laughter in every direction, and finding a place to put our towels and things was not easy. I felt like every eye there was following our progress as we weeded our way around towels pool toys and people, at least all the girls eyes. I always felt like girls were more apt than boys to size each other up, and once we found a suitable spot and I had my towel spread I realized that, at least this time, the feeling was not in my imagination. It was as if someone had hit the pause button somewhere as at least ten girls were staring at me. I turned my back and tried to act nonchalant as I unbuttoned my shorts and started to slide them down over my thighs. I was wearing a black bikini with white polka Yanas. I was suddenly wishing I had opted for the baby blue one piece instead.

"Cameron, where in the world have you been?" It was a shrill female voice. I turned quickly, a little too quickly, as I was just in time to see the pretty blond stand up on tiptoes to kiss Cam on the cheek. Two other girls were there as well, also blond. Great, another reason to be self-conscious, my hair was a cross between brown and blond, my daddy called it "dishwater" blond, now that sounded attractive.

I looked away then as I slipped the tee shirt over my head. I was feeling exposed, embarrassed, annoyed and jealous, none of which were good emotions. I heard Cam reply to the blond, "Hey Courtney. I've been a little busy." As he said that he slipped his arm around my waist and propelled me to turn around. I have to admit I was extremely tense, but the feel of his bare arm against the bare skin around my mid-section ran through me like an electric current. I shuddered, even stumbled a little. Instinctively I leaned in closer to Cam for support. "Courtney, Julie, and Paige, this is Andi..Andrea Sanders."

I felt myself blushing under the scrutiny of their eyes. Somehow I allowed my mouth to curve into a smile as I extended my hand sweetly. The three girls only looked at my hand. But, before I could draw it back a guy I had not noticed joined us and grabbed it. I expected a hand shake, instead he lifted my hand to his lips and kissed it, his eyes took in every inch of me as he did so. Cam pulled me closer to his chest, catching the guy off guard, my hand slipped out of his grasp. "Drake," That was the only word that passed between the two boys, but there was a lot between the lines.

That was the day that my summer dream died. Things changed in the space of a short few minutes. The safe world Cam and I had created where he and I were the stars, was infiltrated by others and I knew somehow that we would not be able to recapture the magic. Considering that I had only been to church a few times in my life and did not spend a lot of time reading the Bible, it was odd that the thought crossed my mind of how great it would have been if Cam and I could have been Adam and Eve. We would never have taken that garden for granted. We could be happy in paradise with only the animals and plants to worry about. But reality smacked me in the face as I watched Courtney ogling Cam, while Drake was ogling me. Things were about to get interesting.

The remainder of that day at the pool was exhausting as I was on the receiving end of fake kindness from Courtney and her friends, and unabashed flirting from Drake and another guy named Bobby. Cam tried really hard to make sure I had nothing to worry about as far as the girls were concerned, and I fell a little more for him because of it.

Cam and I stayed at the pool until it closed at five. It would be another half hour before my mom came to get me so he stayed with me. We walked to the bench swings at the center of the park and sat down on one. The day still had plenty of light, but most of the park patrons had gone home for the day, so we were alone for the most part. I loved being close to Cam, so I could have sat there on that swing forever. I pulled my feet up off the ground to rest them on the edge of the swing in front of me, as Cam gently pushed against the ground until the swing swayed slightly. I laid my head against his chest as he lifted his arm to rest it across my shoulders. We just sat like that for a few minutes, silent.

Cam's fingers were rubbing my shoulder tenderly, and as usual his touch was making me feel strange in the best kind of way. I wished that I could hold on to that feeling; capture it somehow, so that I could draw from it while he was gone.

After a few silent minutes Cam shifted to turn his body toward mine, at the same time he lifted his arm off my shoulders then grabbed my hand. I could actually feel his body tensing up beside me and I wondered what was wrong. My own pulse quickened, maybe in fear, but mostly, I think, in anticipation. Cam captured my eyes with his own, his lips parted as if he were about to speak. Instead he clamped them shut again. "Cam, what's wrong?" I finally asked almost in a whisper.

He lifted his free hand to my face and gently rubbed his thumb across my bottom lip, "Do you ever wonder what it would be like to kiss me? I find myself thinking about kissing you a lot."

Considering that we both were fair skinned and had not put on sun screen that day, it was hard to tell where the sunburn stopped and the blushing began. I leaned my face closer to his hand and smiled, his thumb still touched my lip. "Yes, I wonder that quite often as well."

He smiled. I smiled a little more. For a moment we just looked at one another. A breeze had begun to blow a little earlier and tendrils of my hair had fallen out of the ponytail to dance around my face. Letting go of my hand, Cam lifted his own hand to cup the side of my face. Then he kissed me. It was a gentle kiss, lips touching lips for the first time, unsure, inexperienced. The kiss lasted a few seconds. Then Cam lifted his head. He almost looked like he was going to cry and my heart was doing somersaults inside my chest as he whispered huskily, "I love you, Andi. I really love you."

I couldn't seem to stop smiling and though I had not responded verbally, inside I was screaming "I love you too!" Before I actually replied, Cam was kissing me again, just a tender touch, lips soft and wet against mine. In a moment he lifted his head again, this time I did not wait to speak, "I love you too, Cam."

There we shared our first kiss, and our second. I felt like I could die right there on that swing with his arms around me and his lips on mine, and that would be enough. I would relive that moment so many times in the future. If only we could know the end of a thing from the beginning, we would catalog things a little better so that we could remember every tiny detail.

few weeks after our first kiss Cam and I settled in to a routine.
We rode different buses, but both of us were on the first load,
which meant that we got to school at least half an hour before
second load students. It didn't take long to figure out that the main
building lobby was the favorite hangout spot for the popular kids, the
redneck kids gathered at the end of the hall where you could branch
off and go to the gym in one direction, and to the science and business
buildings in the other. The business building was the least populated in
the mornings so we always went there and sat on the stair well where
few people ever ventured through. It was the best way to begin each day;
together, talking, sometimes doing last minute homework, and always
slipping in at least one small kiss just before we had to go to get to class
before the bell rang.

I tried really hard to avoid Courtney and her friends, as well as
Drake and Bobby, which was hard considering that I had English with
Bobby and Accounting with Courtney. I tried to keep my mouth shut
around Courtney because I was more than content with the ways things
were going for Cam and me, and I sure didn't want anyone to ruin it.
Unfortunately she sought me out even more frequently than Drake, who
continued to let me know that he liked the way I looked. At first I thought

Courtney wanted Cam for herself, but eventually I realized that she was actually running interference for another girl named Cheryl.

Cheryl was one of those girls that I wanted to hate because she had a thing for my boyfriend, but she was so genuinely sweet that I just couldn't. No one could. The teachers all loved her, as did most of the student body. I secretly feared that one day Cam would realize that I was not so great a catch and return her affections. It didn't help that they were both sophomores and had two classes together. I didn't have any classes with Cam.

Instead of becoming more confident in Cam I gradually began to have doubts, which all came to a head one Friday night. Cam was supposed to meet me in the parking lot after work, but he never showed up. He never called or anything, he just wasn't there. I had a sick feeling in my stomach because I knew there was a big party going on at one of the football players houses that night. Cam and I had been invited to go, but I was not about to go without him. I was not one to get drunk and neither was Cam, so I couldn't imagine that he had decided to go…especially without me, but I didn't have any other explanation.

A couple of weeks earlier I had finally been able to get a car. It was a black Mustang with a 302 Boss Engine, whatever that meant. All I knew was that it sounded good, it ran good, and it would go pretty fast. That Friday night I drove my car around and around Oakdale, scrutinizing every car I passed to see if Cam was in it. I had a midnight curfew and no reason to break it on that particular night, so I decided one last lap around McDonalds and I would just go home. I would regret that decision to take one more lap many times in the coming months, but how can a person avoid something they have no clue is about to come?

I turned in on the upper side of the parking lot and started around the building, I suddenly felt like I needed something to drink, so I pulled into a parking spot and got out of my car. Three or four trucks were parked in the corner, about ten or so parking spots past where I had parked. A crowd of boys and a few girls were loitering around them, I pretended not to hear when some of the boys started to whistle and yell obscene things. I think I even heard one of the girls call me a name that I had never done anything to deserve, at least not to her in particular. I quickened my pace because I didn't want to be a part of any trouble. Finally inside the building, I figured I would go to the restroom before I ordered a sweet tea, just to kill time. I was hoping the kids outside would get bored and leave before I came back out.

There were only a few patrons in the restaurant as I weaved my way through tables toward the restroom. When I got to the door and reached for the handle it suddenly opened causing me to step, almost stumbling backwards. All the color drained from my face when I realized that it was Courtney and Julie who exited the restroom. "Oh, Courtney, look who's here?" Julie's words were slurred slightly.

Courtney moved past Julie to stand in front of me, "Well if it isn't *"Andi"*. She said sarcastically, "And Cameron nowhere in sight. Where is lover boy?"

Instead of responding I went to walk past her, but Julie blocked my way, the two of them shared a look. Then Courtney spoke again, "Oh, that's right, your lover boy is back at the party with Cheryl. Isn't that right Julie?"

Julie smiled maliciously and nodded as she replied, "Yeah, those two couldn't keep their hands off each other."

"They have a history you know?" Courtney said, looking directly in my eyes. "And they will have a future if you will leave Cameron alone. I know he is handsome, and he is sweet, that's why he hasn't already told you to shove off. He is just too kind."

"You are such a liar." I said coldly.

"Oh no, honey, I have no reason to lie. Cameron told everyone at the party how he felt sorry for you when you showed up in Oakdale in the summer. He and Cheryl had been arguing over silly things and you were a distraction for him. But he is back where he belongs now." Courtney's steady voice and cold stare were melting my resolve to believe that she was lying. Maybe she wasn't. And that tiny speck of doubt was all it took.

"What makes you think I would believe you, Courtney? Cheryl is your friend and she has been flirting with Cam every chance she has had, and he hasn't left me for her." I hoped my words sounded more confident than I felt.

But Courtney had me in her web, and she was more than happy to destroy me at any cost. "Well, if *"Cam"* is so in love with you, where is he?"

I hated the way she mockingly said Cam's name. I hated that I could not answer her question. I hated that I was starting to tremble and might just pass out at any moment. But, mostly I hated that I was starting to believe her, and something inside me started to die right there in front of the restroom door in McDonalds.

5

✿

I don't remember leaving McDonald's and I don't remember driving home, but I do remember how I felt when I woke up on Saturday morning. I felt dead. At least I imagined that was what death felt like. I didn't have the energy, nor the will to breathe, had my brain not told the rest of my organs what to do, I would have died and never woke up that morning. For the first time since I had gotten my job I called in sick. I did not want to see anyone. I especially didn't want to face even the slightest possibility of seeing anyone from school. I spent the entire day in my bedroom. It was a gorgeous fall day, in mid-October, but the beautiful colors beckoning from outside my bedroom window did not entice me to come outside.

Sometime during that day I remembered the gold ID bracelet on my right wrist. It had been there since the first day of school. Cam had given it to me. It was engraved, "Andi and Cam" on the front and "You Are My Love" on the back. I took it off so I could read and reread those words. I was confused as Courtney's taunting voice and Julie's malicious smile competed with the words on the bracelet. If they were lying why wasn't Cam waiting in the parking lot Friday night? Or, at least why had I not heard from him? I guess I was just a distraction for him until he and Cheryl patched things up. I guess Courtney hadn't been lying. That's what

I chose to believe. Just a few weeks later I would wonder why I could find it so easy to believe that I wasn't worthy of being loved, and so hard to believe that I truly had been loved all along.

By the time Monday morning arrived I was not the same girl. I'm not sure why it happened so naturally for me to dress more provocatively than was normal for me, but that day I did. In fact, I slipped a sweatshirt on over the low cut top I was wearing just to get out of the house. Since I didn't have to ride the bus anymore I waited until the last minute to go in. I was determined to avoid the stairwell in the business building at all costs. I barely made it into my English class before the bell rang. I had already removed the sweat shirt, even though it was pretty cold. I did not miss the surprised, yet appreciative stares from most of the boys in my class, which included Bobby. There were a few looks from the girls as well, not quite as appreciative though.

Bobby could not wait for the bell to ring that day, he came straight up to me as I leaned over my desk to pick up my books that were lying in the floor, I was not bothering to hide cleavage and he wasn't shy about noticing. I was a little surprised at my sudden ability to flirt as I gave a wink and smile.

"Hey, I heard that you are on the market. Is it true…well, from the looks of you it must be?" His words cut like a knife, I'm sure a shadow passed over my face, but I quickly composed myself and replied sweetly, "I may be on the market, but, you're not really my type." I laid my hand on his forearm and slowly slid it up to where his arm bent at the elbow, I'm sure he was affected by my touch. Then I walked past him, smiling sweetly as I went. I could feel his eyes on me as we both exited the classroom, until I weaved my way into the crowd of students hurrying to their next class.

That first day was the hardest as I made sure to keep a smile on my face and some sass in my words, on the inside I was screaming so much I had no more left. I did a good job avoiding any of the places where Cam and I used to meet between classes, and I even had agreed to a date with a guy named Curt who was in my Accounting class. We sat two to a table in that class, I was at the table behind Curt. Courtney shared his table, so it was a matter of self-defense in my mind to accept his offer of dinner and a movie. Courtney had not spoken a word to me during class, which was a relief, but she got in a good jab as we were leaving for third period, "Well, I see I was right about you all along. Nice blouse. Are you even wearing a bra? Oh, I guess it doesn't matter anymore, not since Cameron finally came to his senses and came back where he belongs. You're just white trash. He was bound to find out sooner or later. Curt, well, he is more your league, have fun with that." Her words were delivered with sweetness which belied there true nature. I was suddenly caught off guard when someone grabbed my arm and spun me around. It was Drake. I rolled my eyes and started past him, but he tightened his grip on my arm. "Wait just a minute, sweetheart. What's this I hear about Cameron and Cheryl? What gives?"

The tardy bell rang before I could answer him, not that I would have anyway, I jerked his hand free and scurried past him.

I wasn't sure how I was going to finish out that day, that week, much less that school year without Cam by my side. I was beginning to remember why I had never let down my guard enough to have a real boyfriend before Cam. I guess I was always afraid that I would get lost in someone else, and somehow I might cease to be. That's exactly how I felt. I still couldn't believe that I had meant so little to Cam that he didn't even call me, didn't come to see me. Well, I had seen him at my work a couple of times, but I hid until he was gone.

6

"I have something to tell you, Sis." My brother David said in the most serious tone I had ever heard from him.

It had been a month since I lost Cam, and though I had gone out with four different boys, I was really just going through the motions of living. I wasn't eating and I had not slept well in all that time. If David had some dreadful news for me I wasn't sure I would be able to handle it. "What is it?" I asked, not really wanting to know.

"I overheard mom and dad arguing last night."

I rolled my eyes, "David, they have been arguing off and on all of my life. I used to worry so much about it, about them, but I just feel numb now." I hated how cold that sounded, but it was true.

"Andi, they were arguing about you and Cam."

"There is no Andi and Cam anymore, besides that wouldn't be the first time they argued about us anyway."

"Andi, do you want to know what I overheard, or not?" David sounded impatient. "I am only telling you because I see you wasting away without Cam, and maybe telling you will make a difference."

David had my full attention now. "What is it David?"

"I heard mom yelling at dad for not telling you..."

"Not telling me what!?" I exclaimed. For the moment the implications of what it meant for mama to actually yell at daddy were lost on me. No one ever yelled at daddy without repercussions.

"Andi, Cam called here, more than once that Friday night, and several times that following Saturday. Dad answered the phone every single time and he told Cam you were not available. And he told Cam that he didn't appreciate the lying that had started when you met him. Of course, dad never told you, and he forbade mama to tell you too."

I'm sure the color drained from my face because I suddenly felt sick deep in the pit of stomach. I didn't even breathe for a minute, until I heard David saying, "Andi, are you ok?" I had not realized that I was crying, but I felt the wetness and tasted the salt as a few tears rolled onto my upper lip. "How could he? David, what have I done? I….what if there was an explanation for all of this mess all along, and I never even gave him a chance? Cam will never forgive me for this."

"You don't know that. Call him. "David advised. "Don't underestimate the kid, he really cared for you."

I wasn't sure exactly how I could make this up to Cam, but a phone call seemed like a good place to start. I was nervous, though, as I dialed the familiar number, because I had no idea how he would respond. The phone was answered on the third ring but it was not Cam who answered, it was his mother. "Hi Mrs. Reagan, this is Andi. Can I…I really need to talk to Cam."

"Andi, where in the world have you been? Cam has been moping around here for the past month. I thought you must have moved back to Clearmont or something!" She didn't sound angry, in fact, she sounded like someone who didn't have a clue about the way things had been with me and Cam all these weeks.

"Oh, no ma'am, I've been busy, I guess. You know, school and a job and all."

"I do understand a bit more since Cam got a job of his own." I had almost forgotten about Cam's job at the gas station. He told me when he got it that he wanted to get me something for Christmas with money he earned himself. It was such a Cam kind of thing to do. He was the kindest, most genuine person I knew. That made it even worse that I had not bothered to speak directly to him about this situation. Maybe this was what Cam had meant when he begged me to not let my scars consume me. I'm pretty sure my low self-esteem was the result of an emotional scar. I'm not sure how long I stood there holding the phone and not speaking, but I finally asked, "Is Cam busy, or could I possibly speak to him?"

"Well, he isn't here right now. Since you guys got out of school early for a teacher's workshop he asked for extra hours at work. He will be there until 9pm. He does get a supper break at 6 if you want to call him then."

"OK, thank you, Mrs. Reagan, I sure will!"

As soon as I hung up the phone I looked to see what time it was, 3:15, it would be a while before I could call. Since I didn't have to work that evening, I figured I could run down to my grandparent's house and visit for a while.

My Granny always seemed to have biscuits fresh from the oven, that day was no exception. Considering that I had lost probably ten pounds in the past month, I could afford to eat one. It helped that I was feeling at least a little hopeful about talking to Cam after the conversation with his mom. Granny got us a biscuit and some honey and we went to sit on her sofa while we ate. Grampa was in the spare room picking his guitar, he loved to play that thing, and I loved to listen.

The biscuit was yummy, but the short few minutes of talking to my granny were just what I needed, I'm not sure why I had waited so long to seek her out. She and Grampa believed in that God stuff as much as Cam and his mom did, so, I'm sure she would have wanted to pray for me. I couldn't go back and change anything, but I could be grateful for these few moments.

By the time we finished our honey and biscuits I was yawning. My sleepless nights were catching up with me too. Granny gently pushed me back onto the soft cushions behind me. She lifted the green afghan off the back of the sofa and gently draped it over me, finishing with a tuck here and there. I didn't need any coaxing, I allowed my eyelids to drift shut, and just like that I was out like a light.

"Fire! Call 9-1-1!" Those were the words that woke me some time later. There was not time to wake up slowly. I was up off the sofa immediately and rushing out onto the back porch where the yelling had come from. As I passed through the kitchen I saw that Grampa was already dialing the number to summon help.

It was my Uncle Dave's house that was on fire, it was up on the hill behind Grannie's house. All I could see was a lot of smoke, no flames, and all I could hear was a lot of confusion and crying from my Aunt Lou Ellen. Fortunately there was no one inside the house, and the fire trucks arrived pretty quickly.

After the commotion died down the fireman who seemed to be in charge came over to where my aunt and uncle were standing, along with the rest of the family that had gathered there. I heard him saying that it looked like the fire had started around the wood stove and that they had contained it to that one room. There was apparently more damage from smoke than flames. We were all so glad that no one got hurt.

By the time they wrapped everything up and left I suddenly realized how dark it had gotten. A look at the clock confirmed that I had missed my chance to call Cam, it was almost 7 already. I was disappointed, but he got off in two hours, surely I could wait that long.

Two hours later I was sitting by the phone. I figured it would take at least fifteen minutes for Cam to get home, so I would wait until 9:15 to call. I was hoping that my dad would stay in front of the TV watching some trashy program that he shouldn't, at least that would give me time to talk to Cam. Since the only phone in the house was hanging on the kitchen wall, and the kitchen was an open floor plan with no doors, I couldn't have real privacy. I was just going over how I could start the conversation with Cam when the phone rang. I almost jumped off the bar stool I was sitting on because it startled me. It rang again before I could react and I heard my dad holler, "Somebody answer that phone!" Of course, he threw in a few expletives, which I hate to even think about much less repeat. Quickly I lifted the receiver, thinking to myself that I hoped it was a wrong number, or that it wasn't David's girlfriend. I might never get to talk to Cam if it was her.

"Hello" I said somewhat impatiently.

"Andi," because I was not expecting it to be Cam on the other end of the line, it took me a second or two to realize it was him. "Andi, are you there?"

"Y—yes, Cam, I'm here." His voice sounded so good in my ear. I had almost forgotten the certain way he had of pronouncing my name.

"Cam, I'm so sorry. I don't know what I was thinking and I know I don't deserve it, but I really hope you will forgive me… if it's not too late." I spewed like a volcano erupting.

After a slight pause Cam replied, "I forgive you Andi."

That was it. He didn't say anything else. And I didn't know what else to say. I had ruined things with the best guy I would ever know and I was not sure we would get back what we had shared. Finally I said, "I'll be sitting in our stairwell tomorrow morning at 7:30, if you don't come I will understand, but I have to at least tell you something…and I don't want to wait until tomorrow….I love you Cam. You make me better and without you I don't even know how to be anymore."

There was no response from his end, but for some reason I didn't lose hope. That was the way Cam was, he never spoke without thinking it through. And he would not say something if he didn't mean it. I was angry at myself for forgetting that long enough to listen to Courtney, even if all she said turned out to be true, I owed it to Cam to hear it from him.

When no response came I was distraught, "I'll be there in the morning." I whispered. I hung up before the sob in my throat could escape. Even if I had a tinge of hope I would still cry myself to sleep that night. It was because I had heard Cam's voice, and partly because I was relieved to have finally told him the truth about how deep my love for him was. That day when we shared our first kiss and we both said those words seemed childlike compared to the way I felt now.

7

I was sitting in the back stairwell of the business building at Oakdale High School at 7:15 the next morning. I wanted to be there before 7:30, just in case Cam did come. I needed that time to get a hold on my emotions, which were all over the place.

I was very glad that there was still very little traffic in the stairwell. I didn't want to see anyone but Cam. In fact, I was prepared to run out to the back lot where I had parked my car and skip school if he didn't show up. I tried to read some in The Scarlett Letter for English, but my heart wasn't in it. So I stuffed it in my backpack and just sat in the echoing silence. I checked the time at least once a minute, so when I heard the door at the top of the stairs open I knew it was 7:27. I didn't turn to look as I heard the footfalls approaching where I sat on the second tier of stairs, I didn't have to. I knew it was Cam, and suddenly I couldn't breathe, I had no idea what was about to happen.

He sat down on the step beside me before he spoke. He also reached for my hand that was resting on my knee. He wrapped his long fingers around it and slowly lifted it to his lips. A flash of Drake doing the same thing back in the summer tried to intrude, but I pushed it away and locked my eyes on the golden blond hair on Cam's head as he leaned forward to kiss my knuckles. He did not stop at one kiss, but pressed four small kisses on each knuckle. I felt myself exhale the breath I had been holding as he released my hand and slipped his arms around me. That was the safest place I had ever been in my life. Years later it would still be the safest place I had ever been in my life. "Andi, I missed you so much. I'm so sorry." He held me so tight it almost hurt, but I would never tell him so, I needed that.

"You don't have anything to be sorry about. I should never have listened to Courtney, she just caught me off guard and you know how I get with my self-esteem issues. I imagine things much worse than they actually are." I spoke against his shoulder. I could feel the warmth of my own breathing between us.

He shifted then, pulling away so he could look me in the eyes. "Andi, I know I have told you before that you imagined some of the things Courtney and her friends said about you, but the truth is you have always been right. Since that day at the pool Courtney has been droning in my ear about how you are not good enough for me, and that Cheryl and I belong together."

He paused, and in his silence I wondered if I was supposed to feel better knowing that, because I didn't. He must have seen a shadow of some emotion cross my face because he brought his hand up to caress my cheek then cup it in his hand. "That must sound terrible, but let me finish. I told Courtney that I don't care what she, or anyone else thinks. What they think does not define me anymore than it does you. And their opinions about whom I should love do not confine me. I know I'm only fifteen, but I cannot imagine ever....ever loving anyone else like I have grown to love you, Andi."

A silent tear slid from the corner of my eye, it rolled down my cheek, stopping against his hand, which still cupped my cheek. My breath caught in my throat for a moment as slowly his head dipped toward mine. Instinctively I tilted my head so that his lips met mine in a tender, sweet kiss. Then he hugged me close again. That was my perfect ending. If only we had been in the pages of one of the Harlequin romance novels I used to read, then this would be the final page, but, of course, this was real life and Cam and could not stay in that stairwell forever. We don't have much time before class, but I have to ask you to do me a favor." Cam asked sudden urgency in his tone.

"I went back to my former position so I could see his face again, "Cam, I will do anything for you."

"Remember when we talked about scars? Well, this thing with Courtney and her friends will scar you if you let it. I don't want you to let it. Promise me that you will not hate her, or Cheryl, or any of them. It gives them too much power over you."

I wanted to promise Cam that I would not hate Courtney, but I wasn't sure I could keep such a promise, so I answered him the best way I knew how, "I don't hate Cheryl. I would be lying to myself if I did not admit that she is a nice person, she lets the others lead her around, but she is nice, I've seen that. And I can't blame her for wanting you. As for Courtney, I can only try..."

"You can't let go of anger and hatred by yourself, Andi, you need God to help you with that." There was God again, the more Cam mentioned him, the more I think I wanted to know, but it was almost time for the bell to ring. I looked at my watch, which he noticed, "I know, it is almost time for the bell."

As I stood up he made me pause by laying his hand on my arm. "One more thing....I need for you to be strong, Andi. Things may get hard. You may think they will destroy you."

The look on his face frightened me, as did the ominous tone of his voice, but I could do anything with Cam by my side. "I can handle those girls, as long as I know you love me there is nothing that will ever hurt me, much less destroy me."

The look in his impossibly blue eyes was hard to read in that moment, I wasn't sure if he wanted to walk out of that building pretending like we were not back together or what. I just wanted him to smile and kiss me again. And I would pretend if that was how he wanted it. "Cam, I won't tell anyone we are together again, I don't care if we have to meet in secret for the rest of forever. We're already keeping this secret from my dad anyway."

He looked hurt for a moment as he replied, "You don't seriously think that I will not proudly walk out of this building holding your hand do you?"

I was so confused by his demeanor that I didn't know how to respond.

"Cam, you're confusing me. What will be hard, ugly stares and nasty words? I don't care what anyone says, I love you more than anything."

"Do you think you could come to church with me tomorrow night? I know Wednesday is your night off? I really want to spend more time with you when we are not confined by time."

I wasn't sure what to make of the change of subject, but I was so relieved I just went with it. "Yes, I will ride the bus to school and go home on the bus with you, if that's ok. I know my mom will cover for me. She has been worried about me losing weight these past few weeks. She will be glad that we made up."

"That sounds great!" His voice was lighter than I could ever remember.

Just as I thought, convincing my mom that I needed to spend time with Cam was easy. I was a little worried about how daddy would react if he found out about our deception, but not worried enough to not go through with it. I did have a kind of adrenalin rush getting on Cam's bus that afternoon, I had the note my mom had written to give to the driver so he would let me on and he didn't even question me.

When we first got to Cam's house there was no one else home, it was the first time he and I had been totally alone before. I have to admit I was a little nervous, even though I wasn't sure why. We got a snack of apples and cheese and sat down at the dining room table. About half way through the snack Cam said abruptly, "I would really like to kiss you right now." I felt my face blush as if I had never been kissed before. At the same time my pulse increased, as I really wanted him to kiss me. I wasn't sure what was supposed to happen next, but Cam seemed to be in control. He stood up, grabbing my hand as he did, he lead me into the living room, where we sat down on the sofa. He turned sideways so that his body was perpendicular to mine, then he used his free hand to lift a strand of my hair, sifting it through his fingers. "We have to be careful, Andi, I could really get lost in you and that really scares me. I'm not the most experienced in these things, but there is something about you that makes my heart do somersaults."

I didn't know how to respond, I was no more experienced than he was with innocent love and the quickening pulse I had was partly afraid of what might happen. "I trust you, Cam." It was the only thing that came to mind, because it was true. If my heart were made of the most fragile glass in the world I would not trust anyone besides Cam to protect it. If I trusted him with that, then I had no trouble trusting him with everything else. I leaned forward, closing the distance between us, and I initiated the kiss for the first time.

His lips were soft and moist and somehow just touching them with mine made them feel soft as well. It was the longest kiss we had ever shared and our arms had naturally sought each other so that we were quite close there on the couch. I could feel Cam caressing my back with a gentleness that became urgent.

Suddenly he broke the contact between us. Standing shakily he moved across the room, as if he wanted to get away from me.

"What's wrong, Cam, did I do something wrong?"

His breathing was deep and unnatural as he shook his head, "No, Andi, you didn't do anything wrong. I just have a responsibility to make sure our relationship is what God wants it to be."

I didn't respond right away because I had never heard anyone talking about how God is concerned with our relationships. "How do you know God even cares what we do? Were we doing something wrong? I love you and you love me, isn't that enough?"

"Actually, no, it isn't enough. I know that it is up to me to lead the right way in this relationship."

I was confused in some ways, but loved Cam even more than I did before. I wasn't quite ready to throw in the towel and believe all this God stuff, but I could sense that Cam loved me in a way that looked totally different than the love I saw between my parents.

"I don't know how you got so wise, Cam, but I'll say it again, I trust you."

The door opened then and Cam's mom came in, she seemed to have no idea what had almost happened right there in her living room. She was genuinely glad to see me.

"Hello Andrea, how nice that you were able to get your dad's permission to come over this afternoon. "I'll be glad to run you home after church tonight, if it is necessary.

I glanced at Cam, I saw the blush that rose to his cheeks. He and I both knew that my dad be angry if he knew I was there, but it just wasn't something we wanted to tell his mom right then.

Mrs. Reagan kept talking as she walked out of the living room, "I would welcome some help getting dinner together."

I stood up and met Cam as he fell in step behind her, he took my hand in his as we walked those few steps, the tiny squeeze he gave my fingers filled me with the best feeling.

We were about half way through preparing dinner when we heard the loud blaring of a horn, which sounded like it was almost in the living room. Cam immediately went to see who it was, and what it was about. He was pale as a ghost when he reentered the kitchen. "Cameron, you look like you've seen a ghost, who is that?" Sally Reagan asked, wiping her hands on a dishtowel and starting toward the door.

"Andi, it's your dad." He almost whispered as the horn blared again.

Instantly I felt sick to my stomach. I had no idea how daddy had figured out I was here, and even more so, I had no idea how he would react. The continually blaring horn was an indication that this was not going to be a good night.

"I'm sorry, Mrs. Reagan!" As I scrambled to get ahead of her, "I guess I forgot to tell daddy I would be here. He is probably a little upset with me. I'll just go on home now."

"Let me at least come out and speak to him." She kept following me.

"Please don't." I said trying hard to keep from sobbing. "It will only make matters worse. It's my fault. I'm sorry." Then I ran out of the house and straight to daddy's truck. He was by himself, which scared me even more, I would have to face him all alone.

I didn't say anything when I got in the truck. I had never defied daddy before I met Cam because I was afraid to. He was liberal with discipline, as he called it. He was also pretty good at making sure the bruises would be covered by clothing so no questions would ever be asked.

It was about a twenty minute drive to our house and I felt like I needed to say something to protect mama from his wrath before we got there. He had to know that she was aware that I had gone home on the bus with Cam. She was the only one who knew, so she had to have told him.

"Daddy, please don't be mad at mama for letting me go to Cam's house today. I just missed him so much and I pressured her into letting me go."

"Don't worry about your mother. But, let me tell you that I will not stand for lies in my house. If you are going to live under my roof, you will live by my rules." His words were cold, angry. I suppose I deserved to be punished because lying was not cool, but that didn't excuse all the other times I had gotten whippings when I tried so hard to be good. I could remember the embarrassment of standing on our front porch as daddy whipped me for some offense that I couldn't even remember, as cars drove by. But no one in Clearmont would ever think anything of that sort of behavior. He whipped me so hard that time that the bruises even extended to my inner thighs. I could only imagine what waited for me at home.

8

Mama was in the kitchen when we walked in with her back facing the door. She never even acknowledged that we were there. I wanted to go to her and hug her and tell her I was so sorry for dragging her into the middle of my deception, but I was afraid of what daddy would do.

"Wait for me in my room." There was no disobeying those words, but I was already thinking of how I could get out of that house. As usual when I had that sort of thought, images of Derrick and Casey crossed my mind. David was pretty much the apple of daddy's eye so he never got into trouble, but if I wasn't there for daddy to vent on, who would take my place?

I did as daddy told me and went into his room. I sat there for only ten minutes, but it seemed like an eternity. When he entered the room and shut the door behind him with a slam, I shrank back a little. I really wanted to stand up to him, but my fear was palpable. It was only three steps from the door to the edge of the bed where I was huddled. As daddy took those steps he was removing his belt. I didn't even realize I was crying until I felt the wet tears sliding down my face. Daddy always seemed angrier when I cried, but I couldn't stop.

When his anger was appeased, I could hear daddy slipping his belt back through the loops on his pants. Then he left the room without saying a word. It wasn't my first whipping, but it may have been the worst. The pain would subside. The wounds would heal, scars would come. But the hurt in my heart would need healing too. After a few minutes I heard the familiar sound of daddy's truck engine, then the spraying of gravel as he spun out of the driveway much too quickly. Who knew where he went after these episodes? He always left without a word and no one acknowledged anything had happened.

I started to lift myself off the bed as the door opened again. I shrank back involuntarily. I knew daddy was gone, but my brain was not exactly rational at the moment. Then mama was there hugging me and apologizing. And I thought, "Why does she always apologize, and why doesn't he?"

Mama's tears mingled with mine as she allowed me to turn toward her and slump against her chest. "Mama, I'm sorry. Did he hit you?" I sobbed.

"No. He saved it all for you. You have to stay away from Cam, I'm so afraid that he will not stop until it is too late one day." Mama was also sobbing.

I didn't say anything, but I knew that I would not lose Cam again, no matter what. I would run away if I had to. Mama was propelling me toward the door. I heard her say, "Let's go get you cleaned up."

Mama was as gentle as she could be cleaning the wounds on my legs and dressing them with ointment and band aids, still I winced a few times. The physical evidence was almost like a badge, but the hurt in my heart was worse by far. Maybe this was one of those scars Cam talked about.

It was late by the time daddy came back home, everyone was in bed. I was too, but I wasn't asleep, though when he opened the door and looked inside I pretended like I was. I don't know why he always did that, but he would leave and return late, and always he would open my bedroom door, and always I would pretend to be asleep. Maybe he wanted to apologize, but by the time morning came he never did.

Mama gave me permission to skip school the next day. She knew I would be sore. But going to school seemed to be the only way I could see Cam. I decided to go anyway.

9

Cam was already there in our spot when I got to school the next morning. I was walking a little slower than usual. I tried to hide the discomfort of my jeans against the wounds on my legs, but Cam knew me so well, he could tell something wasn't right. "Baby, I was so worried about you last night, what did your dad do?" He had never called me "baby" before and I wasn't sure if I liked it, but I did like that his voice sounded so tender and genuine.

"It wasn't too bad. I'm used to it." I couldn't look him in the eye when I said that because I didn't want the tears that had been lodged in my throat for so long to start, I knew I wouldn't be able to staunch them, and I would end up in the guidance counselors office. I sure didn't want to tell her my hidden secrets.

Cam took me by the hand as I stood two steps below the one where he was sitting. He propelled me forward into his embrace. I knelt in front of him and just let him hold me. Nothing had ever felt so good before. For a few minutes we didn't speak, he caressed my hair and dropped a few kisses into the hair on top of my head. Finally he spoke, "Andi, those scars we talked about before…have you thought any more about them?"

I still hadn't told him about the day in Wayne's house. I had also seen other thing and had things happen to me that I knew I would never speak of with Cam. So many things I had buried so deeply that to dig them up would hurt far more than to just leave them where they were. Somehow I knew that Cam was not equipped to help me with those dark memories anyway.

I shuddered as a shiver traveled up my spine, but not the good kind.

"What is it, Andi, you can tell me, I want to help you carry those burdens. I know they are there because I see the shadow of them in your eyes every once and a while."

But I didn't want Cam to think I was dirty, which is how I thought of myself, so I wouldn't tell him about those things, not yet. "Nothing Cam, it's a memory that I'm not strong enough to share yet."

The next few weeks passed by relatively free of drama for me and Cam. Our time together had been reduced to just seeing each other at school and talking on the phone, he insisted we keep it that way because he was afraid that my daddy might react in anger again. We were trying to play by daddy's rules in hopes that he would allow us to spend some time together over our Christmas break from school.

We were scheduled to get out of school on December 21, a Wednesday, but that Tuesday Cam was anxious when I met him in the stairwell. He said he had to see me after school if we could manage it. I had to work that night so I wasn't sure how we were going to manage it, but his urgency honestly scared me, so I knew we had to figure something out. I called mama at her work, something I had never done before, and I had told myself that I wasn't going to involve her in my secret meetings with Cam anymore, but I didn't know what else to do. She was reluctant, but when I told her that Cam was adamant she said she would cover for me this one more time. I told her I would take my Algebra homework to Cam's house and get him to help me with it so we could honestly say I was studying with a friend. I just hoped daddy wouldn't ask who.

It was 9:20 when I got to Cam's house, and though it was a cold December night he was sitting on the porch swing waiting for me. As I climbed out of my car to go join him I suddenly felt so afraid of what Cam had to say to me that I almost turned back. I couldn't do that though, I trusted Cam with everything inside me.

He was on his feet by the time I stepped onto the porch, with his hands stuffed into the pocket on the front of the hoodie he was wearing, he looked so young, like a tall little boy. A lock of the golden blond hair that I loved so much had fallen across the corner of his eye. I knew he would be getting a haircut soon since he didn't like it too long. "It's too cold to talk out here, I asked mom if we could sit in my bedroom for a while, is that ok?"

"Of course," I replied.

I followed him into the house, as we entered the living room I remembered the last time I was here. We hadn't been in a position to get as close physically as we had that day, but I had thought about it often. Truthfully I longed to be held and touched by Cam in intimate ways, but monsters from my past kept crowding my mind and Cam had told me during the past few weeks a lot about what the Bible said about that sort of thing and I was really quite confused.

"Hello Andrea, how are you?" Sally said. Cam's dad had his face buried behind a newspaper and barely grunted a greeting. I spoke briefly with them then followed Cam toward his bedroom. I felt a little awkward just to go into his intimate space with his parents sitting in the next room.

I had never been in Cam's room before, so I distracted myself by surveying the space. It was fairly large, especially compared to mine, he had a desk and two dressers and a futon instead of a regular bed, and at the moment it was in the "sofa position", he allowed me to sit down first, then he did, making sure to sit as far away as possible. I had a knot in my stomach that had been there since that morning when Cam was so serious about us getting together to talk. I hoped he would get to the point in a hurry.

My mouth was so dry that I couldn't have formed a word if I needed to. Maybe his was too, because the silence stretched a little. We didn't even look at each other. I was not accustomed to things being this way with Cam. I feared that Cheryl had come back into the picture and perhaps Cam was trying to figure out how to break up with me. I didn't settle on that thought too long as if not thinking would keep it from being true.

Finally Cam broke the silence, "My dad used to drink a lot, and he sometimes got mean when he did. Maybe that is why he and your dad don't like each other. They probably had their share of fist fights." He paused, leaning forward with his elbows propped on his knees, head drooped down.

When I didn't say anything he continued' "He often acted out in anger, but my mom and Clayton always tried to protect me."

I have to admit that I was surprised. Cam's dad was not the friendliest person I had ever met, but I would not imagine him even raising his voice, much less hitting someone. "I'm sorry, Cam. It hurts much deeper than the bruises." I wasn't even aware that my hand went to my leg. Cam, as usual didn't miss the movement. He reached to cover my hand with his.

"Can I see?" He whispered.

I had worn a dress to school that day because my drama class had a performance which I had to dress up for, and I hadn't had time to go home and change before work, so I slowly lifted the thick material to just above my right knee where the worst cut had been, it was a harsh pink scar at this point. He traced along the ragged edge of the scar with his long finger, careful not to push too hard, I guess he was afraid he would hurt me. "I'm so sorry Andi." I gasped in something like wonder that someone could be so careful with me. "Did I hurt you?" He asked.

"No, Cam, I…think somehow you have saved me."

He sat back up and slid across the futon, closing the gap between us. "I didn't want to touch you, but I just need to," as he spoke he drew me into his embrace. I didn't mind at all. After all this is the one place where I felt like I was safe.

"I'm going to tell you a story about how I met God and how He is changing me and my family slowly but surely. It may take a few minutes, but please bear with me."

I settled closer to him, my head resting just below his chin, I could feel his breath in my hair. This was a good place to hear his story, if I could concentrate over the beating of his heart.

"We never went to church a lot when I was younger, mostly Christmas and Easter, and I really didn't pay a lot of attention to the preacher when I was there. It was only Mama, Clayton and I who went, Daddy never did. He drank a lot in those days, and his angry outbursts were increasing. I suppose mama thought we needed God's help, so she told me one Saturday that we would be going to church the next morning. Clayton was fourteen, and by then he was already running with a rough crowd, drinking just like daddy, only Clayton was also using drugs. He laughed in mama's face when she mentioned church to him. So the next morning, after a tough night that left mama with a busted lip, me and her went to church just like she said we would. I didn't know how those people would treat us with mama's face bruised up and her lip swollen. As it turned out, they hugged us, prayed over us and cried with us. I was mesmerized by that. I couldn't stop thinking about it all that afternoon, I guess mama couldn't either because at 5:30 she said, "get your jacket, we are going back to church." I still remember the verses the preacher read that night and how he explained them. It was Luke 13 verses 10-17, it was a story about a woman who had been sick for 18 years. The thing making her sick was an evil spirit, and her illness was so severe that she was bent over and could not straighten up, when Jesus saw her he set her free from the evil spirit and she was healed from her disease. I thought that was the coolest thing. But then Preacher James went on to explain things a little deeper, I don't remember everything he said, but I do remember that at some point he said, "There may be someone in here tonight bearing a heavy weight in your life because of evil. If that is you I am here to tell you that you don't have to let things stay the way they are. God has made a way for you through Jesus just like He did for the woman we read about. You can to ask Him to save you from this evil and He has the ability to give you the power you need to tell that evil spirit to leave you. If you feel your heart about to beat out of your chest and maybe even a little lightheaded, there is a good chance that is God talking to you through His Holy Spirit. Don't be afraid, and don't leave this place tonight without praying. The pianist will play and if you feel the need, meet me right here at the altar."

I was already moving toward the end of the bench before the music began, by the first note I was in the aisle, by the third or fourth note I was at the altar, I didn't walk, I ran. I hit the floor so hard on my knees that it jarred me, but I didn't care. I had started to cry, but I didn't even realize it until the tears started dripping off the end of my nose. I suppose I was trying to pray, but I don't even know what I was saying, I was just crying out for help. I felt hands rubbing my back and I heard a lot of people praying and crying, I must have stayed there for twenty minutes, then all of a sudden I felt a peaceful warmth that I can't really explain. It was just like my heart heard God say I was forgiven, I was clean and I was empowered. When I opened my eyes I saw that mama was there beside me on her knees, eyes still wet with tears. Then she hugged me and I felt like the two of us could take on any army."

"So did the stuff with your dad stop after that?" I asked, hoping the answer was yes so I could possibly believe all that Cam had told me.

Cam shifted his position on the futon, letting me go from his embrace, which suddenly left me feeling cold. "He did not stop right away, that Sunday night when I was getting ready to go to sleep mama came into my room and said, "Starting tonight we are doing battle for our family in prayer." She went on to ask God to take the desire for alcohol and drugs away from daddy and Clayton and replace it with a desire to know Him. She also prayed that our house would be cleansed from evil spirits and that no more could return. We have been praying that same prayer together every night for a little over five years. About six months after we started praying the angry outbursts just stopped, that is four and half years ago. He also stopped drinking alcohol last year. He still doesn't go to church but he has let mama lead a Bible study here. As for Clayton, he is still using drugs and challenging us to keep praying, but he will change one day; we have faith that he will."

I looked down at the scar on my leg; scars really, some were just a little more faded than the others, and of course those scars Cam had asked me about months ago were always hovering in my mind. I just couldn't get past some of them. I wanted to believe everything Cam had told me; that his daddy changed because they prayed, but it just seemed too good to be true. Besides I had all those dark things in my past that were nothing like the things Cam had told me. Maybe my stuff was too dirty even for God to clean up. I decided to share as much of those ghosts with Cam as I could before I left his house. If he really loved me it would be ok.

I stood up from the futon and went to the window, of course, it was dark outside but there was string of Christmas lights outlining the window which illuminated the yard a little, I fixed my eyes on an Oak tree as I began to speak. I told Cam about Wayne and the nasty magazines he made me look at, and about finding some that were even worse under my daddy's mattress. He sounded sympathetic behind me, but I didn't want to see his face, just in case there was disgust in his eyes. I had something far worse to tell him, something I had never spoken of since daddy told me not to four years before.

It was harder than I thought it would be to tell Cam about the things that had happened to me when I was fourteen. That was just two years before, seemed like so much longer than that.

It was hard, and embarrassing for me to remember the night my daddy tried to force me to go on a date with a man who had already tried to hurt me, and was older than my mom. How is a girl supposed to feel about herself when the person who should be protecting her chooses not to?

"I know I have a warped sense of my identity because of the battle that goes on in my mind so often. Cam, how are we supposed to fight the memories anyway? Does God have an answer for that?"

I turned to face Cam again. I saw sadness mingled with love in his eyes. I couldn't understand how he would care so much for me when I barely cared for myself at all.

"I gained a lot of weight after that, maybe in self-defense. Then I started to feel worthless because I had no boyfriend, so I had to lose the weight. I practically stopped eating and dropped the weight I had gained and quite a bit more until my mom got worried about me and took me to see a doctor. I had to retrain my body to eat. After that I felt like I needed to be punished and since I could not hurt myself by withholding food any more I had to do something, I resorted to self- harm…"

I left those words hanging in the air and waited to see how Cam would respond. I had dumped a lot of junk on the shoulders of a fifteen year old boy.

"I'm sorry isn't strong enough, Andi. I'm angry that your dad chose to protect that man over you. I'm sad that you were hurt so deeply. But mostly I'm sorry that you blamed yourself and tried to punish yourself. I'm at a loss to know what to say right now to help that wounding scar to become a healing scar instead. I want to hold you, but I don't know if it is ok." Cam was almost in tears, which made me love him even more. I know mama would have been on my side if I had told her everything, but I couldn't. Having Cam to feel all those emotions on my behalf was humbling.

"My mom was never brave or strong enough to stand up to daddy… except for that night when daddy basically set me up for that date. That night she dared to get right in daddy's face and told him I was not going anywhere with a man who was more than twice my age. When he showed up to get me he had his brother with him. My mama marched onto the front porch and told them to leave and never set foot on our property again. Daddy just left for a few hours and never said anything to me about it. No apology or anything. I think daddy was so shocked that Mama had been so brave that he never tried to force that issue again."

I heard the movement as Cam got up and came across the room to stand behind me. It was a natural reaction for my body to lean back into his as he put his arms around me. I laid my head against his chest, feeling that heartbeat again, I sighed, more at peace than I had been in a long time.

"I had no idea Andi, I'm sorry. Did it help you to think better of yourself because at least your mom stood up for you?"

"I wish I could honestly say it did, but no. I always knew she loves me, but I feel like I'm swimming upstream in a flood swollen river trying to get daddy to love me...choose me. The truth is, that whole incident just brought more confusion in my mind. I mean, is that love? Is that all a woman is good for?"

Cam spun me around and held me at arms-length so he could look me in the eye, "Absolutely not! God has so much love for you and a beautiful plan. The Bible even calls girls the daughters of the King. You are wonderful in His eyes. It's true, but you have to believe it. Andi, surrender your heart to Him so He can help you see yourself through His eyes."

I heard the desperation in his plea, and again I wanted all of this to be true, but I could not get past the fact that I had to go home very soon to the same feelings and struggles. I couldn't see how it would make a real difference for me to say I believed that Jesus died on a cross and came back to life to pay for my sins.

Cam and I were both startled by a sudden knock at his bedroom door just before it opened, his mom stuck her head and said, "I don't want you to get into trouble, Dear, just wanted to tell you it is almost 11 o'clock."

It was a small gesture, but just hearing her call me "Dear" made me feel warm inside. "Thank you, Mrs. Reagan."

She smiled then retreating, closing the door again. As soon as she was gone Cam pulled me against his chest, seemed like I had spent a good deal of this time there. That didn't bother me, except the way Cam was acting was scaring me just a little. His arms encircled me in a grip so tight I almost couldn't breathe. I slipped my arms around his waist and hugged him back, I never wanted this moment to end, but I really had to go home. If I came in too late and daddy found out I had been at Cam's he might never let me out of his sight again.

Finally I tried to pull away, but Cam wouldn't let me go. "Cam, I have to go. It will make things even harder for us if I push my luck too much tonight."

He rested his chin on top of my head, and I heard him say. "Andi, remember that promise you made months ago about not letting the scars destroy you? Well, as long as there is life there are going to be scars, just make sure you find a way someday for yours to be symbols of healing."

"I'll try." I said, huskily, I wasn't sure why but suddenly there was a lump in my throat that was really just a wad of tears that wanted to escape.

Cam walked me out to my car after I told his parents good night. Just before I opened the door he gently pushed my back against the car and leaned in to kiss me. Eagerly I raised my head to meet his as I thought, I hope our kisses always feel this way. He kissed me softly a couple of times. Finally he lifted his head and said, "I love you, Andi, right now and for all of forever….never forget that."

"I love you too, Cam. I'll see you at school tomorrow, early dismissal for Christmas break. I can't wait to spend it with you!" I stood on tiptoe and quickly kissed him on the chin, "Sleep well." Then I got into my car and went home.

10

The next morning Cam called just before I walked out the door to tell me that he wasn't coming to school because his great-grandparents had a couple of pine trees in their front yard that they suddenly thought needed lights on them. So, Cam, being the great guy he was agreed to do it for them before he went to work at the gas station.

I almost stayed home too, but I didn't want to make any explanations as to why, so I went anyway. It was only a half day after all.

It was a wasted morning except that someone in my Accounting class brought a little cardboard box filled with several bundles of mistletoe. He said anyone who wanted to get a special Christmas kiss could have some. I didn't hurry toward the box after class, but I did secretly hope there would be some left, I could make a short stop at the gas station later and surprise Cam. Fortunately he had brought plenty so I scooped up a bundle and mumbled, "Thanks" as I hurried out of the classroom.

Since it was Wednesday I was off work, but I remembered that it was my payday so I planned to go see Cam then go get my paycheck, but I realized that my gas needle was sitting just above empty and I had no money to get gas until I got my check and could get it cashed. So I asked my mom if she would take me to get my check. I didn't bother to mention that I also wanted to stop and see Cam. I could wait until we were on the way, then she wouldn't have to deceive daddy.

Mama agreed to take me, but she said we had to wait until after she fixed some dinner. That afternoon was impossibly slow, I did all my normal household tasks and even cooked most of the dinner myself just to keep busy so the hours would pass more quickly. Finally dinner was over and the dishes were washed and mama, Casey and I headed down the driveway. I was clutching the mistletoe in my hand which was stuffed in my coat pocket when I broached the subject of stopping by the gas station.

"Mama, I got some mistletoe at school today, and I was wondering if we could stop by the gas station so I can get a Christmas kiss from Cam. He didn't come to school today, so he doesn't know, it would be a surprise."

"Sounds romantic, you know I'm a push over for that sort of thing. Let's go get the check first then stop by on the way back. Either way was fine with me.

There were two different routes to get the department store where I worked, one passed right by Cam's work, the other bypassed downtown. Mama took a right on the rout that bypassed town on the way

Mama also had to get a few things from the grocery store, which was in the same plaza where I worked. Our trip took longer than I would have liked. But I had no choice but to be patient, I tried not to get mouthy with mama, I was afraid she might change her mind about taking me to see Cam.

An hour and fifteen minutes later we started back toward town, but there was a police car parked crossways in the road with its lights flashing, mama stopped and rolled down her window as an officer walked up and told us that Main Street was closed because an accident had it blocked. He told us we had to detour around on the bypass. I was disappointed, but then I said, "We can just come from the other end of Main Street. The gas station is closer to that end anyway.

As it turned out when we got to the stop sign where the road fed back into Main Street, there was another police car directing us to turn left, which was away from the gas station.

Since we really had no choice, mama turned the car toward home. I didn't want to go home though, so I asked her if I could get out at my aunt and uncle's house, my Uncle Bradley was a good friend of Cam's dads and he was the reason we met, so I was pretty partial to him. Our house was on the hill about one hundred yards above their house, so I knew I could just walk home when I got ready.

Aunt Susan was just putting a late dinner on the table when I went in. Of course, she invited me to sit down and join them. I had barely touched my dinner at home so I was glad she asked. I didn't even think to mention the accident downtown as we started eating. My aunt was an amazing cook and her food you always wanted to savor. About a third of the way through our meal the phone rang, and my cousin James automatically got up to go answer it, but Uncle Bradley told him to sit back down and let the answering machine get it. The ringing stopped, then shortly after the phone rang again. This was repeated a third time, when Uncle Bradley told James it must be important so he could answer it.

Shortly after he left to answer the phone, James came back into the dining room and he was so pale he looked as if he had seen a ghost. "What's wrong, son?" I heard Aunt Susan ask, "You're as pale as a ghost."

James didn't answer her, instead he collapsed into the chair he had just left a few minutes earlier, I thought he would pass out and I could barely hear him whisper, "Daddy, you need to go get the phone." Uncle Bradley was out of his seat and across the room quicker than I would have thought possible. James's little sister, Janna said, "What in the world is wrong James, you're scaring me!"

Tears were streaming down James's face by this time, and suddenly he was scaring me too. I couldn't wait to hear what was going on so I jumped and ran into the living room. There I found Uncle Bradley, one hand propped him up against the back of the couch, as if he would fall otherwise, while the other hung limply at his side, still clutching the phone's receiver.

"Uncle Bradley, what is wrong!?" I screamed.

His reply was to call out to Aunt Susan asking her to come to the living room. When she came in it was evident that James had said something after I ran out, because she stepped in front of me and said, "Andi, honey, I need for you to sit down. I have…" Her voice broke on a sob as she pressed a hand against her lips.

"I don't want to sit down, just tell me what is going on!" I didn't mean to scream so loudly right in Aunt Susan's face, but I could feel terror somewhere inside me that told me I wasn't going to like what I heard, but I needed to get it over with. In my peripheral vision I saw James run out the front door, pulling on his coat as he went. "Where is James going?"

Then Janna was there in the living room crying like a baby and hovering over me, I thought I was going to explode if someone didn't tell me what was going on, and soon.

I was not aware that Uncle Bradley had crossed the room until he stepped between me and Aunt Susan and grasped me by the shoulders, "It's Cameron, there was an accident at the gas station, Andi…..he didn't make it."

I wasn't sure I heard him right, so I shook my head and tried to force a laugh. Uncle Bradley was quite the jokester and I was sure this was just a sick attempt at a joke. But the colorless skin covering his face told me that he was a serious as he could be. But I was not going to give up on Cam that easily. I pulled out of his grasp and went to sit on the edge of the sofa. I didn't even recognize my own voice when I spoke. I just heard the words. "I don't believe it. I don't know why all of you are crying and carrying on, if Cam was…" I gulped, "If Cam was dead I would know it."

Then I turned my face toward the window nearest the couch and looked out, as if I could see through the darkness that had gathered outside. But I didn't cry, because I was convinced that there was a terrible mistake and tears would be wasted.

To me the next few hours seemed like slow motion, but in truth things were happening quickly. Uncle Bradley rode down town to see what details he could find. He asked me if I wanted to go, but I just sat, looking into the darkness. I had no idea that the darkness was just beginning for me.

James had gone to get my mama, when she came in she looked like she was about to throw up. She came straight to me and tried to put her arms around me, but I literally pushed her away as I said coldly, "This is a waste of time. Uncle Bradley will be back soon to tell all of you to dry up your tears. I'm not wasting mine, Cam and I will be chuckling about this by tomorrow."

The look that settled into every pair of eyes in that room turned toward me was suddenly nothing more than pity, and I hated that. I wanted to call them all liars and run out into the night, run to Cam's house and sit on his futon, just like last night.

Mama and Aunt Susan didn't really know what to do with me because I was being unreasonable. They finally decided to just stop trying to comfort someone who didn't even realize yet that she was grieving. I heard James and Janna start talking about "remember whens" from time they had spent together with Cam and his family, they tried to evoke some sort of emotion in me, but I was hJamieing myself in those moments. The longer Uncle Bradley was gone the more the truth tried to seep into my mind, but I shook it off and thought about how I knew Cam was going to love the new sweater I had bought to give him for Christmas. I couldn't remember if it was wrapped or not and it was starting to annoy me.

Finally the front door opened and Uncle Bradley came in looking like a messenger with a message he would rather not give. Actually he just looked drained, like every bit of color had left his face. He glanced at me, still sitting where I had been when he left, he turned to where the others were basically huddled, supporting one another.

"Oh no, it's true, isn't it? Aunt Susan whispered, her shoulders suddenly slumped forward as if someone just placed a heavy load on them.

The nod of Uncle Bradley's head was almost imperceptible, as if not fully admitting the truth could change it. Everyone's tears came in earnest then, still I sat dry eyed. James came over to where I was sitting and plopped down beside me, "Andi, you heard what dad said, Cameron is gone, you have to accept that. I turned to look at him, the first time I had shifted my gaze in over an hour, "I don't have to believe any of this. I will not accept this until I see him."

"Andi, you will not be able to see him, I'm afraid." Uncle Bradley sounded so sad. "It was a violent accident, an explosion. He didn't suffer, he was gone too quickly, but he is...you just won't be able to see him."

I just stared at him for a moment, trying to make myself keep breathing. Who knew that something I usually did without thinking would suddenly become so hard. I could hear myself dragging air into my lungs and almost choking as it came back out. And though my eyes were looking at Uncle Bradley I wasn't seeing him at all. Mama was kneeling in front of me now, begging me with her eyes to stay calm. I still didn't want her to put her arms around me, I was afraid I would just lose myself if I clung to anyone. With all the effort I could gather I took a deep, ragged breath, holding it for a few seconds, when I finally released the air it was much smoother than it had been, and my former resolve of unbelief took over again.

"I can't believe you all would lie to me about Cam, is daddy behind this? I know he hates Cam and will do anything to keep me from him." My words didn't make sense, but I was not exactly in my right mind.

"Honey, no one is lying to you. This is a horrible tragedy and we don't understand for a moment why God allowed it to happen."

"God," I interrupted mama, "I don't want to hear anything about Him, I never said I even believe in Him, and if I did, I wouldn't now, why would he take the one person in the world who loved me enough to make me feel something!?" It was the first time since my initial screams that I raised my voice, but I didn't care.

Mama looked so hurt by my words, and I was sorry somewhere deep inside, but it sure wasn't enough to make me apologize. She stood and walked to the opposite side of the room, motioning for Uncle Bradley and Aunt Susan to follow. They formed a small huddle and all I could hear were whispers. I didn't care what they were talking about. All I knew was that I suddenly felt like I had to get out of there.

Uncle Bradley was on me before I made it to the door, and mama had picked up the phone. I knew she was talking to daddy when she said, "I need you to come down here and help me with Andi."

I didn't even think daddy would come so I never thought to hope that he didn't, besides I didn't know what mama was planning that she would need help. I found out soon enough. When daddy got there he was different than I had ever seen him before. He took Uncle Bradley's place by me and as awkwardly as anything I had ever seen he put his arms around me. I wanted no part of that, I didn't want his pity, I wanted him to be fair to Cam, and if all that Uncle Bradley had told me was true, it was too late for that. I started to squirm and struggle to get out of his grasp, but he tightened his hold on me, I ceased all movement and went limp in his arms. I suppose he thought he had won some type of battle as his body relaxed a bit, but my heart was dead inside my chest and nothing he or anyone did or said would change that. He finally pushed me back to arms-length and looked me in the eye. I'm sure he saw something that frightened him because he immediately turned to mama and said, "Let's go, she is gonna need something."

I decided that struggling against daddy was not a good idea, so I willingly walked out with him, and mama followed close behind. I immediately noticed that daddy had driven down the hill, and had even left the truck running. I climbed through the driver's door and slid all the way across to the other side, leaning my head against the cold, dark glass, I closed my eyes. As soon as mama had gotten belted in beside me and I heard daddy's door close we started to move. I expected to feel the vehicle turning so that we could head back up the hill, but instead daddy gunned the engine and sped down the road. The left turn at the end of the cove where we lived would take us toward down town. Surely daddy would not take me to the gas station.

Daddy took the left turn, my eyes wide open now, I could feel panic rising up inside me, but I was pretty good at stuffing such feelings down. I didn't say a word. I just sat stoically, swallowing whatever emotion tried to escape. I closed my eyes again.

A few minutes later the truck stopped, I heard daddy get out and felt the emptiness as mama slid out behind him. I didn't move. I almost fell out when the door I was leaning on suddenly opened, I wasn't wearing a seat belt, if daddy had not caught me I would most likely have face planted on the ground. Of course, my eyes flew open as I was falling sideways, and I knew immediately that we were at the hospital. Did they think I was losing my mind or something? Maybe I was, but I really didn't want to go into that emergency room. When my feet finally hit the ground I started to pull away, but daddy had anticipated that and he gripped my hand so hard it hurt my wrist. I still didn't say anything, but the walk across the parking lot was punctuated with my unsuccessful attempts to wrench free of daddy's grip. Mama had went ahead of us in through the double sliding doors, now I saw her coming back toward us accompanied by someone from the hospital, judging by the way he was dressed. He rushed over to help daddy subdue me and the two of them were more than I could fight against, so I finally stopped trying. They practically dragged me inside the doors. There were several people in the waiting area, I noticed one man holding his hand, obviously cut pretty bad considering the brown stained towel it was wrapped in. A couple more were hacking and coughing, I expected to be forced to take a seat alongside them, but the guy helping daddy bring me in asked the guy with the injury if he could take me on back since his bleeding was under control. I was at least glad for that, I couldn't stand the looks of pity on their faces. They didn't have a clue that I was a dead girl walking. At least that is how I felt. Like my heart had decided to quit beating, but my brain had not gotten the memo yet.

There was already a nurse in the exam room where they took me, she was holding a syringe, of course, I knew it was for me. The hospital guy and daddy maneuvered me onto the table in the center of the room, but they didn't release me instead they both gripped me a little tighter. "Don't move." The hospital guy ordered. I hated needles and I wanted to get the shot over with, whatever it was, so I sat perfectly still. The nurse told me there would be a little stick then she thrust the needle into the flesh on the outside of my upper arm. It pinched, but I didn't move a muscle, somehow that little bit of pain reminded me that I was actually still alive. I heard mama asking the nurse what was in the syringe, it was valium, to calm me down.

We stayed in the emergency room for about three hours, a doctor came in and tried to get inside my head, but even the relaxing valium wasn't strong enough to make me let my guard down. I said what I thought they all wanted to hear. "Yes, I understand that Cam is gone and I will never see him again. No, I will not go off the deep end. No, I will not hurt myself."

It was almost 2 a.m. when we got home, and after two doses the Valium they gave me at the hospital really had relaxed me, so I went to sleep almost as soon as my head hit the pillow.

11

felt like I had been hit by a truck when I woke up. It actually took me a few seconds to remember where I was. Images of Cam hit me like a wave and I suddenly felt the need to throw up. I flung the covers back and made a quick move to get up, which was a mistake, as my vision immediately closed in and I felt myself falling forward. Someone broke my fall somewhat, which kept me from busting my face on the floor. "Slow down!" Mama exclaimed. Then another pair of hands joined her in helping me back on to the bed. "I need to throw up!" I cried, afraid I would right there. A sudden movement toward the garbage can told me that the other person in the room was my cousin, Jamie, who also was one of my only real girl-friends. She was back by the bed in a flash with the garbage can, and not a moment too soon as my body began to heave. Of course, there wasn't much in my stomach so it was bile that filled my mouth and spilled into the garbage can. I was sick for two or three minutes before I finally felt subdued, tears were streaming down my face and now my throat felt raw. I lay back on the pillow and closed my eyes, then draped my arm across my face. I just wanted to go back to sleep and dream that all of this reality was just a nightmare.

"He's gone, isn't he?" I whispered hoarsely.

"Yes, honey, I'm so sorry." Mama's voice sounded wobbly.

The tears increased, flowing out from under my arm that covered my face, then sliding down my face and into my ears, just like that day on the porch swing after Granny Sanders died. "Why? It's not fair?" I sobbed.

Both mama and Jamie gathered me in a hug. I sensed that they were crying with me. I had a sudden thought of Cam's mom, she must be devastated. I gulped the tears down and asked, "How is Mrs. Reagan? I need to go see her."

"I haven't seen her, but she called here yesterday while you were still asleep to tell us the visitation and funeral begin this afternoon at 1."

There was something so wrong about hearing mama talk about Cam's funeral in such a calm voice, something so wrong. "I have to get up and take a shower."

"You need to take it slow, maybe you could eat something?" Jamie sounded almost like my mother.

"I don't think I can eat, obviously nothing will stay in my stomach."

"Ok, just be careful. Let us help you to the bathroom."

It was painstakingly slow showering without passing out, my vision kept trying to close in on me. If I could think of anything positive about the situation it was that I was so distracted that I had not had time to think about Cam. Once I was showered and dressed all I had to do was sit and think, I felt like I was being sucked into a black hole, and if it swallowed me I might never make it out alive. I suppose mama could tell something wasn't right because she brought a valium in pill form for me to take, but I refused. I didn't want to risk falling asleep and missing the last chance to ever say good bye to Cam.

Jamie had the most beautiful singing voice, and just started to sing unexpectedly. I don't even know what the songs were that she sang, something folky, but her sweet voice managed to soothe me until it was finally time to go to the funeral.

The church where I had gone with Cam and his mom a few times was back off the main road with an entrance road, about a half mile long. I saw immediately as mama turned toward the church that there were cars lining both sides of the road. I imagined the church, which was really not that big, if all these cars were here for Cam, then we might not make it in at all, much less on time.

Instead of finding a spot to park, mama maneuvered her little car between the two rows of cars toward the church. "You don't think there will be room to park closer do you?" Jamie asked the question I was thinking.

"No, Mama answered, "But I spoke with Sally earlier and she told me to bring Andi right to the front of the church and let her out. She is waiting to bring Andi in with her, then you and I can go park and walk back up."

Fresh tears rolled down my cheeks as I thought of Cam's mom, going through the worse thing a parent could possibly face and she was concerned about me. I couldn't understand that, considering that I could only think of my own breaking heart.

A few moments later mama stopped the car right beside the church steps. There were so many people that I couldn't even see Mrs. Reagan among them until she appeared at the bottom of the steps. For a few seconds I couldn't make myself move to open the door, I almost thought that if I didn't go into that church and listen to those words of goodbye that maybe somehow Cam would still be alive. I knew that was irrational, but honestly I was grasping for anything to save myself at that moment.

Three hours later the funeral was finally beginning, I was beyond thankful for the chairs the funeral home had provided at the front of the church for family to sit it. I know I wasn't family, but Cam's mom treated me as if I were. Cam's dad was in pitiful shape. A few times I was sure he was going to pass out on the spot. Somehow we all made it through the many expressions of sympathy, even Courtney and Julie came through the line, hugging Cam's parents and siblings, ignoring me. Oh well, I didn't need them anyway. I had been caught off guard when Cheryl was standing right in front of me. She was crying harder than anyone else who had passed by and she didn't just pass me by. In fact, she pulled me into a hug that was so tight I almost couldn't breathe. I heard her whisper in my ear, "I'm sorry for the time you lost with Cameron because of me. I did love him too, but his heart was yours." I began to shake when she spoke so kindly to me, then she continued, "I had forgotten to consider

God in all of that, I got caught up in my friend's quest to win Cameron, steal him from you. I'm truly sorry."

There he was again, God. I had decided that I wasn't so sure he even existed and if he did, he was not on my list of favorites, and might never be.

I didn't recognize the songs that were sung at the funeral, something about strolling over heaven together, which didn't register with me. Then Preacher James got up and started his sermon, somewhere in its message was an invitation to come to Jesus and receive forgiveness and let God become your Comforter. I felt like squirming in my seat, but I forced myself to sit still, if Cam was here and could choose the message for his funeral sermon this would be it. It came rushing back to my mind all those times in the past months when he had almost begged me to believe and accept this stuff. I did feel something, but I was in such grief that I was not sure what I felt.

When Preacher James finished with a prayer and the piano began to play Cam's dad almost levitated off the pew. It was only a couple of feet to the altar and the casket from that front row seat, so he was on his knees immediately. Quickly others piled in beside him, behind him and all around until the altar was full. Cam's mom had gone to join her husband in prayer there. I glanced across the space separating me and Clayton, he was looking at me, I think he was sober. The redness in his eyes this time was from the tears he had cried. It seemed like we sat looking at one another for a long time, one almost daring the other to join the praying throng. Finally I felt myself get up and move the few steps to Cam's casket, it seemed as if the people crowded there had left a spot just big enough for me. I knelt and tried to pray, but somehow my words didn't move past the casket I was leaning on. I think I was praying for Cam to save me, and, of course, he couldn't. If he could have, he would have months ago. So all that time there on my knees I just cried and cried, hoping to extinguish some bitterness, but the more I cried out bitter tears, the more there were. When it was all over and the last of us on our knees had gotten back to our pews the service was completed and we prepared to go to the cemetery.

The sun that had been trying so hard to shine through when we entered the church was nowhere in sight as we came out to get into the waiting limousine, in fact, a cold drizzle of rain had replaced it, which seemed fitting.

I did not go sit under the tent that was set up for the family over the hole where Cam's casket had magically appeared, waiting to be lowered. I stood several yards away from the group thronged around, huddling, perhaps for comfort, or maybe for warmth. Mrs. Reagan had told mama she would take me to her house for a while after the service, so mama and Jamie had not came to the cemetery. I stood alone. I was sure that Mrs. Reagan thought I had some kind of epiphany on my knees beside Cam's casket with his picture sitting on top. I suppose she thought I was one of them now; a Christian. But I knew I wasn't. As for Cam's dad, I hoped he had found whatever peace he could at that altar.

The icy drizzle smacking me in the face didn't affect me as I stood there. The cold wetness mingled with the warmth of my tears until you really couldn't tell one from the other. My hands were numb, which was good considering that I had bitten my nails so far down that all but my thumbs had been bleeding. I knew the pain would make me feel something when the feeling came back after I got warm again. I stuffed them into my coat pockets, out of habit really. My fingers brushed across something scratchy deep inside my pocket. I grasped it between my thumb and first two fingers. I knew before I pulled it out that it was the mistletoe I had hoped to use for a magical Christmas kiss. I felt the bile rise up in my throat again and I turned, sliding across the ice that was starting to slicken the ground, I hurried to a nearby tree and leaned against its trunk as the bile came spewing out of my mouth. I didn't know if anyone saw me or not, didn't really seem to care, because I had just remembered that sometimes you have to feel pain because nothing else can even register. I needed to feel something. So, here I was now with the biggest scar of my life and the deepest pain I had ever felt, and I didn't even have Cam there to talk me through it. How would I ever live without him?

I spent the rest of that day with Cam's family, except Clayton, who had left the cemetery with a couple of guys I didn't recognize. I imagined they might be friends who would take him and get him high so he would not have to feel the horrible emptiness in the world that used to be occupied by Cam. A part of me wished they would invite me to come too.

There was a steady stream of people in and out of the Reagan house all the way into the early evening hours. I know Cam's parents were exhausted but they were so gracious to everyone I could not understand where they were getting such strength. Especially Mr. Reagan, he really must have gotten something special at that altar. As I sat in a corner chair, away from the crowd, I closed my eyes and tried really hard to believe all that Cam had ever told me about God, but there seemed to be a voice screaming in my head about how God, if he existed, was not so great to have taken Cam away from us. No Davider how hard I tried to not hear that voice, I just could not make it go away. When Mr. Reagan finally drove me home a little after 9 I was beyond exhausted. He offered to walk me up to the house but I knew that could be an awkward situation if my dad happened to come outside. I had my seatbelt undone and was opening the door before we had come to a complete stop, as soon as it was safe I dropped my foot onto the ground and started climbing out, "Thank you Mr. Reagan, I can see myself to the door. Thank you for inviting me to spend time with you guys." I slammed the door shut and started walking away because my chin was already quivering and I didn't want to break out in tears in front of him. I'm pretty sure I had seen tears glistening on his cheeks when we drove into the driveway and the street light flooded the interior of the car.

It was after he drove away, and I was left standing there in just the faint light that I realized that I didn't have a clue what to expect inside the house. I had not even seen my dad since the day Cam died, and I hated to admit it, but it was a relief. But I noticed right away that his truck was parked beside my mom's car, so I couldn't avoid him. I was getting shaky on my feet again, though I had tried to eat some from the mountain of food people had left at Cam's house. When I could not put it off any longer I walked up the steps to the walkway then on up to the porch. I could hear the television blaring on the other side of the door before I even opened it, maybe I could use that to my advantage to slip in unnoticed.

As quietly as I could I opened the door, which took me into the room just beside the kitchen, I suppose it was meant to be a dining room, but the only furniture we had in there was a piano and some chairs. As soon as I stepped through the door my mom was coming in from the living room. "There you are. I was just going to call Sally and see if I could come get you."

I didn't respond, I just shut the door and started to walk past her. She would have none of that, as she grabbed my arm as I started by her. "Did you ever eat anything? I've been worried about you."

I wanted to accept her kindness but I was too tired, angry and lonely, I barely replied, "Yeah, I ate. I just need to go to bed now." Then I walked away. If I had not been so self-absorbed I might have noticed the tears glistening in mama's eyes. I didn't even realize I was missing out on the comfort she wanted to give.

The next week at home was excruciating, and it was mostly my fault. Between mama, David and his girlfriend, Madison, Derrick and Casey, they tried everything they could think of to communicate with me, make me smile, even make me mad, any kind of reaction, but I had closed my heart off to them. For once Daddy was my favorite person in the house because he left me alone, and I adopted his angry, bitter attitude. The worst part about the whole thing was that the very thing Cam had spoken to me about last summer was happening....my scars were consuming me.

12

❧

The funny thing about grief and brokenness is that it can cause you to harden yourself more and more as the days go by. And it can cause you to push away the people you need to be clinging to. I was a prime example of those things. Every day I hardened my heart just a little more, I wouldn't even return Mrs. Reagan calls, or go visit them. It would be much too difficult to hold onto the hard exterior if I went to the last place I had ever seen Cam alive. That was the place where he had held me and kissed me and tried somehow to let me know that I was going to be facing horrible days. But, no matter how a person hardens themselves there is no getting around the fact that people crave people. That's why it was so easy for me to accept the invitation to a party at my co-workers apartment. His name was Jeff, he was in college, and he seemed to be everything that Cam had not been. Even his looks were totally opposite. Where Cam had been blond blue-eyed and beautifully handsome, Jeff had black hair and dark features and he was ruggedly attractive. The word "cute" would never apply to Jeff. It wasn't the first time he had invited me to a party. In fact, he had flirted with me constantly since I started my job. Once I had Cam to be my reason for turning him down, now I had none. The Saturday evening after Cam's funeral I was looking for any distraction, so when Jeff came out of the stock room to invite me to his party I did not hesitate to tell him I would be there. He wrote the directions on the back of a receipt which he pulled out of his pocket, and he winked at me when he handed it to me, smiling around the toothpick in his mouth. "You won't be sorry." He walked away after that, leaving me with the strange thought about how he never dropped that toothpick when he was talking.

The three hours remaining before we closed went by quickly, I guess because I was actually nervous about having agreed to go to Jeff's apartment. I had read over the directions a couple of times, and curiosity made me flip the receipt over, that's when I discovered it was for beer, a lot of beer. I had not had much to do with alcohol, except the time when I was 11 and I went with my cousin to babysit and she knew where the key to the liquor cabinet was. She introduced me to vodka and orange juice that night and I hated it! Three quick swallows was all I had choked down. The thought that I might consume some beer in a little while was scary and thrilling at the same time because I figured at least getting drunk might help me turn off the voices in my head, and just maybe I could stop missing Cam for a few minutes.

The stock crew always left right at closing time, but the floor employees had to straighten their departments and count up tills if they had a register that night, so Jeff left before I did. As I was straightening up the shelves in the housewares department I decided that I was not going to show up at his apartment by myself. There was a good chance that there would be some kids from school there, and everyone knew I didn't fit in with that gang. The other partiers would no doubt be Jeff's college friends, no way was I going to go walking in there like a special guest. I was ready to just go home and lock myself in my room.

Twenty minutes later when I walked across the parking lot toward my mustang I noticed a small Toyota truck parked beside me. I didn't know who it was until I got closer. Jeff was climbing out as I walked up, "I thought you would never come out. I waited so you can follow me to my place." He smiled, but something about his face made me shiver in a way I had never experienced with Cam, maybe it was the cold late December wind. I barely heard him continue when he said, "I didn't want you to chicken out on me."

"I would have if you had not waited." I admitted. I found that there was a tiny thrill in me somewhere because he wanted me to be there enough to wait. "You lead, I'll follow."

The Towers Apartment Complex was not too far away from the department store, it was a small town after all. I realized right away that it was on an alternate route that would take me home. When I pulled into the parking lot I was glad to see a lot of cars, it would be easier to blend in that way on the off chance that one of my parents drove by. I had called my mom and told her I was going to Jamie's for a while. Then I called Jamie to tell her she was my cover story. Of course she wanted to know where I was really going, but I lied as easily to her as I had to my mom.

It was a dark night and there was not a lot of illumination in the parking lot, the lone street light was at the opposite end of the complex, which made it almost impossible to recognize any vehicles, so I was going "blind" into this party. By the time I got out and walked a couple of spaces over to where Jeff had parked, he was already out and reaching across the side of his truck to get the boxes of beer he had bought. Seemingly from nowhere a couple of guys showed up and gathered some of the boxes that Jeff couldn't carry. I told them I could carry some, but one of the guys laughed and said, "Babe, the first time is free. No buying, no carrying, just drinking. The next time you will have to chip in a few dollars."

The three of them started walking toward the last apartment on the end lower level, which was the obvious choice, considering there was music blaring from its depths and the door was standing open. It was like a flood light in a small radius. I stayed right on Jeff's heels feeling anxious, and a bit like I might throw up. When we got inside I saw that the place was packed. Immediately I saw Drake and Bobby and I wanted to turn around and leave. But Jeff had already set down the three twelve packs of beer and was suddenly at my side with his arm draped across my shoulder. "Gang, in case you don't know, this is Andrea and she is my guest. Looks like my good old roommate got things started before we got here, hats off!" He said tipping an imaginary hat with his free hand. A guy I had never seen before gave a little salute and started walking in our direction.

"Andrea, this is Ted, the greatest roommate ever, besides me, of course, now, get this girl a beer!

Almost magically a chilled can was thrust into my hand, with the tab already gone. I hesitated before taking a sip because I was not sure how it would taste, and I really did not want to embarrass myself by not being able to handle it.

"Well, look who the cat dragged in."

I spun around quickly and probably would have fallen if Jeff had not been anchoring me with his arm around me. As I knew before I looked, Courtney and Julie had just walked in. I figured Paige was around somewhere too. Courtney walked over to stand right in front of me and Jeff, "What are *you* doing here?" She asked disdainfully. Before I could answer she continued, "What would sweet Cameron think if he saw you here?"

I felt sick to my stomach, I couldn't believe that anyone would be so insensitive, not even Courtney. It took every ounce of self-control I could muster to ignore her. Turning away I brought the beer to my mouth and tilted my head back, my throat moved impulsively to swallow the liquid. I gulped at least four times before Jeff pulled the beer away and said, "Slow down, I don't want you throwing up!" Around the room a few people were chanting "Chug! Chug!"

I decided to listen to Jeff and I drank the remainder of the beer a little slower. I discovered pretty quickly that I did not really like the taste, but the heady rush that I could feel beginning somewhere was delicious. I eagerly accepted the next chilled can that was pushed into my hand.

I lost count of how many cans of beer I drank. It got to the point where I actually thought it tasted pretty good. My head was buzzing excessively as I mingled through the apartment. Even in my light drunken state I was glad that I had arrived at the party as Jeff's guest because I'm sure Drake or Bobby would have been a nuisance otherwise. Courtney seemed to be giving me a wide berth after the altercation earlier so I was feeling alright. At some point people started to leave, and in what seemed like a matter of minutes everyone was gone except me and Jeff. Even Ted had disappeared. I stood up from the couch a little too fast as I was getting ready to go home. I swayed backwards and plopped right back onto the couch. Almost immediately Jeff was there beside me, "You aren't leaving yet, are you? You were my special guest this evening. Don't you think I at least deserve a kiss?"

Suddenly I felt repulsed by him, he still had the same smoldering good looks, but in that moment my mind was screaming that he was dangerous and he stood for everything that Cam had not. When he slid his arms around me and leaned his head to kiss me I squirmed to get out of his embrace. Suddenly I was transported back to a picnic table in the dark with a fumbling man trying to do unspeakable things to me. But Jeff's lips were soft and my head was in such a haze that I lost the will to struggle against him. I went limp in his arms as he kept kissing me. I'm not sure how things happened as quickly as they did, but the next cognizant thought I had we had progressed to a bedroom, and the door suddenly opened and I heard Ted say, "Oh, excuse me, I didn't realize you were..ummm, busy." He chuckled just before I heard the door shut again. I was humiliated and feeling so dirty in that moment, I was not fighting against Jeff at all, but inside I was screaming for him to stop. A tear slid from the corner of my eye and I finally whispered, "Please stop." Maybe he paused for a moment, but then he said, "Oh, sweetheart, it's too late for that. You know you want this as much as I do."

13

✤

A few weeks after that night at Jeff's apartment I was in a rhythm of school, work and parties. The problem was I wasn't putting much effort into school and my grades were suffering because of it. I was faithful to show up at work because I had the car payment, but things were getting difficult there because I felt some kind of way that I could not really explain after my encounter with Jeff, yet I had gone back to his apartment a couple of times, and one drink would always lead to another until I had no reservations about anything that happened behind closed doors. Some mornings after I would still be in a hazy buzz and wouldn't even remember the night before, but when the buzz wore off I always felt dirty and ashamed. Sometimes I would imagine Cam's voice talking to me about scars and somewhere inside I knew that a scar had happened in my life with Jeff, but I felt like I had no power over it, but it sure had power over me. I pushed those thoughts of Cam away as quickly as I could every time they tried to fill my mind because I could not stand to think of what he would think of me if he were alive. That inevitably led me to me to think that if he were still alive I would not be drunk every weekend and doing all those things that I would never do sober. So I surmised that it was all God's fault because He let Cam die, every time that thought came to mind I moved farther and farther away from Him.

I hated the way I felt every day, and to make Daviders worse, Lucy, one of my friends from work who was older and already out of high school, developed a thing for Jeff, so I was on her blacklist. There were days when I went to work that no one spoke to me except the manager.

I quit my job at the department store the day before Valentine's Day, no notice, I just laid my name tag on the counter as I walked out that night and told Mr. McCormick, the manager on duty, that I would not be back. It seemed like everything in my life was in shambles, where I had friends at work before, I just felt so alone. Honestly, I thought back to the days following Cam's death when my mom and Jamie had me on suicide watch, and I wondered if that might be the best thing I could do. To make matters worse the trouble with my dad was escalating, if I happened to be off on a weekend when he was home, he and I could not even be in the same room without emotions running over like a volcano erupting. I started going to Jamie's house every time her mom and dad said I could. Her dad was my mom's brother Paul, he was one of the nicest people I had ever met, I often wondered why my dad couldn't be more like him.

It was a Friday when I quit my job, the next morning when I told my parents that I had quit, daddy went through the roof. That was our worst encounter since the evening he came to Cam's house and picked me up. Mama was so afraid for me that she called Uncle Paul and asked him to discuss with Aunt Janet the possibility of me moving in with them for a little while. That Sunday morning I packed a few things and drove to their house, which was only about two miles away. That night I confided in Jamie and I felt for a few minutes like I had a real best friend. She listened to me pour out my heart for three hours and she didn't judge me for the things I had been doing, and she didn't think that I deserved to be treated the way daddy treated me. I think that time with Jamie should have been a turning point in my life, but I had become pretty good at sabotaging myself, so it was only a matter of time before I would mess up this chance. It didn't make things any easier that Jamie and her family were church goers, and it I was under their roof that meant I had to go too. Between trying to hide my secrets and not wanting Jamie to become like me I figured it would only be a short while before I would need to find another place to stay, or go back home.

Fortunately I was able to get another job pretty quickly, at a local seafood restaurant called Pauly's. I had somehow managed to keep all my grades above failing, except English, so I had something to work toward.

My first day of work at was the Wednesday after I walked out of the department store, I had no intention of going to Jeff's house anymore, considering that I had heard that he actually took Lucy out on Valentine's Day, and apparently he really liked her, that hurt just a little, but they could have each other for all I cared. Even my attempt at indifference did not stop the scar from digging a deeper hole in my heart.

There was only one other high school student who worked at Pauly's, her name was Beverly, she was a sweet girl, who had only been working there for a week the day I started. The manager's name was Ilyana, but she told me to call her Yana, there were three other employees, Ethel, Janice and Jack. Ethel was 58 years old and was the best cook in the place, Janice was her 35 year old daughter, who had never been married, and Jack was her 27 year old son, who had also never been married. They were an unusual bunch, but I needed the job, so I decided I was just unusual enough to fit right in with them. I suspected right away that Jack might be gay, which was ok with me. I mean who was I to judge anyone? He seemed nice enough and willing to mind his own business, so I could look the other way when he and his 'friend' had a rendezvous in the corner booth.

One of the best things about working at Pauly's was that none of my coworkers knew anything about me, Beverly went to a rival high school in the neighboring town, so she didn't know many people from my school, which made it easier for me to put the months since Cam behind me. I could pretend that the nights with Jeff had never happened, and since I was living with Uncle Paul's family I most likely would not have bruises to explain. I thought this was the best thing to happen in my life in a long time, that's why it really caught me off guard when the train I was riding started to get shaky on its new track.

The second Friday night after I began working at Pauly's Yana invited me and Beverly to go hang out with her after work. I suppose we should have thought that was a strange invitation, considering that Yana was 36 years old, the same age as my mom, but Beverly didn't seem to have many friends, and though Jamie and I were close, she was actually dating a nice guy and spent most weekend evenings with his family. That is how

Beverly and I ended up going with Yana to a party at a fraternity house at Stockwell University, she had several cases of beer in the back of her car, it suddenly made sense to me why so many students, especially guys, from Stockwell, stopped by Pauly's so often. Of course I had partied with a few people from Oakdale Community College, but I was a nervous wreck when Yana parked in front of the huge house with a wide front porch that spanned the front and disappeared around both corners. When Beverly grabbed my hand and whispered, "Please don't leave me alone in there!" I realized that she was more afraid than I was.

End of Part 1

Part 2

14

I wasn't sure if the room was as dark and smoky as I thought it was, or if it was the effects of the alcohol I had consumed. One thing I was sure of was that the music blaring from speakers I had yet to see was much too loud. The hangover headache I had grown accustomed to over the past five months was hitting even before the drunkenness wore off. Through the haze of my intoxication, and the dimly lit atmosphere in the frat house great room my eyes scanned. I was looking for Beverly, or Yana. Beverly and I had been initiated into the college party life by Yana Finch a few months earlier. She was our boss at Pauly's so we had willingly gone, but we had no idea that we would find ourselves in this predicament. When I didn't see Yana or Beverly I decided to just go outside and try to clear my head.

I literally staggered across the room, bumping into the occasional partier. I noticed a girl whose name I could not remember, she was dancing on the bar. I had been in that same spot a few times myself. I wanted to shake that image though, because I had given too much of myself away in this place. I'm not even sure why I kept coming back, except Yana seemed to expect it.

Finally I made it outside onto the wide porch. It was a nice May night, no clouds to block the light from the full moon. I walked around the corner, following the porch, which actually encircled three sides of the sprawling two story cabin-like house. I thought, again, of the wealth of most of the guys at the fraternity. It was the most prestigious fraternity at Stockwell University. The guys were well known for philanthropic endeavors in the community, as well their full engagement in campus life through sports, the arts and other areas. The sad thing was that those same guys were using their position to rob a lot of young girls of their innocence. Of course, most of them didn't bother to ask how old you were when you showed up at their parties. If you had the right looks they didn't even care who invited you, or if you were just crashing.

I eventually found a lounge chair all the way at the far end of the backside of the house. It was in the shadows enough that I could almost hide there. I settled back against the cushion and swung my legs up on the seat. A wave of nausea swept over me. I closed my eyes and willed the wave to pass. I hated to throw up. Just the thought of it took me back five months to that December day when Cam was buried. And there he was right back inside my head where he still lived. I had tried to let him die more times than I could count, doing everything I could think of to kill his memory. The very fact that I was sitting there in a drunken haze would destroy him if he knew. Absent mindedly my right hand went to the upper part of my left forearm, rubbing furiously at the scars there. I did not cut myself anymore because those scars are much too visible for prying eyes. Instead I wounded myself with my own words and attitude about myself. I did a great job of avoiding Courtney and her entourage for the most part. But she did get in a good jab the few times I did see her. And I let myself believe the ugly things she said about me, even doing everything in my power to make them true. The scars were building and I was reminded once again of the conversations Cam and I had shared about scars. I suppose it was inevitable for him to be right back in my mind. He was there even during those nights when I got so dangerously intoxicated that it was a miracle I was still alive. I had lost count of how many times I had woken up draped across my bed, still clothed and wondering how I even made it home. Always crowding behind that was how much I still needed Cam. I had not thought about God much at all.

On this particular night at the frat house I had stopped drinking before I lost cognitive ability. I suppose I wanted to remember and try to figure out how I got here.

The first three weeks after Cam died I was basically on suicide watch. Between my mom and Jamie I never even had a minute alone. One or the other of them literally went to the bathroom with me, even sat on the toilet when I took a shower. I guess they had good reason to worry because I did try. I suppose I should be grateful that they cared enough to be there for me. A light breeze blew across my shoulders; I shivered.

"Hey, are you cold?"

I almost jumped off the lounge chair. I didn't realize there was anyone around. "No, I just, no, I'm not cold."

"I've seen you a lot recently at the house haven't I?"

When I didn't respond he continued in a smooth baritone, "I guess I should introduce myself, just in case you don't talk to strangers. My name is Andrew Harrison, call me Andrew." He extended his hand, which was visible, illuminated by the moonlight.

I thought for an instant of my brother, David, and how he had rescued me more than once in recent months. Maybe I should call him to come and get me now. Reluctantly I took the strangers hand, still not verbally responding as he spoke again, "You're one of Yana's girls, aren't you?"

"My name is Andrea, and I'm not anyone's girl, whatever that means." My reply sounded cold to my own ears, but I didn't care. I had come outside to be alone, and I didn't want any smooth talking Casanova interrupting my solitude.

"Hey, I didn't mean anything by it. You do come here with Yana, don't you? I've noticed you...a lot."

Despite my resolve to not be affected by a handsome guy's obvious attention, I couldn't deny the adrenalin rush that made my pulse begin to race. For some reason that I could not comprehend I had no trouble attracting the attention of boys, and yes, men. Many of the guys in the fraternity were at least 21 years old, and I had even noticed men who had to be near my dad's age. I was not yet 17, so I could really cause trouble for the fraternity if I told the right people.

"I'm not really interested in being noticed tonight. I don't have a ride until Yana is ready to go, so I found this quiet place to be alone." In my words I basically admitted that I was one of "Yana's girls."

He didn't reply right away, but he didn't walk either. Instead he stood there looking down at me while I was looking up at him in the dim light. Finally he said, "Are you sure you don't want to come back inside? There are more private places in there than party central in the great room."

I was very well aware of the "private places" inside that house and the thought of revisiting any of them made nausea rise up inside me. "I'm not interested, and I'm not sure if I am supposed to thank you for whatever this is, but I really just want to be alone right now."

"Ok, I get it. I could drive you somewhere to get you away from here. I haven't been drinking this evening, so I think you will be safe with me."

The thought of getting away from this place was just what I wanted so I didn't hesitate, "I would owe you one if you could just take me to my car. I left it at Pauly's."

"Pauly's it is, with perhaps a stop by Holy Grounds Coffee House to have a strong black coffee." He said brightly.

I had heard of Holy Grounds before, but I did not go there. I knew it was a hangout for church people, or I thought it was anyway. It seemed odd leaving a party where underage drinking, among other illegal activities were happening to go to a Christian coffee house. But I found that I was intrigued by Andrew Harrison, and I realized that since he had been talking to me I had not once thought of how much I missed Cam.

I told Andrew that I didn't even want to go back inside to tell Yana and Beverly I was leaving so he said he would make sure someone let them know. Honestly I didn't care if they knew or not. The more I had thought about how Andrew referred to me as "one of Yana's girls" the less comfortable I was feeling about it. It almost made me feel as if Yana was running some kind of escort service. I shook off that thought as Andrew returned. I had far too many other things to occupy my mind than to start creating new stuff.

Within ten minutes Andrew and I were headed down the long, winding drive that separated the fraternity house from the main road. His vehicle was a Jeep Wrangler and he had removed the top since the weather was nice and mild for May. The wind whipping through my hair actually seemed to be helping my head clear.

At the end of the driveway Andrew turned left toward Oakdale, which was only about 10 miles away from Stockwell. An open-topped

Jeep was not the best place for conversation so neither of us spoke as the miles disappeared beneath the wheels. A short time later Andrew braked to a halt in a parking spot very near the entrance to Holy Grounds. I didn't move as he hopped out and walked around the front of the Jeep toward the door, he looked back over his shoulder, "Aren't you coming? I think coffee would be good for you before you drive yourself home."

"I'm not so sure about this place. I'm not exactly a church girl, you know." I was glad for the cover of night because I could feel the blush coloring my cheeks.

"That doesn't matter. Come on. There won't be a lot of people here this time of night anyway." He had walked closer and now extended his hand to help me out of the Jeep.

I reached out and grasped his fingers and it felt like electricity. I would have thought that I imagined it, except his sudden intake of breath told me that he had felt it too. All of a sudden I didn't know where this was going, but I was curious enough to wait and see.

The interior of the coffee house was bright compared to the dim light outside. I actually expected it to be dimmer, but the rest of the atmosphere was about what one would expect. There were sofas everywhere, as well as coffee tables and oversized footstools. Several area rugs marked different seating sections. A pool table dominated one corner, where I saw two guys obviously enjoying a game. I saw a bar along the back wall, though the menu on the wall behind it had no alcoholic beverages to offer.

Andrew had been right about there not being many people there, besides the two playing pool, two were seated on barstools in a stage area strumming guitars. The only others I saw were three girls on a sofa near the back. I heard several of them greet Andrew and I realized that he was no stranger to this place. I found myself wondering if he might be a Christian like Cam had been. I wasn't sure if I hoped he was, or hoped he wasn't. I felt a pang of guilt then because that was the first time I had thought of Cam since I met Andrew Harrison.

Andrew ordered two straight black coffees, when they produced two steaming cups he took them both and lead the way to the most secluded spot in the place. It was a café table with a couple of chairs. Andrew quickly set the mugs down and pulled one of the chairs out for me. I was taken off guard by his kindness and tears started to form at the back of my eyes. I blinked several times to keep them at bay. I was confused by this guy who had come out of nowhere and awakened something in me that I had not felt since Cam. He had rekindled to ability to feel something, I still wasn't exactly sure what I was feeling, but I felt myself smiling as I said, "Thank you." I had not smiled in months.

"So, Andrea, tell me about you." Andrew said between sips of coffee.

I really wasn't ready to spill my life story there at Holy Grounds so I diverted the request back to him, "You first."

My hands were hugging the mug of coffee sitting on the table in front of me, it was almost slow motion as I watched Andrew's hand slide across the table. He extended his index finger and rubbed it across the side of my hand. There was that electricity again. I had to concentrate to keep from grabbing his hand, I was suddenly feeling vulnerable, like I might be about to lose myself in someone else yet again. I didn't think I would even be alive this long after Cam died, so the thought of putting that much of myself into another person scared me to death.

Andrew Harrison, senior at SU, set to graduate in two weeks, and I am employed by the college as well." As he spoke his finger continued to caress my hand. It was hard to keep my focus on what he was saying. I was not proud of the things I had done since Cam died. I had willingly done a lot of things I was not proud of at that frat house. Of course, that was made easier by the fact that Jeff had so easily stolen my innocence with no regard for how it would affect my emotions. That was something I could not get back and I hated to think of what Cam would think of me if he were alive. But if he was alive I would not be doing the things I was doing. I might even believe the stuff in the Bible Cam had shared with me. Instead all I thought about God was if he was real I did not like him very much.

Suddenly it seemed as if Andrew Harrison was pushing me toward dangerous territory. It was probably wrong, as Cam would say, according to Gods standards to be so free with my body, but it was almost easy when you were emotionally detached as I was. If Andrew was interested I would probably not put up much of a fight. Even as I thought that I wondered if a lightning bolt would strike me as I sat in Holy Grounds, about as close to church as I was going to get.

I finally responded to Andrew, "Wow, you're a senior, that's cool! What do you do at the college?"

"I'm a student recruiter actually." He replied.

"Student Recruiter…is it appropriate for you to hang out at frat parties where underage kids are drinking alcohol, and a lot of other stuff is going on? I mean those guys are not as squeaky clean as the image they project." I was very frank.

"Did you ever think that maybe I was there to rescue someone… maybe even you?" He gently loosened my fingers from the mug and grasped them in his hands. I didn't know what to think of this guy in this moment. Cam had been a kid. Andrew was a man, probably 23 or 24, that frightened me somehow.

"So you don't live there? I asked, trying to stay in the moment, and not imagine his lips on mine.

"Not anymore. I have a house down by the Oakdale River."

"Hmmm, sounds nice."

He suddenly let go of my fingers and grasped the sides of his chair to slide it closer to mine. A small shiver traveled up my spine as he settled himself. He was so close I could feel his breath on my face, yet he leaned in even closer. "I am intrigued by you, Andrea, and I want to get to know you better. Honestly, I want to kiss you, but this is not the time, nor the place. I also don't think this feeling is one sided."

I blushed under his scrutiny as his eyes held mine, "You should know something about me." I whispered, I was going to tell him I was only sixteen, but I heard myself saying, "I'm seventeen, but I will be eighteen soon, just thought you needed to know that."

My admission did not seem to affect him.

After that we finished our coffee and he took me to Pauly's to get my car. By then my buzz had worn off so driving home would not be a problem. I was sure Andrew would kiss me before we said our goodbyes. I had not decided if that thrilled me or terrified me. I guess I would find out.

When we pulled into Pauly's parking lot I saw that mine and Beverly's cars were not the only two there. In the spot right beside my Mustang was Jack's truck. I wondered why it was there, but it only registered briefly as Andrew carefully turned into the spot on the other side of my car. He was out of the jeep and on my side to help me out in no time. I felt special for the attention he was giving me.

As I climbed out of the jeep and feet hit the ground I was standing face to face with him, of course, he was quite tall compared to my short frame, so I tilted my head back to look at him, "Thank you for the ride, the conversation and the coffee."

The street light in front of my car was shining right down on us and I did not miss the movement as his head dipped toward me. His lips found mine, unresisting and ready. It was the first kiss I had meant since the last one I shared with Cam.

Just as quickly as the kiss began it was over, Andrew hugged me against his chest for a moment then pulled away. "Until next time", he said. He pressed a piece of paper into my hand, "Call me, I'll be waiting."

I clutched the paper in my hand, maybe I would call him, maybe not, but I didn't want to lose the only chance I had if I decided I wanted to. Andrew climbed into his jeep as I slid into my Mustang. Then he was gone. I sat there for a moment, trying to decide if the past couple of hours had actually happened, or I had imagined them.

I was startled when a shadow appeared in my peripheral vision. I turned to see Jack standing by my car. I let the window down, "Jack, you scared me to death! What are you doing hanging around in the parking lot?"

"I ssaw you."

His speech was slurred so I knew he had been drinking, and he had not gotten coffee to sober up. "You saw me? What are you talking about?"

"I saw you giving that pretty boy a kissss. Why don't you ever give me a kiss?" His hands were reaching into my car window. "Jack you're my boss! I don't think this is appropriate." I exclaimed.

"Like all that stuff you do at the frat house isss?" He sounded like a hissing snake.

"I thought you were gay?" I asked, thinking of his special friend named Justin who often came into the restaurant. The two of them would sit in a corner booth holding hands across the table and whispering.

"Oh, we're not exclusive. Justin and I have an open relationship. Guys, girls, it doesn't matter. I've had my eye on you since you started working here." By this time he was practically climbing through my window.

I shrank back into the seat as far as possible. The smell of alcohol wafting between us with every breath was making me gag. "Jack, I don't want to see you lose your job. Get out of here and we will pretend this never happened."

"Oh honey, I'm not gonna lose my job. But you best be getting home now, too late for a pretty girl like you to be out and about by yourself." He pulled himself back out of the window, stumbled backwards. I thought he would fall down, but somehow he righted himself. "I've got my eye on you little girl. This isss not the last of thisss."

I quickly put the window and started the engine. Keeping my eye on him I backed out of the parking spot and headed home. With the coffee, the sweet kiss from Andrew and strange encounter with Jack, I was completely sober.

Going to sleep proved to be a problem as I could not stop thinking of Andrew Harrison and that kiss. Of course I thought a little about how to handle what happened with Jack, but that was not pleasant thinking so I left it alone.

I don't know how long I lay there thinking, but sometime in the predawn hours I realized that Cam had not been on my mind since Andrew approached me on the porch at the frat house. I reached in the darkness to the nightstand where I had left the paper with Andrew's number written on it. I suppose I just wanted to make sure it was still there. I was pretty certain that I would call him sometime.

15

I was a little apprehensive when I went to work the next day. I didn't know if Jack would be working. I was not eager to see him after last night. I hoped he would not mention it, because I had decided I wouldn't.

As it turned out he wasn't there, but it was almost as hard facing Beverly and Yana considering the way I had skipped out of the frat house last night.

"I'm surprised to see that you chose to show up for work." I guess I deserved the sarcasm dripping from Yana's words.

Beverly was quieter than usual. She hung out by the cash register even during the lull in business that came just before closing. After I finished cleaning the deep fryer I went to talk to her. "Hey Beverly, you're quiet. Are you ok?"

I thought she was going to burst into tears as we stood there. Instead she shook her head and pushed past me and hurried down the hall toward the bathroom.

I was almost afraid to find out what had happened to upset her so much. She was better at holding out than I was and for the most part her innocence was still intact. I often wondered why Yana continued to insist that she go to the frat house. I suddenly felt the need to know what had her so upset so I headed to Yana's office to ask her. The door was ajar as I approached and I heard Yana talking to someone, on the phone I surmised. Something made me hesitate outside the door to listen.

"I know she is inexperienced, but she is fast learner. I suppose Eric figured that out last night after the hour he and Beverly had together."

I had a sick feeling in my stomach when I heard those words. I started to storm into the office, but Yana started talking again, so I paused mid-step. "I know Andrea was part of the deal, but you better control the guys who show up at those parties if you want me to keep bringing my girls. It was one of your former frat brothers who left with her, you know?"

In my peripheral vision I saw Beverly come out of the bathroom and move toward the front of the restaurant. I knew she needed me, so I would get an explanation from Yana later. I spun around and hurried to Beverly.

She was getting her purse from under the counter when I stepped up beside her. "What happened last night Beverly, I need to know. I'm sorry I left without saying anything, but I just had to get away from that place."

There were no tears in the brown eyes that turned to look back at me, but there was a sad lack of life. Whatever happened had devastated her. "Eric…." She whispered in a hauntingly sad voice.

"What about Eric? Did he hurt you? If he did we have to tell Yana?"

"Tell Yana what?" I was startled to hear Yana's voice. She had approached without a sound. "There is nothing to tell, except that Beverly and Eric…got acquainted last night."

I knew exactly what Yana was implying I also perceived that Beverly had not consented to anything. I was angry at myself for ever letting things get this far. "Yana, how can you cater to those guys? Look at Beverly. Do you see what this has done to her?"

"Why don't we change the subject and you tell us where you disappeared to? Maybe your friend would not be in this predicament had you not left her to fend for herself."

I blushed and angry red, how dare she turn this on me. She was the adult who had taken a 16 year old girl and 17 year old girl to a party where drugs, alcohol and sex freely flowed.

"Please tell me you don't think I am responsible for what happened." I said to Beverly.

She never replied as her eyes diverted to look at the floor.

"I had to get out of that place Beverly. I felt like I was drowning. I'm so sorry. I think I'm done with frat partying."

"You have no idea how much trouble I can cause for you if you don't settle yourself down, little girl." The malice in Yana's tone chilled me to the bone.

"Yana what is going on here? I feel like I've stepped into the Twilight Zone."

"Don't you know that we are Yana's girls? We have been for months. It's just that the customers have decided to step up the services they want rendered." Beverly said flatly. I blushed when she said that because I knew that the guys I spent time with were getting anything they could possibly want. A part of me wanted Beverly to believe that I was still holding out as she had been. She was a year older than me, but even with that fact, nothing that went on inside that frat house was right.

That phrase from last night went through my mind again as I remembered Andrew asking if I was one of Yana's girls. The blood drained from my face as realization hit me. Beverly and I, and no telling how many of the other girls at those parties, were nothing more than escorts. I often wondered how I got myself into such situations. Was I really that naïve, or just plain stupid?

Whatever we had become a part of I was ready to confront Yana. She was the one who had taken us down this path.

"Yana, you let Eric take advantage of Beverly. How could you do such a thing? What about the problems we could cause for you? You've been taking two minor girls to wild parties for months now, even encouraging us to get drunk. Not to mention what goes on behind closed bedroom doors. I'm pretty sure you have broken a lot of laws."

"You don't know anything sweetheart. You are one of those girls who somehow attract men like flies. I don't think you even realize the effect you have, but I do. The only thing holding you back is a bent toward shyness. The alcohol and occasional pills take care of that, though I don't want a junkie on my hands. The way I see it I am helping you as much as you are helping me. Besides I am a respected business owner and very involved in community affairs. I'm not worried about any kind of trouble you think you can cause for me."

"Owner," Beverly and I said at the same time. "Yes, I not only manage this place, I own it, and I have connections in the community. I really don't want anyone to get hurt, and no one has to. This is just an arrangement among friends."

If Yana really thought Beverly and I were not getting hurt she was lying to herself.

Beverly and I looked at each after a short pause, the question hanging in the air between us of how did we get involved in something like this? Oakdale was a small town where you just did not expect to get caught up in some sex-for-hire ring, especially not when you were still in high school.

Yana turned and walked away. I suppose she was satisfied that neither of us would say anything about the illegal activities she had dragged us into. I guessed that she was right, neither Beverly, nor I knew enough about the law to be sure we would not end up in jail. Just thinking such a thing made me uncomfortable, and unfortunately, my next thought was that I just wanted to get drunk or high, anything to get my mind somewhere else.

"Do you want to go hang out? I asked Beverly because I didn't know what else to say.

"No, I just want to go home and pretend the weekend never happened. Actually I would like to pretend the past few weekends had never happened. I can't believe Yana got us involved in such a horrible mess. I want to ask my parents for help, but now I feel so ashamed and dirty. If my mom knew what happened last night it would kill her, and my dad would be ready to go after Eric."

My instinct was to put my arms around her as she finally shed a few tears, but when I tried she pulled away. "I can't....just don't. I have to figure out how to process this on my own."

After that we finished the closing process and left, walking out together, yet so far apart. Now the only person who could be an ally for me was pushing me away and creating her own little shell.

Sleep did not come easily that night as my mind raced with scenarios that could get us out of the predicament that held us captive.

16

The next few weeks passed in much the same way as the previous weeks. Every weekend we were taken to the frat house and expected to perform in whatever way the guys wanted us to. I lost count of how many guys I was with, some of whom I never even knew their name. It also did not take long to figure out that not all of Yana's "clients" were students. The deception ran deep in that house.

Once I thought back to my first time with Jeff, I never saw him anymore and I was sure he had no idea how much damage he had done to me. Maybe he wouldn't care if he did know. If I had not still been reeling from the loss of Cam the whole scene may have never happened. Or maybe God knew I was that kind of girl and that it was only a matter of time before I hurt Cam. I surmised that God was probably just protecting Cam from me by letting him die. So it really was my fault he was gone after all. Shame tinged my cheeks with color as I recalled that night at Jeff's. When Ted opened the door I so hoped he would put a stop to what was happening. Of course he didn't, his laughter still rung in my ears. When it was over Jeff made me get dressed right away and told me to leave, but not before he convinced me that I had been willing. Just thinking about it all reminded me that the formation of another scar was formed that night, and it hardened my heart more and more. I could barely hear Cam anymore, pleading with me to believe God. A sudden strange memory of a story Cam had told me came to my mind. It was about a woman who was a prostitute, but God forgave her and gave her a new life. I think I really needed that, but I just could not believe.

The complicated things going on in my life made it almost impossible to be normal in any way. Things became strained at Uncle Paul's, mostly with Aunt Janet who wanted to put me into the same mold with Jamie and her brothers. They were all good students and never gave their parents any trouble. Then one Saturday night Jamies's boyfriend was out of town and she wanted to hang out with me after work. I told her to just wait outside and I would come out as quickly as I could, but she came in to go to the ladies room. I didn't want Jamie to meet anyone I worked with, especially Yana. I didn't want her to find out about the frat parties, I was so ashamed. Yana was standing out front when Jamie came out of the restroom. She stopped to talk to me, "I hope you have an idea about what we can do tonight. I've already seen both movies that are playing.

"Just wait outside, I'll be out soon." I was trying to get her out of there.

But she turned to speak to Yana because she was nice like that. "Hi, my name is Jamie, you must be Andi' boss."

"Yes, I am Yana Finch." She smiled. Looking like a barracuda. "Aren't you lovely?"

"Jamie, please wait outside. I'll be out soon." As I spoke I took her hand and propelled her toward the door.

"Andi, you're being rude." Jamie protested.

To my consternation Yana was following us step for step toward the door. "Jamie, would you be interested in a job here at Pauly's?"

"No, she doesn't have time to work with her class load and sports, right Jamie?" I quickly replied.

Jamie gave me an angry look before conceding that I was right, "Andi may be rude, but she is correct. I couldn't possibly get a job now. But thank you for the kind offer."

"If you change your mind," Yana said as she produced a business card from her pocket.

"Thank you. Andi, I'll be waiting outside."

Finally Jamie was gone and I could breathe again. But Yana was not finished. "A new girl, she would go over well at the frat house."

I clinched my fists so tight my hands hurt. "You won't be able to get to Jamie. She has a boyfriend and she is very close with her parents. If you try to drag her into your schemes my Uncle Paul will intervene."

Yana did not reply she just gave me a chilling look then turned to walk away. I relaxed my hands even as I wondered why I could not stand up for myself as I had done for Jamie. I suppose it was because I did not think I was worth it. I decided that night to go back home. I had been at Uncle Paul's for three months and had rarely seen daddy during that time. Maybe he and I could have a fresh start. But I knew for sure that I would do whatever it took to protect Jamie from Yana.

The next morning was Saturday and I figured that was a good time to go home. I got up early, while everyone else was still sleeping. I stuffed my clothes in a bag and walked out of Jamie's room. Before I left I found a piece of paper and wrote Jamie and all the family a note. I thanked them for letting me stay a while then I lied and wrote that daddy had apologized and really wanted me to come home. I attached the note to the refrigerator with one of Aunt Janet's magnets and then I was gone.

I drove the two miles home quickly and tiptoed into the house. Daddy was a flea market junky and I was glad to see his truck was already gone. Everyone else was still sleeping when I slipped in so I went straight to my room and crawled into my bed. The familiar blue comforter reminded me of the picnic Cam and I had shared one time. I had packed a basket, grabbed this very comforter and we walked through the woods behind my house until we found a clear, secluded spot. We had that time without fear because my dad had been gone out of town. We spent quite a bit of time just talking and laughing and holding hands. I could see it all so clearly, and I imagined I could smell Cam on the comforter even though it had been washed. I buried my face in my pillow to cry. It was the first time I had let myself cry like that since Cam's funeral. I cried until my throat hurt, and I thought I might be dehydrated because eventually my tears stopped flowing. I knew that my face was red and swollen from all of that crying, in fact my eyes would barely stay open they were so swollen. So I just closed them and lay there, exhausted and craving someone to come and tell me that December 21 had been a horrible dream. But, of course, that would never happen. Finally I slept. Real deep sleep, which rarely came to me without nightmares, but this time I may as well have been dead because I knew nothing.

When I woke up I was surprised to find mama lying on the bed beside me. She had pulled my head on to her shoulder and her arm was wrapped securely around me. I stirred, and would have moved, but she pressed my head back down and put her lips against my hair, "I'm sorry I'm not stronger. I should be able to protect you and to help you heal, but some days I'm barely holding on myself."

I gulped. I was not used to such honesty from mama, because I never got still long enough to allow her to be tender. I felt much too vulnerable, I grabbed her hand in mind and whispered, "Mama, none of this is your fault. It just is what it is. I hope it is ok that I came home. I will try my best to stay out of daddy's way and not make him mad. I just couldn't stay at Uncle Paul's anymore."

"I missed you very much. So did Casey and Derrick. David did too. I think perhaps your dad missed you too. He just has some demons he is dealing with and for some reason they rise up whenever you are around."

"Do you think I am evil Mama?" I asked, afraid she might say yes.

She pulled her hand free of mind and stroked my cheek, "Absolutely not. I don't think your dad is either, but there is something that both of you have to deal with. The hard part is figuring out what it is." She paused as if choosing her next words carefully, "I don't think either of you will be truly alright unless you allow God into your life."

I stiffened in her embrace. The last thing I wanted to hear about was God. If he was real, and as good as some people seemed to think he was why wasn't he helping me? Of course my next thought was that I would not let him help me if he tried. I pushed that thought away, broadening the scar tissue covering my heart a little further. "I don't need God, Mama. I just need some new friends."

Mama sighed heavily after I said that, then she kissed me on the head and released me as she sat up, "I won't push the issue. But you better believe I am praying for you."

Mama got up from the bed and started for the door, pulling back at the last minute she produced a slip of paper out of her pocket and held it out toward me. "I found this on your nightstand a few weeks ago, I don't know why I took it. Maybe this phone number belongs to someone who can be a new friend."

I took the paper and nodded at mama. She opened the door and went out, leaving me alone again. I unfolded the paper, knowing already that is was Andrew Harrison's phone number. I wondered if he had thought of me at all since that night in May. I remembered he told me that night that he was graduating in two weeks, it was August now, I figured he was a college graduate well on his way with the career he had begun at the university.. As for me, I had barely passed all my junior classes, and would be starting senior year in just over a week. Did I even dare call him now? I had looked for him at the frat house every weekend since the night we met, but he had never been there. Finally I crumpled the piece of paper and tossed it toward the trash can across the room. It hit the rim and bounced onto the floor behind the can. That is where I left it.

The remainder of August passed by quickly. I had decided I wanted to try harder at school. I still had to keep my job to pay for my car, so I kept going to Pauly's and playing Yana's games. No matter how I tried to avoid making daddy angry, that was one part of my life that was inevitable. He was more verbally abusive than he had been before, and the physical outbursts continued as well. Between the cuts and abrasions he gave me and the faint evidence of the cutting I used to do I was somewhat covered in scars. It was ironic to me that Cam had been so desperate to make sure I would not let my scars destroy me. The fact was every new scar was the only thing that made me feel alive anymore. I still tried to push aside thoughts of Cam, now thoughts of Andrew were there too; he was just another impossible dream. To be honest, I don't know what kept me from taking a hand full of sleeping pills and walking into the woods for an eternal sleep. Somewhere inside me there had to be a voice screaming, "There is always hope!" The question was, would I survive until hope revealed itself.

17

When football season began at Stockwell University home game Saturday's, business was extremely busy. One such day in late September I was working the kitchen while Beverly was running the front, the flow of hungry customers was nonstop. I peeked out the serving window every now and then to see if there were any breaks. At one point I was taken off guard when I saw Andrew Harrison looking right back at me from the other side of the window. I almost dropped the shrimp dinner I had in my hand. I saw Andrew mouthing something to me, but I wasn't exactly sure what, so I told Jack I needed a quick break. I set the shrimp dinner in the pick-up window and hurried toward the door which opened into the hallway. I hated to see Andrew while I was wearing the ugly brown uniform required at Pauly's. I was glad that we had the option of a cap instead of a hair net.

I walked down the hallway, half afraid that Andrew would meet me there, and the other half afraid he wouldn't. Then suddenly he was right there in the middle of the hallway in front of me.

"Hey there, aren't you a sight for sore eyes?" He smiled and my pulse quickened. I'm sure he could see the artery in my neck moving as his nearness made me giddy.

"Hi." My voice came out in a husky whisper, which was unintentionally alluring. I could tell by the look on his face that Andrew was feeling the same emotions that were surging through me. He wants to kiss me right here in the hallway at Pauly's, I thought. Or maybe I want him to kiss me would seem more accurate.

"I really hoped you would call." He sounded disappointed.

"I...I wanted to, but things have gotten hectic around here." In that moment I felt so ashamed for the time I had spent at the frat house. My mind raced, wondering if I really had had no choice about doing the things Yana expected of me.

"What time do you get off?" He asked.

"We close at 9 o'clock. Clean-up usually takes about 45 minutes, so it will be close to 10."

"I'll be waiting in the parking lot if you want to talk." Immediately after he said that Andrew leaned down and kissed me on the cheek and whispered in my ear, "I can still taste your lips." Then he was gone. I wasn't sure how I was going to make it through the next hour and a half with such anticipation.

I saw Andrew's jeep parked beside my Mustang in the farthest corner of the parking lot as soon as I came out of the restaurant. I had deliberately hurried out ahead of the others. I really hoped Andrew would want to get out of the parking lot before anyone even realized we were gone. I was glad that Yana was not working that night, and Jack had a late evening planned with Justin, which kept his mind off of me. I wondered if I would ever get the place where there was not so much chaos in my life. Maybe Andrew represented a start.

I practically ran across the parking lot, carrying my boots because I didn't even take time to put them on. Andrew was climbing out of his jeep as I hurried up. I quickly opened my door and threw my work clothes inside as I said breathlessly, "Could we go somewhere else to talk? I don't want to hang around here."

"Sure, get in." He replied.

I scrambled around the front of the jeep and hopped in the passenger side almost toppling over into the driver's seat in my haste.

Andrew chuckled a little and asked, "Whoa, are you in a hurry to get out of here because you don't want to be seen with me?"

"Oh, that's not it at all. I just don't have anything in my life right now that isn't someone else's business, and I sure I would like to have something that no one else knows about."

"I can understand that." He replied as he started the engine and sped out of the parking lot.

I didn't ask where we were going because I really did not care. I was willing to go anywhere to get away from Pauly's and everything, and everyone that reminded me of my life for the past nine months. I did not want to invite thoughts of Cam back into my mind either. First I would start to miss him, and I could not take the ache. Or I would feel dirty and guilty, and shameful because of the person I had become, I just wanted to get away.

A few minutes and a few turns later I realized we were headed toward the Oakdale River. I remembered Andrew telling me he had a house down by the river. I was, at once, excited and afraid that he was taking me there. Of course there was nothing innocent left in me, but I was hoping that getting me into bed was not the first thing on his mind. As much as I remembered his sweet kiss, and wanted more of them, I knew I needed to distance myself from any of the things I had been doing.

The road by the river was very dark that September night, the moon was hidden behind thick clouds, so the only light came from the headlights on the jeep. My eyes stayed focused on that light as it splashed in front of us on the road. I did not want to let that darkness get to me. It was silent inside the jeep, I wasn't sure if Andrew wanted to talk yet, and I had no idea how to start a conversation.

We turned left on a narrow gravel road, which was almost hidden by trees. I assumed it was his driveway. It was somewhat of an inclined road which went on for about a half mile. Suddenly we drove out of the trees into a wide open place where a neat house sat perched atop a small knoll. There were outside lights which illuminated the house enough to where I could get a good look at it. There was a staircase ascending from the circular drive where we had stopped. It led to a porch that stretched all the way across the front of the house. We took our time going up the stairs, still not speaking. As we stepped onto the wide porch I noticed two wicker chairs and a sofa. Andrew grasped my elbow lightly and led me toward the half glass front door. We paused as he produced a key and unlocked the door. "I'm glad I put a couple of logs on the fire before I left earlier. It's nice and toasty in here." Andrew finally broke our silence.

My eyes wondered around the room, it was very nice, with lots of wood and stone. It was furnished with brown leather furniture. I was impressed with his taste. The enclosed glass fireplace was situated in the center of the room and was usable from both sides. I had never seen anything so nice and I suddenly felt out of my league.

I had moved to stand near the fireplace, letting the warmth seep into my bones. I was not aware that Andrew had moved to stand right behind me until I felt his arms come around me, pulling me back against him. I felt my pulse quicken and suddenly I did need not the fireplace to warm me up. I closed my eyes and just enjoyed the sensation for a minute until Andrew released me without warning.

I swayed on my feet and almost fell backwards before I caught my balance.

"I'm sorry Andrea. I did not bring you here to take advantage of you. I really do want to talk, to get to know you. You have not been far from my mind since we met."

I turned to face him. I needed to see his face. I had learned a few things about reading people in the past few months, and I just wanted him to be telling the truth. What I saw on his face told me that he meant what he said.

"Why didn't you call? I was sure we had made a connection that night, but when I didn't hear from you I figured I had been wrong. Now here we stand and I can see your heart beating in your throat, and I can see you as a vulnerable little girl whom I want to hold and protect…and eventually love. I know you feel something too."

I swallowed the lump that had formed in my throat and stifled the tears that threatened. It was futile, but I couldn't help thinking how much I wished I could go back to the day after that night and call him. I couldn't believe where I had allowed myself to get to. I was afraid that when I told him how very used I was he would send me away and never want to see me again. It never occurred to me before that moment to wonder if I was part of the reason he had not been back to the frat house since the night we met.

"I'm not a little girl." I finally said.

"Of course you're not." He said, "I just meant that you seem fragile somehow, as if you need someone to protect you."

"Is that what you want to do? Protect me." I asked.

Andrew extended his hand toward me. Without hesitation I slipped my fingers into his. I wasn't sure if I wanted to admit that he was right about me needing a protector, but his strong hand felt good holding mine.

"Come, sit down." He said, gently pulling me toward the sofa nearest the fireplace.

After we were seated I commented, "I haven't seen you at the frat house since the night we met."

"I haven't been back there since that night."

"Why?"

"Because I kept thinking about your comment about how inappropriate it was for me to be there, in that setting, with other non-students. As an employee of the college I need to act with more wisdom than that."

I pondered that for a moment, wanting to reply with the right words. Finally I settled on a straight forward approach, "Not going there yourself is not enough. Aren't you accountable for what you know? And you know all sorts of laws are being broken behind those walls."

"I'm not judge and jury. I can only control myself. Therefore, I will not be going back there. I managed to graduate with honors and I got a decent raise in pay at my job. I don't plan on jeopardizing my career just as it is set to take off."

I could tell I had offended him, and I really wished I could take my words back, except I knew I was right. Someone needed to put a stop to the junk Yana was exposing us girls to, someone with more credibility than me. I figured this was as good a time as any to tell Andrew how far things had gone.

"If you really want to protect me then you will do something about Yana. It seems like she has me by the throat, and I have no choice but to do whatever she tells me to. But it isn't just me, Beverly, and no telling how many other girls are being used there every weekend."

"How did this conversation take a turn like this? I wanted to get to know you to see if we have a connection. Can't we just forget about frat parties and illegal activities for a while?" He sounded frustrated.

"I wish I could forget. Actually I wish I could erase all that has happened. But, of course, wishes are for fairytales. I don't know what you think you are going to find out about me, but let me just begin with a cold dose of the ugly truth. "My pulse had risen as I willed myself to maintain eye contact with him. I wanted to see his reaction when I spilled out the ugliness. "I lost my virginity to a guy I used to work with. He has barely spoken to me, except for a few words the other nights I spent in his bed. The night I met you I was looking for some way to change the direction my life was heading. I was sick and tired of losing more and more of my self-respect inside that frat house. After you took me away that night, Beverly....well, I can't go there, but let's just say her innocence died somewhere in that house. After that Yana became much more aggressive in the way she presented us at the frat parties. I truly never realized that we had become "call girls", but I have lost more pieces of myself in that horrible place than I can count. I'm not proud of any of it. Honestly I could throw up thinking about it. I suppose the only good thing is that I never invested my heart at all. I don't think I am exactly the girl you are looking for."

I had watched Andrew's face the entire time I was spewing out that information. I saw more than one emotion displayed amidst his expressions, but I honestly could not read him, and I had no idea how he was going to respond.

Silence hung in the air, even as all I had confessed seemed to crowd between us on the sofa. I tried to tear my eyes away from his face, but I needed to know if I was going to find the redemption I was longing for in him.

After a few moments he closed the distance between us, except all that stuff was still there, threatening to suffocate me. He never said a word as he cupped my face in both hands, then his head dipped toward mine and I knew he was going to kiss me. I wasn't sure how that was supposed to make me feel, but that primal instinct that had become such a part of me pushed any rational thoughts from my mind. When his lips touched mine they responded. I think he was caught off guard. Maybe he thought I would kiss like a proper seventeen year old girl should, but my experience overrode my age.

It began with a kiss by the fireplace, the next thing I knew I was waking up beside him in his bed. He was sound asleep. I just lay there looking at his face. Tears stung the back of my eyes because I wanted to think that being with him was different than all those other times with other guys. On the surface I began to believe that delusion, but deep down I knew this was not going anywhere good. The question was how long would it take for it all to fall apart.

I guess Andrew felt my eyes on him because he woke up suddenly. I quickly averted my eyes, feeling strangely shy.

"Hey there," He said lifting his arm to invite me closer. I accepted his invitation, sliding close to nestle my head on his shoulder. He pressed his lips against the top of my head and whispered, "You are amazing, and I would like to just keep you here, but I'm sure I better get you back to your car so you can get home before your parents send out a search party.

I didn't move to get up right away, neither of us did, we just enjoyed a few moments. If I could have frozen time right there it would have been fine with me. I knew he didn't love me, and I wasn't even sure I had the capacity to love any more, but it was easy to pretend, even for a few moments that I was exactly where I belonged. I had not felt anything close to happy since I lost Cam, but in that moment at least I felt content.

Finally I shifted up to lean on my elbows, "Will I ever be back here again Andrew?" I asked, afraid to hear his answer.

He stroked my shoulder with his fingers, allowing them to slide down my arm to trace the light pattern of scars just above my elbow. I tensed. I was afraid he would want to know about those scars. But he never asked. I was glad too, because those scars were mine and Cam's conversation. I wasn't willing to share that with anyone.

We got up and got dressed after that and he drove me back to Pauly's to get my car. Neither of us said much during the drive. I wondered if his thoughts were similar to mine in any way.

I expected him to drive away as soon as I got out of his jeep. Instead he got out and came around to meet me before I even got my door open. Reaching down he took my wrist and turned it so that my palm was facing upward. He dropped a piece of paper then closed my fingers around it, "Here's my number again. If you don't hear from me, use it this time." He lifted my hand and kissed my knuckles, "Until next time." His breath felt tingly on my skin as he spoke.

I was at a loss for words as he walked backwards to his jeep and climbed in. I said, "Until next time." I shoved the paper into my front pocket. He started his engine and began to pull away. "I won't be going to the frat house anymore. I don't care what Yana says." My words were drowned out by the roar of his engine, but I really wasn't saying them for his benefit. Those were a promise I wanted to keep for myself.

It was almost 4am when I slipped in through the door at home. My nose twitched as I detected the faint scent of cigarette smoke, not like smoke that had settled, more like smoke still hanging in the air. I was afraid for a moment that my dad would step out of the shadows and ask where I had been, or just start hitting me. But he didn't, so I tiptoed down the hall to my bedroom. I was glad it was Sunday and I didn't have to work, I was exhausted for a lot of reasons.

18

I was still tired on Monday when I went to school, but I was in a different frame of mind. I had been a straight student all the way through ninth grade, but I had neglected my studies so much I barely passed eleventh grade, and things were not great this far into my senior year, but at least I could finish strong.

Beverly was, of course, a year older than me, but her parents had asked for her to be held back in first grade, so she was in her senior year as well, and had transferred to my school. She and I had first period together. She was already in the classroom when I walked in. With a few minutes before the bell would ring I hurried to the seat in front of hers. She almost looked nervous to see me. "Hey Beverly, we need to talk sometime today."

"You bet we do," she whispered urgently, "Something is different about you. I can see it in your eyes. I just don't want to get caught in the crossfire if it has anything to do with Yana."

"You won't," I said with more confidence than I had a right to.

Beverly and I planned to meet in the parking lot after school. She and I both had work that evening, and I really wanted to talk to her before we got there. If I didn't have a car payment I wouldn't even go back to Pauly's. I was sure Yana would not give me a good reference for another job, so I was stuck there. But I would not continue on with things as they had been for the past months.

"Where did you go after work the other night? Yana was not too happy when you didn't show up at the party. She had some new guy lined up for you." I had just walked up beside Beverly's car when she asked.

I had decided to tell her enough about that to keep her quiet, but I wasn't sure I could truly trust her and I did not want to cause trouble for Andrew.

"I went to that Christian coffee house with that Andrew guy again."

Beverly chuckled sarcastically, "Christian place! Weren't you worried that the ceiling might cave in on you?"

"Yeah," I agreed with a fake chuckle of my own. "And I decided that I am not going back to that frat house any more. If I ever want a nice guy like Andrew to like me I have to make some changes. I don't care what Yana says either. I know I probably can't make any real trouble for her, but I can squeal so loud that I become a nuisance for her to have to deal with."

Beverly looked incredulously at my face, her look almost made me lose my confidence, but I knew as sure as I was standing there that I would rather die than go back to that awful place.

"You don't think she will let you walk away with no questions asked, do you?"

"Of course not, I plan to tell her that I'll keep my mouth shut if she will just leave me alone. As far as I see it we are all responsible for our own salvation from this situation Beverly. I'll be here for you if you decide to walk away too."

Beverly chewed on her lower lip, a habit I had noticed in her when she was nervous or upset. "Don't worry. I won't let Yana know that you knew about my plan. I don't want to see you get hurt, but I am going straight to her office as soon as I get to Pauly's, if nothing else, just wish me luck."

I hugged Beverly then. In other circumstances she and I may have been normal teenage friends going to the mall and blushing over stories of our first kiss. But Yana had stolen such things from us. I did not want to be responsible for getting Beverly out of this mess, but I did want her to be ok too.

Less than an hour after my talk with Beverly I was sitting in Yana's office, with only her desk to separate us. My palms were sweaty and itchy as nerves almost got the best of me. From somewhere in the past I remembered how much Cam believed in prayer. Of course, I had no right to pray. I didn't even know how, but I gave it my best effort as I thought, rather than said, "God, if you're there please help me be brave."

Without pausing then to notice Yana's stern face, I plunged ahead, "I am not going back to the frat house anymore. I want more for my life than I see happening right now, and, as I see it, I am the only one who can do anything about it. I am not interested in causing you any trouble, though I can squeal pretty loudly and be a big fat nuisance if I have to. The truth is, though, I don't have the energy to do that. I'm just tired of existing the way things have been. It's that simple. I am done."

I was breathing heavy, my chest rising and falling noticeably when I finished talking. I could not read the expression on Yana's face, so I wasn't really sure what I would hear. Her response took me by surprise.

"I have no problem with your decision."

I almost fell out of my chair at her calmness. It never occurred to me to give God the credit for it.

That was it. Nothing else was said on the subject. Yana just told me to get to work because my shift was already fifteen minutes old. There were not words to describe how I was feeling as I worked that shift. The closest thing was that I figured this was how it felt to be a normal teenager with an after school job. I knew I had homework, and for the first time in a long time I was focused on getting home to work on it.

I could tell Beverly wanted to ask me what had happened, but she was so afraid that Yana would get angry that she never approached me. Part of me wanted to tell her to go boldly into the office and tell Yana the same thing I had, but I needed time to get my own feet firmly on the ground. I needed to learn how to be strong. After all, the killer in horror movies often appeared to be dealt with only to rise again at the very end. I would not feel like I was out of the woods until time passed.

19

The next few months were the most pleasant I had known since the summer I spent with Cam. I still ached every time I thought of him, and I probably always would. But I had seen Andrew at least one day out of every weekend since the night he took me to his house the first time. For those moments Cam was not at the forefront of my mind. It seemed that we ended up sharing Andrew's bed every time we were together. But I was good at convincing myself that it was ok, because our feelings were so strong for one another. How could it be wrong?

I had been working really hard at school and earning good grades, but I still had no real direction for my future. I was just enjoying the time with Andrew and cruising through every day. I could think about the future another day.

It was the first weekend in May when Andrew told me he wanted to host a cookout at his house and actually invite some of his friends so I could start getting to know them. I was anxiously excited as the weekend approached. I bought myself a new outfit, a pretty skirt with a strapless blouse. Of course, I also got a thin sweater to wear because I didn't want Andrew's friends to see any trace of the faint scars on my arms. Time was causing them to fade, but I knew if anyone saw them and asked about them I would feel all those old pains all over again.

I drove to Andrew's house a little early to help him prepare for the cookout. I was in a happy place as we worked side by side, singing along to every song that came on the radio, that was something that he and I shared, we both loved to sing. I had never been brave enough to let anyone hear me sing until one day when Andrew and I were riding in his jeep and I was harmonizing with the singer on the radio. Andrew turned the volume down to just loud enough for me to hear, he encouraged me to continue so he could hear me. He was so encouraging and many times after that day he and I spent some of our time together singing. He even taught me a couple of songs that he learned at church. He and I sounded pretty good together. I was even thinking I wanted to go to church with him. It was the first time I had thought about God in any way for a while. I also thought then of Cam and I remembered that long ago day when he and I had been alone at his house and anything in the world could have happened. I was certainly willing because I loved Cam very much. But he had pushed me away after a passionate kiss explaining to me that God had a good plan for sexual relationships. I didn't understand, though he tried to explain that it was meant for married couples only to share with one another. I suddenly felt ashamed and guilty standing there in Andrew's kitchen, only feet from his bedroom where we usually ended our dates. I was confused because Andrew went to church, he talked about it sometimes. So I could not understand why Cam wanted to save our purity while Andrew had no such desire. How could two Christians feel so differently on the same issue?

I did not realize Andrew was behind me until I felt his breath in my hair as he lightly kissed the top of my head. I felt a familiar shiver go through my body. I swayed back closer against him.

"We could take a quick run through the bedroom before the others get here." Andrew whispered in my ear. Again I shivered, only this time it was different because I really wanted to just be in his company with good conversation, food and friends. Why did it always have to come to this?

I slid away from the counter where I had been preparing a salad and was out of his reach before he could react. I moved to the opposite side of the island and faced him across it. "I was thinking about church." I said nervously.

I wondered if I imagined the color draining from his face, or if it really had, as he broke eye contact with me. "What about church?"

"I want to go with you some time. We could sing the song we have practiced together so many times. I think we have great harmony."

He still did not look at me. Instead he focused his attention on the knife I had been using to make the salad. He picked it up and began slicing a cucumber. I watched the knife slice through easily and thought of the scars on my arms again. I wondered, not for the first time, why Andrew had never asked about them. I usually did a good job of keeping them covered, but I was sure he had seen them. . Maybe I had never really meant enough to him that he would even notice.

"Yeah, sure, that would be great." He finally replied, though he did not sound convincing. I decided to believe him anyway, so maybe one day it would happen.

A short time later I heard the sound of vehicles approaching. Suddenly my stomach was aflutter with nerves.

The next three hours were some of the hardest I had ever endured. It didn't take long to figure out that I did not fit in with Andrew's friends. They were all older, all but one had already graduated from college, and the other would soon. They all obviously went to church with Andrew as well. When that subject came around Andrew blushed, the brightest red I had ever seen when I said, "I hope to join you guys at church sometime." The only response was a changing of the subject.

The rest of the evening was a blur for me. I couldn't wait for it to be over. By the time his friends left around 10, I had already washed the dishes and cleaned the kitchen.

Andrew came into the kitchen. I was pretending to wipe the sink to avoid turning to face him. He came up behind me as he had done earlier. I shoved him backwards as I spun around, not willing to let him touch me. Part of me wanted to make him talk to me, but the other part dreaded what he would say.

He stumbled a bit when I shoved him because it caught him off guard, by the time I got across the room he had righted himself. "So, this is it. I suppose I've been expecting this for some time now. After all, you and I are from two different worlds aren't we?"

"Are you breaking up with me?" I asked, as stone-faced as I could muster.

"Breaking up? Hmmm, I hardly think we can call it that. Have I really ever committed myself to an actual relationship with you?"

I digested his question, searching my mind for every moment we had spent together. I had to admit that he was right. No relationship had truly been established. It just hurt so badly to realize that I had only been a good time physically for him. "How can you say that? Maybe you never actually asked me to be your girlfriend, but what else could we call what we've been doing. You call me up and invite me over. You cook for me. We sing together, and you lead me to believe that I could come to church with you and sing."

"Come on Andrea, you had to know that none of that was going to happen. I enjoyed our time together and may even call you in the future. But, well, to be honest you can't really sing great anyway. You would just embarrass yourself."

I could not believe the coldness in his tone, and the harshness of his words. Just like that my heart received another scar. What nerve he had to suggest that he might call me again in the future!

"Oh, by the way, so you won't find out some other way, "I have been seeing someone for a few weeks. She is a great girl. My mother introduced us." He said smugly.

"What? Why did you even ask me to come here this evening? You've been seeing someone for weeks? How many times have I been in your bed since you met this great girl?" I willed myself not to cry.

He actually blushed at that. I locked my eyes with his and almost dared him to look away.

"I honestly don't know why I asked you to come…if things were just different, it might work for us. But you are 17 and struggling to even finish high school. I just graduated from college, with honors, and I have a job on staff at the college. How could we ever make this work?"

"Did you think I would give you one more good time for the road?" My chest was heaving with anger mixed with pain, and the effort of not crying.

There was no verbal reply, just two sets of eyes locked in confusion. As odd as it seems I felt compassion, or pity for him in that moment, which took me by surprise. But I could see the war going on in his eyes, and only imagined the turmoil in his mind. I think I knew then that I would feel the sting of this for a while. And it may keep me from trusting my heart to someone again, at least for a while, but he was going to be stuck with the decisions he made based on what his parents and everyone else thought. I was thinking that his prison was going to be more confining than mine in the long run.

I left after that and it would be the last time I ever walked into that house. Strangely I felt a resolve inside that I could do something with my life. I don't think I would have gotten to that point if this whole scenario had not happened.

With only a month left in my senior year, I finally went to the guidance counselor's office to see what options a girl like me might have for going to college. I half expected to find out that I had no options and be sent away. I was more than pleasantly surprised to find out that Miss Conway truly wanted to help students get somewhere with their lives. She even told me a little about herself and how she got through college with a lot of hard work in the classroom, as well as working a clerical position at the college she attended to pay her own way.

I have to admit it never occurred to me that I could get away from Pauly's until Miss Conway told me she would help me get my foot in the door at Oakdale Community College. She told me that was my best option for getting the first two years of college until I decided exactly what degree I wanted to pursue.

20

It was over a year later when I fully realized what a difference that one conversation with Miss Conway had made. If I could go back and talk to her right after Cam died I would, but I really had no time for regrets. Life was going to happen whether I was ready for it or not. Somewhere along the way I had begun to understand the conversations with Cam about scars. It had taken almost two years to begin to realize that I played a big part in how much the scars of life would control me. I often wondered if Cam had some sense that he was not going to be around to protect me.

A month into my sophomore year at Oakdale Community College I was doing better than I ever imagined. I was getting good grades and had found a job on campus, which got me away from Pauly's for good. I had made some new friends, but none too close, I had to protect my own heart and I was determined to keep the rest of it intact. Despite all the good changes I still had struggles. I could not get past the way Andrew had hurt me. I wanted to admit that I was as much to blame as he was, except I really didn't believe that. I had given him all of the heart I had left after Cam and he had rejected it. I had struggled to get back enough heart to live life and try to get better. But the truth was that hurt would mar every attempt at a relationship I might make. Of course, I had not tried to pursue anything of a romantic nature since the night I walked out of his house. I thought I had a handle on the drinking that I had used to numb me during the frat party months, but I found that at least once a week I retreated to alcohol for a few moments of forgetting. On those days I sometimes also sought out a guy to be with. That was not usually a problem. There were always college guys ready for a good time with no strings attached. I was glad not to invest my heart.

I figured if I could just keep working hard at school that maybe my momentary lapses in judgment with alcohol and men would not hinder my future hopes of getting scholarship money to continue my education. I was hoping to get a Business degree, though sometimes I wondered who I was kidding to think I could actually accomplish such a thing. I rarely spent any time with my family, which seemed to be the best thing for everyone. For some reason I was a trigger for my dad and he often got so angry when I was around that he just had to let it out. I had gained a few more scars from those moments. But I would do whatever was needed to keep daddy from turning his anger on anyone else. I was happy for David, who had started working for a building contractor and was doing really well. He was still dating Madison, who had been a constant in his life for almost three years. I hoped she and David would build a life together.

I was lost in thought as I walked across campus heading toward my English class when I realized I was running late. Professor McGinty always started class on time whether you were there or not. I picked up my pace a little. I was practically running when I reached the door of the Thomas C Morgan English Building. I reached for the handle just as the door swung open from the other side. I suppose my forward momentum crashing into the moving door was all it took to knock me off my feet, because the next thing I knew I was on the ground. I literally shook my head for a moment, trying to figure out what just happened. Then I felt a masculine hand touching my arm, and I heard an unfamiliar voice, "I'm so sorry! Are you okay?"

I shrugged his hand off of my arm as I struggled to my feet. In an effort to help me, the stranger was just making my progress slower. "Just get out of my way. I can get up myself!" I exclaimed.

When I had righted myself I finally looked at the guy who had knocked me down. To my surprise he was grinning like the proverbial Cheshire cat, in fact he seemed about ready to burst into laughter.

"I'm glad you see the humor in this situation. First you knock me over, and now," I glanced at my watch, "You have succeeded in making me late for class."

He tried to tone down the grin that was obnoxiously covering his face, but it wasn't working.

"I am sorry, I really am. But, hey since you're late for class already, and I am guilty as charged, maybe I could buy you a coffee to make up for it."

I couldn't help noticing the dimples that creased his freshly shaven cheeks, and the even white teeth that were probably courtesy of an orthodontist. For a slight moment I wanted to accept his invitation, but then Andrew's handsome face was swimming in front of my eyes, and I felt my emotions closing in.

"That won't be necessary. I can go into class late. I don't want to make a habit of skipping class. I've worked too hard to get where I am now."

I started to walk past him then, but his hand reached to gently touch my arm. I jerked away, as if he had touched me with a hot branding iron, which startled him. "I'm sorry, you didn't hurt your arm when you fell did you?"

The sound of genuine concern, paired with the look on his face almost melted my resolve, but the scar covering my heart would not be forgotten that easily.

"No, I'm fine, I just need to go."

"Can I at least ask your name before you go?"

"Andrea," I said on a sigh. "My name is Andrea, and I am very late for class now."

He smiled again. "Hi Andrea, my name is Sully." I almost laughed out loud as the big blue Sully from some kids movie flashed in my mind. I suppose he got that a lot because he said, "No, I'm not a monster."

I suddenly felt like I was allowing myself to get too familiar with this handsome dark-haired, brown-eyed guy. "Well, if you will excuse me, I'm going to the library to do some studying since I'm much too late to be fashionable now."

"You know that offer of a coffee still stands…I mean, if you aren't going to class anyway." I thought I detected hope in his voice.

I'm not sure where the thought came from, but it was there all the same, *"he is just hoping to get you into his bed later."*

I tried to dismiss it, but there was Andrew Harrison in my face all over again. I decided to be rude was the only way to get out of the situation. "I am not interested in having coffee with you. I just want to get back to my day. Maybe I can salvage something."

"Sully," We both turned at the shrill voice.

It was a blond girl, a very pretty blond girl, who made me keenly aware of the fact that I had on no make-up and had thrown on a large tee shirt and baggy jeans, and my own drab hair was in a messy bun. I did not like the self- conscious feeling, so I took the opportunity to get away. "It seems you have a willing coffee date right there." I said it sarcastically then I spun around and walked away.

"Sully, sweetie, I've been looking for you since yesterday afternoon. Didn't your roommate tell you I came by your apartment?"

I heard her words trailing off as I hurried away.

It was easy to walk away, but forgetting the encounter was a different story. I just could not get those dimples out of my mind. My thoughts waffled from thinking he wanted sex, worrying that he didn't and wondering why I didn't offer. He was definitely good looking, and obviously he was interested in me, at least he had wanted to buy me a coffee.

As the days passed I found myself looking for him on campus, or at least hoping we would "bump" into each other again. After a month I was a wreck. I feared that my grades would begin to suffer if I didn't find a distraction to get him out of my mind. I was off work from my job at the campus print shop the third Friday of every month, that day I also got out of my last class an hour early, I should have been grateful for the extra time off, but I just wondered how to fill the time without regressing to my old ways.

I remembered that my mom had an invitation to visit an old high school friend that weekend. With David also going out of town with Madison, and daddy going hunting, I decided to offer to keep Derrick and Casey for her. I knew she had planned to take them with her, but I imagined she would welcome a change of plans.

With those thoughts in mind, I practically skipped to my car. I was already planning a trip to the zoo with the kiddos for the next day. I didn't know why I had not already offered to keep them.

I was humming the song on the radio as I came up our long driveway, humming is the only way I enjoyed music now days since Andrew Harrison crushed my confidence. I shrugged off thoughts of him as I parked my Mustang. I expected to see mama's car, but the only vehicle there was daddy's old truck. I was surprised that he wasn't gone yet. Then I thought I remembered hearing him tell mama one of his buddies was going hunting too. I assumed they had ridden together.

I was a little disappointed to think that mama and the kids had already left. So now I was dreading a long weekend of trying to say sober and not make any bad choices.

I expected to find a note on the counter when I went inside. But there was no note. I tossed my key ring onto the kitchen table as I came in, I watched as it skidded all the way off the farthest edge. "I'll pick it up later." I thought as I went to the refrigerator to grab a bottle of water. I surveyed what was inside while I was getting the water, not much to fix for supper. I would probably go out and get something. After I shut the fridge door I screwed the cap off my water and tilted my head back as I took a drink, I was already walking toward the hallway as I did so. I decided I would take a shower before I figured out what to do. I was half way down the hallway when I realized I should grab some fresh clothes. I turned back to go to my room, a few short minutes later I was headed back toward the bathroom. I was humming the tune to some song that had gotten stuck in my head, when I suddenly realized that I could hear something moving around in my parent's room. Immediately the hairs stood up on my arm as fear twisted the pit of my stomach, but then I thought I was being irrational. It was probably daddy. I covered the distance from the bathroom door to the bedroom door, which was standing ajar. I reached forward to push it open as I spoke, "Daddy, is that.....you" The question died in my throat.

The next few minutes were like a blur as I turned to flee the delicate situation I had seen in my parent's room. I had never seen daddy like that.

Everything was happening so quickly as Daddy came behind me down the hall. I had never seen him in such a bad way before. I had noticed several beer cans on the floor when I opened the bedroom door. I was certain that Daddy was intoxicated. He was completely out of control. All I could think of was getting as far away from him as I could, and quickly. Unfortunately he was determined to not let that happen.

I hurried to the dining room table where I usually tossed my keys when I came in. Grasping for them, I remembered how they had skidded right off the far edge just a few minutes earlier. I leaned forward in a desperate attempt to get those keys. I felt daddy grasp my shoulders from behind.

The next thing I knew was the feeling of my head crashing against the underside of the table. It was like the lights went out as I lost consciousness.

21

It was dark and a little chilly when I woke up. It took me a few minutes to realize where I was. The pounding in my head reminded me soon enough of what had happened between me and my dad. I wondered where he was now. I moved slowly. I was lying in the kitchen floor, right where I must have fallen when I lost consciousness. A slight touch with my hand told me that I had quite a knot on my head. I also felt sticky liquid around my mouth and seeping down the side of my face. Tentatively I touched my lip with my tongue. I knew it was cut. I was almost afraid to touch myself anywhere else. Who knows what other injuries I might find? I had no idea what had gone on after I was knocked out. Now I was terrified that daddy would hear me moving around and come back. I couldn't just lay there, I had to move.

At a snail's pace I tried to get to my feet, I heard the clank of keys. I had reached them just before my head hit the table. I realized I was still clutching them in my hand. After what seemed like an eternity I made it outside to my car. Every moment I expected daddy to grab me from behind and drag me back into the house, but he never did. Once inside my car, I locked the doors and leaned my head against the steering wheel for a brief moment. I was in no shape to drive, but I knew I could not stay where I was.

I cranked my car and painfully pushed the clutch to shift into reverse. My mind was racing as I wondered where I could go. I could go to Jamie's house, but I really did not want to drag any other family members into this horrid mess. Somewhere in the back of my mind I remembered conversations with my friend Natalie. She was always inviting me to join her at the campus church or something. She offered once to let me move and share her apartment on campus. I had been there a few times. Maybe I could find my way there with my head pounding. I decided to take a chance that I would find her at home on a Friday night.

A drive that should have taken me fifteen minutes ended up being almost thirty. It hurt to press the clutch to change the gears and I was constantly looking in my rearview mirror. I was terrified that daddy would follow me. When I finally got to the apartment complex I had to search to find a parking spot and trying to remember which apartment was Natalie's was only making my head hurt worse. Though I really did not know the first thing about it, I had begun to whisper prayers that I would find her at home.

Through the haze in my brain I remembered her apartment number was 112. I slowly walked to the door and began to pound against it with my fist. When she opened the door on the second knock I almost fell into her arms. "Andrea?" It was a question rather than a greeting. I suppose in my current state I was hardly recognizable, I nodded.

"What in the world happened to you? Oh my goodness, let's get you inside." I heard the concern in her voice.

I didn't realize I was shaking until her arms wrapped around me. Then I almost shook us both to the floor. Somehow Natalie managed to guide me to the sofa and there she sat me down. Sinking onto her knees in front of me she said, "Honey, you're a mess. What happened to you?"

I couldn't take the tenderness in her voice, I started to cry. I cried so hard I almost lost my breath, and she let me. I'm not sure how long I cried, but I do know that there was a lot of pain released there in her apartment. Not that I would leave it there. I knew myself well enough to know that I would pick it all back up eventually. But in that moment I had no capacity to hold it.

After a while my tears stopped, and my shaking was under control. Natalie had wrapped her thin arms around me and they felt like a safe place to be, so when she shifted and started to release me, I grabbed her and held on tight. I heard her speaking above my head, "Andrea, I need to get you some medical attention. Your face is a mess of bruises and cuts, and I can feel a huge knot on your head. You might have a concussion. I'm just going to go get my neighbor, Julie. She is a nursing student at Stockwell."

Reluctantly I loosened my grip, embarrassed now that I had even come here and let down my guard. But I was here now, and I did need some help, so I was in no position to argue. Before going to get her friend Natalie brought me a wet cloth. I noticed a faint brown stain on her shoulder where I had rested my head against her, "I'm sorry I ruined your shirt," I said as she extended the cloth to me.

"Oh it's nothing. I can wash it. Why don't you try to clean up a little while I go get Julie?"

A short time later a petite brunette named Julie was examining my wounds. "Did you lose consciousness when you hit your head?"

I nodded.

Her fingers probed my head. Then she was touching my face, I tried not to, but I winced when her fingers grazed the raw skin at the side of my mouth. I think that was where the first punch landed. I knew she was going to tell me I needed to go to the hospital, and I knew there would be questions which I would not answer.

Just as I thought, Julie said, "You have to get to the hospital, I'm certain you have a concussion, at least a mild one. And a couple of these lacerations on your face need some attention."

I thought about protesting, but I just didn't have the strength. "Okay, I will go." I said as I immediately started to stand, "did you see where I put my keys?" I asked Natalie.

"You are not driving yourself. I will take you." Natalie replied.

"I'll come too, since I examined you first. They may want to question me. "Julie offered.

"I'm sorry I came here and got you both involved. It's Friday night, I'm sure you have better things to do than hang out at the hospital."

"That's what friends are for. I am still curious about what….or who, happened to you." Natalie said.

"I'm not answering any questions here, or at the hospital. There is no law saying I have to." I said stubbornly. Not that I wouldn't want to see my dad punished for his actions, but I didn't want to drag mama and the rest of the family through a mess.

Neither of the girls pushed the issue after that, and soon we were on our way to the hospital.

The ER waiting room as not very crowded, but I sought out a chair as far in the corner as possible. I did not want pitying glances or nosy questions. Natalie went with me to sit down while Julie went to sign me in. Of course, I had barely gotten seated when they called me to the desk to answer insurance questions. Already I regretted coming here, and I just wanted it to be over with.

I noticed that Natalie had walked away while I was answering questions, "Where did Natalie go?" I asked Julie.

"She had to make a phone call. She will be back in a minute."

"Who is she calling?" I was immediately suspicious, and nervous. What if she called the sheriff, what would I do?

Julie must have detected the alarm in my eyes. She laid her hand on my forearm and said, "She is calling her friend Sullivan Jeffries. She is really concerned about you and she knows that Sullivan will pray. That's what he does."

I suppose that information calmed me down a bit, except now I wondered why a stranger I didn't even know would be willing to pray for me. But, now, my head was pounding and I didn't even seem to care what Natalie was doing.

A few hours later we were back at Natalie's. It was early Saturday morning, and I felt so bad for having taken so much of the girls' time. They both assured me they were glad to have been there for me. Natalie insisted that I get some sleep in her bed. I was exhausted so I did not protest. Though she would be waking me every hour or so since I had been diagnosed with a concussion. I had stitches above my lip and my left eye. I had gasped when I finally saw my reflection in the mirror. I knew I needed to call mama and let her know something, but I needed sleep first.

As it turned out I slept all day Saturday and into Sunday morning, except for the wake up calls from Natalie. It was almost 11am when I opened my eyes, squinting against the light streaming through the thinly curtained window. It took a moment to remember what had happened, but soon enough the scene was flashing in my mind.

I finally decided to sit up and try my feet on the floor. I was not expecting to be so sore. I felt like I had been hit by the proverbial train.

Slowly I made my way out of Natalie's room. It was not a large apartment. The living area and kitchen were totally open, separated only by a small island. I saw Natalie sitting on a stool by the island as soon as I came into the room. She must have heard, or sensed that I was there because she lifted her eyes from the book she was reading. Immediately she shifted the foot that had been perched against the stool. She stood up. "Hey Andrea, how are you feeling?"

I didn't respond right away. I lifted my hand to my face and felt the thick bandages, with the slightest bit of pressure I winced. "I'm sore." I finally admitted. "Thank you....for the hospital, the bed...everything."

"I can't tell you how glad I am that you showed up on my doorstep Friday night. By the way you had a phone call on your cell last night. It was your mom calling. I didn't tell her much, because I didn't know much, but she was already frantic. She knows something happened. She wanted to come get you but I talked her into letting you rest here."

"I suppose I will have to keep on thanking you....and I'm sorry. I know you deserve some explanations, but I can't give you much right now." I paused. I needed to find out if my mom had mentioned my dad. Mostly I wanted to find out if he was at home. I didn't want to think about him hurting mama or anyone else. "Did...did my mom mention my dad?"

"Come, sit down, we can talk. You look a little pale." She took a few steps toward me and said, "Let's sit on the sofa. These stools are hard to navigate on a good day. I imagine it would be painful for you to climb up there today."

After we were settled on the sofa Natalie spoke, "Your mom said that your dad called to tell her that you had been hurt, though he gave her no explanation as to how. She wanted to know if you had told me anything. I'm just going to ask you outright....did your dad do this to you?"

I averted my eyes immediately. I was glad for the partial covering of the bandages on my face to disguise the angry blush I knew was there. I decided quickly to tell her at least part of the truth. I needed to let out a little of my emotions before I self-destructed. Getting high had crossed my mind already, and I knew that was not the direction I needed to go. "What is said here has to stay here."

I waited until she replied, "of course."

"My dad has a temper problem, and for some reason he sometimes unleashes it on me. Most of the time I have no idea what sets him off so I have no way to prevent his outbursts. He has hit me a few times." I paused, I knew I was downplaying the situation, but just sharing a little was difficult. "Yesterday I....well, I was in the wrong place at the wrong time, and daddy had been drinking. One thing led to another and the next thing I know I was waking up on the kitchen floor in the dark. I vaguely remember the cracking sound as my head hit that table..." I trailed off.

I noticed tears in Natalie's eyes. She reached to take my hands in hers. I had the goofy thought that it was like her hands were hugging mine.

"I'm sorry. I don't know what else to say."

"That's enough. I just don't want dad to hurt mama or Casey, my little sister. He never seems to get aggressive with my brothers."

After a short moment of silence Natalie suggested that I call mama while she fixed me something to eat. I thought mama had been anxious long enough so I took Natalie's advice.

It was awkward talking to mama. I didn't know what daddy had told her, and I really didn't want to go through the ugly story myself. As it turned out daddy told mama that he had lost his temper and hit me a little too hard. He told her he just left after that. He failed to mention that I was unconscious when he left; to be fair, maybe he didn't realize I had been knocked out.

After our conversation I knew I could not go home for a few days. Mama would be shocked to see me in my current condition. I had no real plan of action. I didn't want to stay in a hotel and cut into the savings account I had been working to build. But at least I had that as an option. I figured I could sneak home on Monday to get some clothes.

Natalie had made a large stack of pancakes by the time I finished talking to mama. Suddenly I realized how very hungry I was. I started to eat as soon as I sat down. Natalie bowed her head briefly before joining me. I was embarrassed. "I'm sorry....I didn't pray, or whatever."

"Well, I imagine God understands how hungry you are. And I'm sure He knows you are grateful for the food."

I appreciated the fact that she was lighthearted and did not try to make me feel ashamed.

After we finished eating I offered to wash the dishes, but Natalie refused to allow that.

"I'll get the dishes. You just sit there and talk to me while I do them."

"I already owe you so much. I'm not sure how I will repay you before I leave."

"Are you planning on going home?" Natalie asked as she sprayed the soap off the plate in her hands.

"I think I will stay away for a few days. I'll get a hotel room. I'm not ready to answer mama's questions."

"No you won't. You will stay right here with me for as long as you want."

I was so humbled by her generosity, and to graciously accept it did not feel natural to me. "Oh, I couldn't do that. I've already cost you two nights of good sleep."

By this time Natalie had finished washing the dishes and she came to sit by me on the sofa again. "In case you did not realize this sofa folds out into quite a comfy bed. If you are worried about me sleeping in my own bed, then you can sleep here."

I felt tears burning the back of my eyes. I blinked a few times to hold them at bay. I knew if I started crying again I might spill my whole ugly story right here in Natalie's kitchen, and I was not ready to let myself be that vulnerable and transparent.

"Why are you being so kind to me? I mean, we are friends, I guess, but it isn't like we have been really close."

"I could give you the "bible answer", she said, making quotes in the air with her fingers. "I do want to be the type of person who helps others as if they were Jesus, but the extra truth here is that I have invested a part of my heart in you as a friend. And I always take care of my friends.

I almost flinched when she mentioned Jesus. I really didn't want to go back down that road again. But I had to admit that it was nice to have someone care about me for whatever reason.

"Since I don't really have any good alternatives I accept your offer, but only if I can buy some food or something to help out."

"We can figure that out when it is necessary. Right now I want to ask you to come with me to the Gathering in the Student Services building."

"I'm not sure what that is, but I don't really feel up to mingling right now." I said, hoping she would not push the issue.

"I don't want to leave you here alone, and I have responsibilities there. So I really need you to come with me. You can talk as little or as much as you want. Besides I really want to introduce you to my friend Sullivan Jeffries."

I don't know if she was trying to make me feel guilty, but that was exactly what I was feeling. She had done so much for me already. I did feel as if I owed her something. This was the second time I had heard the name Sullivan Jeffries. I wasn't sure why the thought of meeting him made me anxious.

I suddenly realized that I really did not have anything to wear besides the clothes I had been wearing when I came here. I was actually wearing Natalie's extra pajamas at the moment.

"Before you say anything, I have a closet full of clothes. My mom owns a boutique and even designs many of the things she sells. Obviously you will fit in them. My jammies are just right on you. But, if you really don't want to go, you are still welcome to stay here."

I had to smile because she was learning to read my mind it seemed. Just the small movement of my mouth reminded me of how I must look. But I knew I needed to stop hiding and take some chances. So I told her I would go with her to the Gathering.

She led me to her closet and told me I could choose anything. I was surprised to see the abundance, and all of them were cute and stylish. After a while I decided on a pale yellow dress with a sash belt overlaid with daisies. I had been wearing my white Converse tennis shoes when I showed up on Natalie's doorstep. I found them by the bed. After a shower, where I was careful not to get the bandages wet, I slipped the dress on. It seemed to me that the scars on my arms were suddenly very noticeable. I went back to Natalie's closet and looked until I found a thin white sweater. It would cover the scars and silence any questions. There was that word again: scars; who knew scars were going to be a part of life? After I borrowed a bit of gel for my unruly curls I finally went to find Natalie.

It was almost 4pm when we arrived at the Student Services building.

I hurried out of Natalie's car in order to keep up with her as she walked toward the entrance. I was feeling out of place and awkward. I just wanted to stay near her.

There were quite a few people inside the building. I recognized a few faces, but no one I had any relationship with. Natalie kept walking past the back row, I wasn't sure I wanted to get any closer. I had no idea what to expect here. I grabbed Natalie's arm as I hesitated mid-step, she turned to look at me, "Are you okay?" She sounded worried.

I briefly thought about telling her that I was feeling sick, but that would have been a lie, I was really just uncomfortable.

We had stopped in the middle of the aisle and people were starting to come in, I said, "I think I will sit back here on the last row, I'll be fine back here. You go on. I'll find a seat."

She looked uncertain, I'm pretty sure she was thinking I might leave. I still felt like I owed her something for the last 48 hours of care. I reassured her that I would not leave before the service. Only then did she leave me to take care of her responsibilities. She turned back after a few steps and said, "I want to introduce you to Sullivan afterwards." Several pairs of eyes looked from her to me. I was embarrassed as I remembered the bandages and bruises covering my face. As quickly as I could I retreated to the far left back corner of the seating area. I tried to act calmer than I felt as several people still looked my way for a moment or two. I was relieved when finally all eyes turned away. Then it was my turn to look around. I noticed all those people, most of them in groups, talking and laughing together. I wondered why my life had not led me on a path of being one of those people who seemed so carefree and able to laugh and talk freely with friends.

As the minutes passed a few people actually came to shake my hand and tell me they were glad I was there. Somehow I relaxed enough to feel good about that.

After a while the lights were dimmed way down as the heavy curtain at the back of the stage slid apart. There were people already in place on the stage. The guy playing the guitar was strumming softly as he spoke into the microphone, "Good afternoon, it is great to see so many of you here to worship God and get to know Him better. Please stand if you want to and join in with the worship in whatever way you want. The words to the songs we will sing will be projected on the screen behind me. Please feel free to sing along."

I really didn't pay a lot of attention to what he was saying, as I was transported back a few weeks to the day when I was literally knocked off of my feet in front of the English building. The guy with the guitar who was onstage speaking was the same guy who had tried so hard to buy me a cup of coffee to make amends for messing up my day.

I realized that everyone was standing as the music began and the hum of voices told me that most of them either knew the words already, or they were reading them on the screen. It was a nice song, nothing like I had ever heard at Cam's church the few times I was there. Nor were they like anything I had ever sung with Andrew. Thoughts of those days effectively stifled any desire I might have to join the song, but I did feel captivated in some way I could not understand. There seemed to be power in those words....

"Pour out Your glory Lord. Reveal the wonder that is You, as we strive to seek Your face, oh let our hearts be true...."

I was so caught up in the words that it took me by surprise when I realized I had lifted my arms above my head like many others in the room. Honestly that confused me a little. Self-consciously I dropped them to my sides. I was not sure what had just happened, but it was foreign enough to make me curious and to make me want to run away at the same time.

I focused my attention on the guy leading the group. I remembered his name was Sully. When I thought of that I also had a light bulb moment. Natalie had told me she wanted me to meet her friend Sullivan Jeffries, the funny thing was I certain I already had.

Three songs later we were asked to sit down. The dimmed lights were brightened somewhat and Sullivan put down his guitar and followed the other band members off the stage. They sat on the front row, of course, as another guy came to the microphone. He was carrying a stool which he used as a table, placing the book in his other hand on top of it.

"Thank you Sully, and praise team, you guys are anointed for this time, in this place."

I heard a few people call out, "Amen!"

Then the speaker continued, "Hey everybody! For anyone who

doesn't know me, my name is Colin Harwood. I am the Associate Pastor at Transform Church. We are located in the Greenbriar Plaza, just a few miles from here. I was invited to come speak to you all tonight by Todd Groves, who as most of you know, is the ministry leader on this campus. I have a message that God just won't let me get away from. At the same time, He has not allowed the freedom to share it until right now. So that tells me that every ear in this place better perk up and listen, because God knew you would be here and He gave me the green light. This is for someone, maybe more than one."

There was silence in the room as Colin thumbed through what I assumed was a bible. As he flipped pages he continued to speak. "I am going to speak to you about four different women. And just so you guys won't feel left out, there will be some men in the text as well. If you have a bible great, if you don't that's fine too. The verses will be projected on the screen for your convenience. We will begin in Genesis chapter 34, the first two verses. Here meet a young woman name Dinah, she was the daughter of Leah and Jacob. We will also meet a man named Shechem. We will see how an innocent young woman is violated in the worst way, and how that affected her future.

In the chapter just before this it tells how Dinah and her family had just arrived in the land of the Shechemites, and Dinah had gone out to meet some of the women. Perhaps she hoped to make some new friends. She must have been a people person, outgoing and probably a happy girl. There is not a physical description of her in the few verses telling her story. But there was something about her that caught the eye of Shechem. I believe she was beautiful to look at outwardly, but she must have had something much deeper. After Shechem had defiled her, which is to say he raped her, the bible says his soul was drawn to her and he actually loved her, at least he called it love. For just a bit of Shechem's background, he was the son of the ruler of the land, and he was spoiled. Whatever he wanted he got using his power, or the power of his father. In fact he asked his father to get Dinah for him to be his wife. The funny thing is there is no mention of him ever asking Dinah if she wanted to be his wife. Why should he anyway? He had already ruined her chances at a proper marriage anyway. The outcome of this for Shechem is a story for another day. For now, keep Dinah in your mind, as we move on to the next woman in our story.

The second woman we will learn about tonight is Gomer. Her story lives in the book of Hosea. Hosea was a prophet of the Lord. His name actually means "Salvation", that is no coincidence. Hosea was chosen by God to show Israel a picture of what salvation looks like. It would not be an easy path for Hosea. Gomer was not a very lovely name for a woman, and indeed she was not a very lovely person. She may have been outwardly beautiful, or had some quality that caused her to be desirable as a prostitute, but loveliness is not equated with the outward appearance. Gomer's very name was association with completion of worshiping false gods. There was nothing praiseworthy about this woman. And it seems she had chosen to live up to the name given to her by her parents because she became a prostitute. As is the way of God, He sent a redeemer to save her out of that lifestyle. That was the calling God gave to Hosea. Possibly the only true godly man around in his day, and God not only made him a prophet, he also told him to marry Gomer. Hosea obeyed and he married her, gave her a home off the streets and took care of her. Can you imagine how grateful she was? All of a sudden she was respectable. But her struggle was real. Maybe it was a bondage that needed to be broken in her spirit, a lying voice that told her that was all she was. For whatever reason, after years of marriage, long enough to have three children, Gomer took off and returned to her old profession.

As the story of Gomer and Hosea continued, there came a time when Gomer left Hosea and the three children she had born to return to her life of harlotry. But God instructed Hosea to pursue after her again, and to buy her back out of the slavery she wound up in. Hosea was instructed to love Gomer as He loved Israel. Hosea acted in obedience, telling Gomer that she must continue to live as his wife and not return to her sins.

Just in case someone in here tonight does not know the significance of God telling Hosea to love Gomer as He loved Israel let me tell you. Israel is God's chosen nation. It would be an entire teaching series to explain it all, but for this moment here is a quick overview. The modern church is a metaphor for Israel, and the wedding is the picture in which God frames the entire picture. You see, He sees those of us who believe in Him as is bride. And here God was telling Hosea to go find a bride among the sinful, and even further He told him to go again and buy her back. Those are shouting words!

Wow, that's yet another deeper message for another day. But, let us look now at the third woman in our scenario. Her name is Mary. She was a virgin daughter who loved and honored her parents. I'm sure she worked hard around the dwelling where the family lived. She was not perfect, because she was human, but she did have the exact attributes that God wanted for the mother of His only Son. Part of it was her lineage, but she had kept herself pure, never knowing that this extravagant moment was coming her way. I want to reference only one verse, it comes after the angel of the Lord had visited Mary to tell her that she had been chosen by God, Luke 1:38, in this one verse Mary acknowledges that she is God's servant, and presents herself willing to follow His will.

Now, before we move on to the fourth woman, let's revisit these three again. Remember Dinah, she was just a new girl in town out looking to make some new friends. Instead her innocence is stolen by a powerful man. She was not perfect either, maybe she even batted her eyelashes at Shechem suggestively, but that would have given him no right or reason to thrust his evil into her life. She was not at fault, but the very act itself was so wrong and dirty that it soiled her. Imagine this, a beautiful winter morning with a fresh blanket of snow covering the land, snow that has not yet been walked on. It is a smooth surface that follows the lay of the land, but it is so clean and white, and because it is covering the land, it is also clean and white. Now imagine an old hound dog taking a walk right across the yard. Everywhere he shuffles through the white blanket he is leaving a noticeable trail. He is disturbing the smooth white surface. No Davider how you try you cannot erase his footsteps. He has effectively desDerricked the pure snow. Only God could really repair the damage by sending another snowfall to smooth the surface over again.

A second look at Gomer makes me wonder if perhaps she thought that old lifestyle had some unbreakable hold on her. It is possible to fool yourself for a time. But true transformation has to come from the inside out. Her wounds, mostly caused by her own actions, were so deeply etched in her that she needed a complete overhaul. Maybe the prospect of truly changing was more than she thought she could do. Why else would she forsake the love of a kind, honest man?

Finally, there was Mary. She was everything that the two other women were not. She was doing everything right. She had not been visited by the sin of another to soil her life. She was chosen. Ironically the thing that could have made her an outcast…her sin was that she became pregnant though she was not married. And it was God's idea. You see sometimes, many times, people will judge a situation, or a person, without having all the facts. In Mary's case she was blameless. Even more, she was chosen. And God found her faithful to accept His outrageous invitation.

The question for all of the ladies here tonight is, which one of these women represents you? You are the fourth woman I want to talk about. Maybe your life has been wrecked by the sin thrust upon you from someone else. You may have acted out and jumped headlong into a life of sin trying to appease the pain and shame you wanted so desperately to be rid of. You may have started out as a "Dinah" and ended up as a "Gomer". If that is you, I can only imagine how fast your heart must be beating right now. Do you even realize that there is the possibility to leave here feeling like a brand new creation? The choice is there, and it is yours to make. You don't have to carry all that junk anymore. And you don't have to find your identity there either. In fact, if you equate yourself with the choices you have made then you have believed a lie. Maybe you are a "Mary" sitting here tonight, and you're thinking I've given everything I am to serving God. How could I ever get any better or closer to Him? Two thoughts for you to consider: 1. There is always room for improvement. 2. If you think you have reached the pinnacle of serving Him you are a victim of pride and arrogance.

Believe it, or not all three of these women have one thing in common, and you have it as well. Guys and gals included, I might add. That commonality is the fact that without God we are empty. Mary's womb was empty before Jesus. Dinah and Gomer's hearts were empty before Jesus. They may have had full, busy lives, but in the only way that mattered, they were empty. Even Mary had a heart that was empty. Just imagine how she felt, carrying the Son of God. The Savior of the world was camping out for nine months in her womb. And she needed His redemptive work just as much as anyone. Redeem is one of those "Christian language" words we use that might go right over your head, basically you can say Jesus compensated for our faults and bad choices in order to regain possession of us. We can choose to be in His grip, possessed by Him, the Son of the One who is defined as Love, the only One who can save us from all that will desDerrick us in our minds. Or we can choose to be the possession of a cold, hard world ruled by a lying spirit that will constantly remind you of how bad your life is, how big your problems are, and how fresh your pain is. It's a no brainer as far as I'm concerned.

The common denominator we need to overcome the emptiness is found only in the person of Jesus Christ. He levels the playing field for all of us. Because God saw humanity struggling with sin, even from the foundation of the world, He knew it was coming. He knew we would return to our failings again and again. He decided that real sin would require something other than words. He made it so that the only way to be redeemed would come through a once and for all blood sacrifice, pure, undefiled blood that could only come from Himself. So He had a plan, to take on human flesh, to live on earth, to feel our pain, to face our temptations, to allow every sin ever to be uploaded onto Himself as He willingly hung on a cross, dying so that we may live, and walk in forgiveness and freedom. Paul put it eloquently when he wrote... *In the beginning was the Word, and the Word was with God, and the Word was God.... The Word became flesh and dwelt among us.* Have you heard the expression "just say the word and I will make it happen"? That is exactly what God did when He became the embodiment of His own Word in the form of Jesus. He was born to die so that His pure, perfect blood could become the final payment...the redemption that would reconcile humanity to God.

No Davider what has happened to you, or what you have done before this moment, it can all be washed away, not just swept under the rug where it may resurface later. It can be gone, you can be new, born again in the spirit...just say the word and Jesus will make it so. You are not here by accident. He is talking to you. Please don't reject Him.

I don't want to leave you guys out of this equation. Think for just a moment of the men in these verses we read. Hosea was a fine man, a prophet of God. And he was willing to do whatever was asked of him. Surely he would have wanted to marry a woman of upstanding character, maybe he hesitated, he wasn't perfect, but the important thing is he surrendered to the Lord. Joseph is the man behind the scenes in Mary's story. He, too, was a fine man who was willing to forsake the approval of men to follow the Lord's plan. Maybe having a visit from an angel was the inspiring factor he needed to choose well. Finally there was Shechem. He was spoiled and selfish. He probably never considered the feelings of other people when he made his decisions. If you guys see any of Shechem's tendencies in yourself you might want to be the first one to hit your knees. Sin is sin, that is for sure, but the thought that your evil invades an innocent life carries a lot of weight. The point is we all, including me, need something, here and now."

Colin stopped speaking then as he moved away from the microphone to come down off the stage. He walked up the aisle, all the way to the back row, the row where I was sitting. I was glad I had slid all the way to the farthest end because when he glanced in my direction I felt like his eyes might literally burn me if I were any closer. He didn't linger, instead he moved back toward the front of the room, looking from one side to the other. I think he was trying to make eye contact with every person there. When he got back to the front he turned to face us, "Remember He already knows about everything in your life. And the only things He won't forgive are the things you won't let Him forgive. He paused again and moved back up onto the stage. Then he continued, "The invitation is threefold. I believe there are two types of sin to deal with, the kind that is perpetuated against you, and the kind you willingly engage in. Dinah and Gomer, and Yes, Shechem, live there. For that "Dinah" sin you simply need to be cleansed. But that "Gomer" sin needs some high horse power forgiveness. The Bible says that God cannot even look at sin. This is why we cannot let any of the mess to stay with us. Just ask God to do the work He knows, and you know needs to be done to close the gap between you. Then every day for the rest of your life choose to turn the other way when your flesh tries to take you back. Finally, for those of you who are living right and doing all you know how, why don't you just humble yourself before the Lord and praise Him because He is the only Way you make good choices. One Psalm proclaims that God inhabits the praises of His people. Could it be that your praises joined together might usher in a greater, stronger presence of the Holy Spirit? And maybe that greater, stronger presence is the remedy some of the others here need, your honest worship and praise Davider."

Though I had not noticed, Sullivan and the other singers had gathered back on the stage behind Colin, and music began to fill the room. The girl who had been singing more back up before stood at the front and began to sing. I didn't know the song, but one thing she kept repeating was "It is well with my soul. I was feeling something in my heart that I had never felt before, something that told me that all was not well with my soul. I remembered kneeling and trying to pray at Cam's funeral, along with his dad and many others. But I had never felt the way I was feeling now. Whatever I might have wanted that day no change had come to my life, if anything I had stood back up angrier at God than I had been before.

I realized that everyone had stood up so I stood too, but my legs were so shaky I wasn't sure they would hold me. I glanced around to see if I sensed anyone else was feeling the way I was. I saw several people moving toward the front of the room where Colin was waiting. I suddenly felt like I needed to move too. I stepped toward the end of the row. Thankfully no one else had sat back so far, so there was a clear path to the aisle. In a few seconds I was at the end of the row, I hesitated a moment as I heard Colin say, "You take the first step toward Him and He will carry you the rest of the way." In that final moment before I took my next step my brain told my legs to turn right toward the entrance instead of left toward Colin. So that is what I did.

I really did not know where I was going as I quickened my pace. In moments I was pushing open the door and stepping outside. It was a little before 7pm, the extra light of spring still illuminated the sky. With no thought of hesitation I turned toward the gardens that were near the entrance to the campus. It was about a mile in distance, but I had begun to run, and I covered the distance quickly. Thankfully there were not many students milling around campus on a Sunday evening so no one bothered me as I entered the gate. I remembered the wooden benches near the center of the garden, so that became my planned destination. With Colin's words ringing in my ears and tears rolling down my face I finally reached a bench and sank down onto the rough surface. Now what? I thought as I continued to ponder all that I had just heard. One part of my brain just wanted to forget it all, but there was a part that wondered if it could be so easy just to say I believed Jesus and all that stuff about dying to give me a new life. Somehow that was hard to grasp. But I didn't want to spend the rest of my life struggling to do the right thing. I leaned forward and rested my head in my hands, the tears continued. Soon I could feel my body shaking as simple crying turned to sobs, the entire time there was a battle raging in my mind, I didn't realize it, but that battle was necessary for me to find peace for my heart.

22

I don't know long I was there on that bench before Natalie and Sullivan showed up. It never occurred to me to wonder how they knew where to find me; they just did.

"Andrea, are you okay?" Natalie asked as she sat down beside me on the bench and gently placed her hand on my shoulder.

I looked up through eyes that were swollen. I could feel the wetness of the bandages on my face and I realized how horrible I must look. At least the sobbing had stopped. No more tears were coming from my eyes. I avoided looking at Sullivan, though I was sure he wouldn't recognize me as the girl he knocked down a few weeks ago. I couldn't have been more wrong, as I would soon find out.

I was looking at the ground in front of where he was standing. I watched as he knelt down in front of me, I shrank back a little on the bench. "Hey Andrea, I'm not going to hurt you." His voice was so tender I couldn't handle it. I closed my eyes and shook my head. I didn't want him to think that I would even consider that he might hurt me.

"Do you remember me Andrea? I think I still owe you a cup of coffee."

"Of course I remember you," I replied, though I didn't want him to know that I had thought a lot about him since that day. I continued, "I know you won't hurt me. I just….this has been the most unexpected thing in my life. Something happened in my heart back there and I'm not sure I understand it all." I opened my eyes and looked at him.

"It's okay, Natalie and I are here to help you understand. Why don't you tell me what you are thinking right now?"

"Umm…I got on my knees at Cam's funeral and I poured out my heart to God, but not because I wanted to admit that I needed a Savior. It was actually pure anger that poured out. When I stood back up I was still angry, and I decided that I didn't want anything to do with God. Everything that has happened in the past three years has just been me running away from Him. I have thought a few times that He might want me to run toward Him, but those thoughts only make me feel so guilty and ashamed. So I ran farther away, anything to feel better." My words were spoken so fast that I wasn't sure they made sense. "I just don't know why God would want to forgive me, and even if am forgiven, how can the past be forgotten? Surely I can't just sweep it into a pile and pretend like it never happened. Pastor Colin even said we can't sweep stuff under the rug…it's too much. It will always come back." I dropped my head into my hands again, though for the moment I had no more tears.

I felt Natalie shift beside me on the bench so that she could lay her hand on my shoulder. I sensed she wanted to say something, but maybe could not find the words. The voice I heard was actually Sullivan as he tentatively put his hand underneath my chin and gently started to lift my head. "I don't know who Cam is, obviously someone you loved very much, perhaps someday you can tell me. But for this moment Andrea, look around, while we still have a bit of light. Tell me what you see."

I turned my head from side to side, allowing my eyes to move around the garden. At first I wasn't sure what Sullivan wanted me to see. Then it hit me. "Cocoons, I see cocoons everywhere." It was true, in the faint light just before darkness I saw that the bench I had settled on was in the butterfly section of the garden.

"Yes, cocoons. So what is inside them?"

"Caterpillars, of course," I replied.

"Do you know what all those caterpillars did before they wove those cocoons around themselves?"

"Yeah, they ate like a bunch of gluttons and fattened up," I replied with a chuckle.

"Right again. Now think about the parallel between them and you," Sullivan began. "You have eaten of worldly things like a glutton for years. All the while you were wrapping yourself in a cocoon of self-preservation. The only problem is you were protecting yourself from the wrong thing. I think most people figure out that God has the power to wreck us in ways that will leave us realizing that we are powerless on our own, and how much we are totally dependent on Him. Truthfully that is what keeps many from ever accepting Him. If we could just get His judgment and condemnation we would be far more comfortable, because His grace just doesn't seem to make sense. We are so good at beating ourselves up for our failures that we cannot fathom such a love that will say I forgive you."

For a moment Sullivan and I looked into each other's eyes. I was trying to process what he had said when the thought I had the day we met came running through my mind. It was that moment when I had thought he just wanted to get me into bed. As the thought surfaced I felt the burn as shame colored my cheeks. I looked away. I suppose that's the way it would always be, if I began to think that I was clean or worthy of real love, the memories of who I had become would always be there to knock me back down. I dropped my chin against my chest.

Sullivan dipped his head forward until it was almost lying on my lap, "I need you to see me Andrea. I need to know that you understand what I am about to tell you."

Uncertainly I lifted my eyes so he could sit back up. Again we looked into each other's eyes. It was then that I noticed in my peripheral vision that Natalie had her head bowed and her eyes were closed. She was whispering softly and I knew that she was praying for me. I wasn't sure how to feel about that, but I didn't dwell on it because I didn't want to miss whatever Sullivan had to say.

"Let me ask you another question about those caterpillars in their cocoons...why are they there?"

I felt like I was in elementary school again talking about caterpillars and cocoons, but I humored Sullivan with an answer. "They are becoming butterflies, of course."

"What is that process called?"

I rolled my eyes, as I was beginning to lose patience with this whole scene, "Metamorphosis, transforming, changing, or whatever you want to call it."

"Yes, Andrea, that is exactly right." He smiled. "That is the best illustration for where you are now. Your cocoon has been invaded by the One who created you, and He will not leave you as He found you. He loves you just as you are, but He has so much to offer you that He will change you. The moment you felt a change in your heart He was nudging you, asking you to allow Him to begin the transformation part. It will be something that happens little by little every single day of your life. Sometimes you might slip backwards, but He will never let you go. Sometimes you will be growing so much in your knowledge of Him that you will feel overwhelmed with His goodness. But the majority of the time you will move forward one step at a time at an even pace, and that will be enough. Of course, you are in the driver's seat. By that I mean, you get to decide if you are going to believe God for all of this or not."

I wanted so much to grab his words and hold onto them, but I still had so much doubt trying to crowd my mind. I hated to admit it, but I really wanted to get high, or drunk, something to get me away from the battle in my mind. But I had learned that checking out for a little while with substance abuse was not a solution. I literally shook my head, hoping that in doing so I could shake off the voice pulling me away from what Sullivan had said. It wasn't easy, of course, but there was just enough resolve in me somewhere to believe, so I blurted out before I lost my nerve, "I believe! I know I cannot fix my own life, and I'm so tired of trying, and failing. And more than anything I am tired of the voice that so often reminds me of all that I have become." I was crying again now as the words spewed out of my mouth.

Instantly Natalie threw her arms around my neck and cried with me. "Thank you Jesus, thank you Jesus." She said over and over again. Then Sullivan had his arms wrapped around both of us and I heard him saying, "We praise You, Father, for this lost one who has been found."

I didn't fully understand all that praise stuff, but I did know how I felt. I felt like someone had lifted a house off of my chest. I hadn't even realized how hard it had been for me to just breathe for so long. Truthfully I could have sat there forever with the arms of two relative strangers wrapped around me.

Of course it doesn't work like that. After a few minutes of crying and hearing their words of praise we separated. My own heart seemed to be screaming out praise of its own that I didn't really know how to put into words. But somehow I trusted that words did not matter right then, and they would come when it was time.

I was finally able to stop crying and Natalie gave me one more hug, speaking against my cheek, "I'm so proud of you for being courageous. I'll be right here with you for the journey."

"Thank you so much Natalie. I can't tell you how much I appreciate your kindness."

"You don't have to. God put me in your life because He knew this moment was coming. I know you have a lot to work through at home. My house is your house if you need it."

By this time darkness had settled over the gJamie with just enough moonlight illuminating the path so we could make our way back. It occurred to me that I had kept Sullivan and Natalie from whatever responsibilities they may have had. I told them I was sorry, but both of them assured me that they would not have been anywhere else in the world than right there in the garden with me and Jesus.

"I just have to go back inside to grab my things." Natalie said as we arrived in front of the building.

"I have to get my things as well, "Sullivan added, "Why don't you come too? I want Colin to meet you."

Even with all that happened in the past few minutes I was still apprehensive about meeting a preacher. Doubt started to flood my mind, and I felt fearful. What if he took one look at me and saw how dirty I was? Would he be able to sense that I had shared the bed of so many men that I had lost count? For the first time ever another voice in my head broke through, this voice told me that I was not that girl anymore and God knew it. That was all that mattered. I had left the old me in the butterfly garden, and I was already in the beginning stages of transformation. I chose to believe that second voice, "Okay, I will go with you."

23

The lights inside the building were very bright after we had been in the darkness for a while, and all that crying had irritated my eyes. I could tell they were swollen and I knew my bandages needed to be changed. I could not imagine what Colin, or anyone we might encounter, would think when they saw me.

The auditorium where we had met was brightly lit now as a few people were still around putting things back in order. Right away Natalie told us she was going backstage to where she had left her things. Then she was gone. Sullivan seemed to feel responsible for me, so he said, "Come on you can help me with my stuff." He gently grasped my elbow to propel me along. That small action was somehow a comfort to me. I didn't hesitate. We were just mounting the stairs to the stage when Colin appeared from behind the heavy curtain. Immediately he saw us and walked in our direction. "There you are Sully. In all the excitement of all God did here this evening I misplaced you."

"Well, the Lord knew where we were. In fact, He led Natalie and me right where we needed to be." Sullivan replied. "Colin, meet Andrea, a new believer, and a new friend!"

"Hallelujah!" Colin exclaimed in true preacher fashion, only I didn't sense anything theatrical about his response. I was certain that he truly was giving God praise. I felt the familiar mist of tears at the back of my eyes as my heart once again swelled with gratitude.

Colin extended his hand and I did likewise. His large hand encompassed my tiny one as he said, "I'm so glad to meet you as a sister. I hope you will feel like joining us at Transform Church. I'm sure we have a place where you can serve. And I know God has gifted you with something that is needed within some congregation. It could be Transform!"

I smiled and gave a small nod, though I found it unnerving to keep eye contact with the charismatic man, who could not have been much older than Sullivan and I. He must have noticed the way my eyes dropped because he said, "I can see that you are somewhat overwhelmed by this new thing in your life. In fact, I continue to be overwhelmed every time God moves as He did here tonight. In case you two didn't hear, there were seven more names added to God's book here, eight counting you. It doesn't get any better than that. All eight of you came here empty and broken, and without hope. All of eight of you are leaving here filled with the Holy Spirit of God, on the mend and filled with hope. But that doesn't mean that whatever brokenness brought you here is going to be gone now. In some cases there will be consequences for choices made, and in some cases there are probably other people involved in the equation. I want to encourage you to be ready for the enemy to try to paralyze you in the battlefield of your mind. He is just smart enough to know he has lost your soul, but he is tenacious enough to try his best to cripple your efforts to bring the message of the hope of Christ in you to the lives of others."

I was looking him in the eye by the time he finished speaking, because I knew the enemy he spoke of had already rose up in my mind. This was not going to be easy, but somehow I knew it was going to be worth it. Colin released my hand, which had remained in his. He turned to Sullivan, "I think we need to pray for our new sister in Christ. Why don't you do the honors, Sully?"

"I would love to." Sullivan smiled. They both bowed their heads toward their chests and I did the same as Sullivan's strong voice began to talk to God about me.

"Father, I'm so thankful that Andrea has come into a relationship with you through Jesus. I don't know all that has hurt her in her life, but I do know that those things do not have to define her anymore. She has scars, God, I can see them, and evidence that there will be others. Please help her see them as places of healing rather than places of hurt from this moment on. And help her, God, when the enemy tries his old schemes in the battlefield of her mind. Create in Andrea a clean heart, and give her a steadfast spirit that is founded and grounded in You, In Jesus name. Amen."

I thought my tears were over for the night, but I felt warm, fresh liquid sliding underneath my eyelids as Sullivan talked to God about my scars. For a moment it felt like Cam was there with us. Why would Sullivan pray specifically about scars? A shiver traveled up my spine as I thought about the possibility that I mattered so much to God that He somehow let Sullivan know. But that was a silly thought, wasn't it? Surely God was too busy to care about little things like that. I suppose Sullivan felt the shiver that went through me because when he finished praying he said, "Are you cold?"

"No, I'm good," I replied, actually I was feeling freer than I had ever felt in my life, and I had peace, which I was afraid would be elusive. I didn't want to get into discussing scars with him…not yet anyway.

"Hey are you ready to go? I know you must be worn out and we need to get those bandages changed." Natalie said as she joined us.

I wished that she had not mentioned the bandages, of course, they were there for all to see, but I was not prepared to talk about any of that right now and I was concerned that Sullivan or Colin might start asking questions. I had a lot of sorting out to do in my head about my dad, and a lot of other things.

"I'm ready." I said quickly and turned to go.

"You should sleep well tonight." Colin called after me as I was walking away. I glanced over my shoulder and smiled. My eye caught Sullivan's expression and for a moment I went weak in the knees. He had a sad sort of look on his face, like he was hurting for me or something. I wasn't sure I understood that, but it made me feel warm inside. "Thank you for praying for me Sullivan." I said.

"You're welcome, and I told you the day we met that you can call me Sully." The look in his eyes lightened and a genuine smile curved his lips.

I smiled back, "But I would rather call you Sullivan. I'm sure I'll see you around."

I went out the door before he could reply.

About an hour later I had showered and Natalie had redressed my wounds, as advised by Julie. Now I was lying on the sofa bed expecting to go to sleep with more ease than I had in a long time. However, that was not the case. Instead I was going over scenarios in my head about how to act and what to say when I went home. I had decided to go the next day instead of waiting any longer. Honesty would have to become a part of me if I expected to change. I did not want to put off telling mama about the attack, and I was excited to tell her about my experience at the Gathering. I would not tell her the things I knew about daddy's porn problem or anything else. That was his demon to deal with. I would pray for him, but I was new at this so I didn't even know how or what to pray. I was on the verge of falling asleep when I realized that I really wanted daddy to feel this peace that I had. It felt strange for me to care about daddy in that way. Suddenly it was about more than just not getting hit anymore. It was about his soul and eternity. I could feel God doing some things in my heart even as I lay there trying to pray for daddy for the first time ever.

I thought about Cam, and though I still had an ache in my heart because of his absence, I was grateful for the time we shared and the first glimpse of Jesus love that Cam had shown me. As I thought of the last night we were together and how he was acting I wondered if he somehow knew he was going to be going to heaven soon. Ultimately his concern had been for my soul. Now that I had accepted Jesus for all that He is and was experiencing that same concern for my dad, I finally understood Cam's urgency. No amount of regretting could turn back the clock. The only thing I could do was to live with the expectation of seeing him again someday.

I prayed again as my thoughts were winding down. I was glad I had asked Natalie to drive me home tomorrow since I would not be released to drive until I saw the doctor again. Finally I felt myself settling in to sleep.

24

My classes went by faster than I could ever remember the next day. I had no downtime in any of them, so, I had no time to think about what I would say when I got home. That was probably a good thing as I would be forced to really rely on God. Natalie would not be out of class until 4:00, which gave me an hour after to wait. I decided to walk to the butterfly garden. I had loved it before, but now I felt like it was my sanctuary.

There were a few students in the garden as I made my way into the center where the bench I claimed as my own was sitting. Usually I tried not to make eye contact with people, but on this sunny day I found myself looking at people, hoping to give away a smile. But then I remembered my bandaged and bruised face, and I was suddenly self-conscious. I dropped my head toward my chest and moved quickly to the bench where I had chosen Jesus last night. Thankfully no one else was there so I sat down. I tilted my head back and closed my eyes, feeling the sun, warm on my skin. It was amazing to me how much different I felt about something as simple as enjoying the sunshine. Somewhere along the way of collecting scars I had lost the ability to just "be" in the moment. I remembered Cam telling me once that it is a good thing to be still and listen to God. I was beginning to understand that now.

I prayed the best way I knew how with the time I had before I would be at home. I guess it was a moment of being still that allowed me to admit that I had been blaming daddy for everything that was wrong in my life when in reality I played a huge part myself. Daddy had hurt me in more ways than one, so had some other people, but I knew that having the victim mentality would not help me at all. I kind of stumbled my way through that prayer as I asked God to change me and to work in daddy's heart because he needed freedom that only God could give. Natalie called as I was finishing my prayer.

A short time later I was climbing into Natalie's car for the short ride home. She assured me that she would be praying and she had asked Sullivan to as well.

It was almost 4:30 when Natalie dropped me off. I had made plans to get my car home later. I thanked my friend then walked up the path to the house.

I knew that everyone was home. At least everyone's car was there. I whispered, "Help me Lord," as I opened the door and walked in.

The television was showing the early evening news. I could see daddy in his chair there in the sunken living room. Then I noticed mama standing by the sink. They both turned to look at me at the same time. I pushed the door shut and leaned back against it, feeling a little weak. For a moment no one spoke. My eyes automatically traveled to the table as I remembered the last time I was here. I glanced at the floor where I had awakened a couple of days earlier. There was no evidence of the terrible scene that had marked my last encounter with daddy, I was glad though, because I did not want to relive that anymore. I forced thoughts of what used to be out of my mind. I remembered Colin talking about battles in my mind the night before. I could almost hear Sullivan praying for me. I smiled at that. David appeared at the end of the hallway at that moment. He broke the silence, "Hey Sis," he paused when he saw my face, then he walked right over and put his arms around me. I closed my eyes and melted into the hug of my big brother. It had been a long time, but I recalled times in the past when he had tried to be my protector. Finally I pulled back and said, "I'm glad everyone is home. I need to talk to all of you. Where are Derrick and Casey? I know they are young, but I want them here too."

"I'll get them. They are playing in Casey's room." David trotted down the hall as I took the few steps separating me and mama. Immediately her hand went to the bandages on my face. I saw the tears that had gathered in her eyes. "Don't cry mama. I am okay. I'm actually more than okay. These wounds will heal too."

In a few minutes the six of us were sitting together in the living room. I could not remember the last time we had sat anywhere all together. I boldly took the TV remote off the arm of daddy's chair and turned the TV off. He never said a word, and since that first moment when he looked at me when I came in, he had not looked at me. I was just thankful he was still sitting there, not making a scene, not scaring Derrick and Casey, not threatening to hit me. In that moment I knew two things…someone was praying and God was answering.

Now that I had everyone's attention I realized that I had no idea how to say what I needed what to say. The direct approach seemed best, "Something happened to me this weekend." I paused and took a seat on the sofa. Casey scurried over to stand in front of me. She reached her tiny fingers to touch the bandages on my face. "Booboo," she said as only a child can. I put my arms around her little body and hugged her, realizing that it had been so long since I had spent real time with my family. I mean real time when I was not detached, depressed or angry. I felt regret and shame, but I only allowed those feelings for a fleeting moment because I knew I could not undo the past. All I could do was change the present and hopefully impact the future.

"Yes. Casey, sissy has a booboo, but it's ok."

I lifted Casey onto my lap as I looked around at my family's faces. Daddy's was the hardest to look at, but I could honestly feel love for him surging inside me. Perhaps some of the hardest mind battles I would have to fight would involve him; but I would love him anyway. That realization brought tears to my eyes. I finally continued as I turned my eyes away from daddy, "This did happen this weekend." I touched the bandages. "But something else happened that is changing me from the inside out. I don't really know how to describe it, because I am thinking it will unfold for the rest of my life. But it began with a prayer in the middle of a butterfly garden last night, and now I am transforming, just like a caterpillar. I am sorry that I have not really been a part of this family in a long time. I would like to say that everything started after Cam died, but the truth is I think…actually I know my issues began long before I met Cam. He just happened to have a wisdom that only God can give, and he recognized that I had things in my life that could, and would, harm me if I ever faced them. But they have to be faced or the potential for them to destroy me will always be a shadow over my life. Last night I took the first steps on a new path, with the only One who can help me face, and survive, myself, and whatever issues have been controlling me."

I stopped speaking then because I really didn't know anything else I could say. I noticed that mama had tears rolling down her cheeks.

"I'm so happy because you know Jesus now," she smiled through her tears. "I have wanted to help you since…as far back as I can remember. But I knew the beginning of your brokenness was too much for even a mama to handle. So I have prayed for you. I'm sorry I have not been a stronger mother to you, but I am so thankful for everything that has brought you to this moment."

I set Casey on her feet and stood to close the gap separating me and mama. She was standing ready to give me a hug by the time I got to her. David came and put his arms around both of us and said, "I made this decision months ago when I first began dating Madison. I'm sorry I have not tried to lead you here."

The three of us were still in our huddle when Casey and Derrick slammed into us and wiggled their way into the middle. It felt so good. I was crying as I said, "Mama you have been all that I would let you be to me, I love you for that. David, I wouldn't have listened anyway. I've been angry at God for a long time. I suppose everything really does have to happen at just the right time."

Casey and Derrick were wiggling around like two monkeys in the middle, so we broke our huddle. I looked around expecting daddy to be glaring at us. I wanted him to be a part of what was happening. But all I saw was his empty chair. Daddy had quietly left the room when no one was looking. I knew there was a lot of praying for him in my future.

25

As with most things change doesn't necessarily come over night. I imagine that spiritual things might be more about the process than most people think. I kept going to class just as I had before, but I focused more on the people around me. I was smart enough to know that the people I chose to spend time with mattered a lot. So I spent as much time as I could with Natalie and gradually her friends became my friends too.

Several weeks had passed since the night in the butterfly garden when my life changed. I was learning to truly let my guard down and making real friends. Sullivan and I were also getting close. I was attracted to him certainly. He was handsome and kind. But I was more drawn to the man he was inside than anything. That was new for me, and even a little scary. When he asked me to go on an actual date I accepted without hesitation, but I started to second guess myself right away. I had not shared much of my history with him, though I had told Natalie a few things. She assured me that God did not care about my past. She said He is interested in your present and future. That is why I decided that the closet was the best place for those skeletons. But if I hoped for any romantic future with Sullivan I would have to tell some of the ugly truth. I was horrified at the thought of him knowing about the girl I used to be, but I couldn't keep such things from him. I had only known him a few weeks, but I had already figured out that he was not the kind of man to just date someone for the sake of dating. He was a man who would want a wife someday; a wife who would love God above everything else. That was a learning process for me too. I was still trying to figure out what my life was supposed to look like if I loved God that much.

Our date was scheduled for a Saturday evening so I had the entire day to prepare. I knew that Jamie was home on break from college so I made arrangements for her to help me get ready. It would give us time to catch up.

We began our morning at Sweet Impressions Kitchen, a local bakery which also offered breakfast sandwiches. "So how are your classes going?" Jamie asked as we settled into a booth at the bakery.

"Classes are good, much better than I ever expected actually. How about you? Do you ever get homesick?"

The waitress arrived with our breakfast so we thanked her and blessed it then we continued our conversation as we ate. "I do miss home, but I love college, the classes the people, all of it."

I wasn't surprised that Jamie liked college life so much. She was such a confident person who was bound to succeed as whatever she attempted. *If only Uncle Paul had been my dad instead of my uncle,* I hated that thought as soon as it entered my mind because it made me a victim all over again. The battle in my mind was all about being a victim. I just could not allow myself to go there anymore. But even having Jesus in my life did not take away the thoughts I wished would evaporate. I had to choose what to think about. I suddenly remembered a message from Pastor Colin from recently. It was called *The Things That Hold Me Captive.* I settled on a verse he referenced that told me I was fearfully and wonderfully made. I was reminded that God loves me. Always has, always will and He was taking me somewhere.

I finally replied, "I knew you would flourish there. I'm glad."

"Well, what else is going on with you? I was thrilled when you wrote to tell me about your salvation experience. I'm sure God is doing some things in your life."

I shifted a little in my seat, feeling strange at the "churchy" sound of my "salvation experience", but honestly there was no better way to describe what had begun in me with that first prayer.

"Actually I joined a church called Transform. I have a lot of friends there. In fact the guy I'm going out with tonight is on the worship team there."

"That's great! What is his name?"

"Sullivan Jeffries. He's a great guy. He also leads a ministry group at Oakdale Community College, though he is a junior at Stockwell. Honestly I'm really nervous about this date." I admitted.

"He sounds great. Worship team, that's cool. Do you remember when we were kids and grampa used to let us into the church building on summer days. We sang our hearts out. Maybe you could join that worship team. But what is it about the date that makes you nervous?"

I was startled at the memory Jamie shared. I had forgotten about those summer days singing with my cousins. Then the memory screaming for attention in my mind was of Andrew Harrison saying "You can't really sing that well. You would only embarrass yourself, and me." Amidst that memory, fighting to get through I recalled another of Pastor Colin's recent messages where he said that the devil is not only a liar, he is also a thief who steals anything good he can from us. But greater than that was the fact that God is the Redeemer and Restorer. Maybe the devil had stolen those long ago sweet memories, and replaced them with Andrew's hurtful words. Why was it so easy to remember the hurtful things and forget the good things?

"I don't sing much these days, and I don't date much either." I replied. "There was a lot of stuff that I did that I am not proud of. I told you about Andrew and Jeff, but there were others. I am about as used as a dirty mop."

Jamie digested that information for a minute before responding. Finally she spoke, "If Sullivan Jeffries is a true worshiper of the One he leads others to worship then he will not judge you for your past."

"I don't think he will judge me, Jamie. My biggest fear is that I will tempt him to have sex with me. I'm sorry to be so blunt, but most of my experience with guys ended with sex, except for Cam, and you know how that ended."

Jamie blushed, a moment passed then she replied, "Andi, I'm so sorry that we even have to have a conversation like this, so much happened in your life that just seems so unfair. But God can use all of it for a good purpose if you will let Him. That may be the whole reason He allowed things to happen as they did. But you can't live your life in fear of how you are going to react to people. You will end up a recluse and always lonely, missing out on the relationships God means for you to have. You have to learn how to face the ugly and change through the process."

I grasped Jamie's hand in mine across the table, "Thank you Jamie, you just reminded me of the butterfly promise. That is what I call my journey with God."

I spent the rest of the day with Jamie at her house. She was great at fixing hair. She had even offered to put some highlights in my drab color. She also gave me a long bob cut. I liked it a lot and told her if the nursing thing fell through she could always change her major.

I had given Sullivan the address at Jamie's and asked him to pick me up there. I was ready in my khaki pants and pale pink sweater when I saw his red truck come into view.

"I think your date is here." Jamie had seen the truck too.

I swallowed hard and wiped my sweaty palms on my pant legs, my fingers were sore as my old habit of nail biting was back with a vengeance. "Yeah, that's him."

I went to give Jamie a hug. I had enjoyed the day together so much. "Thank you, thank you Jamie, for everything. Have a safe trip back to school. I love you so much."

"I love you too Andi. Everything will work out for you. Don't imagine it any other way."

By the time the two of us separated Sullivan had gotten out of his truck and was knocking on the glass patio door.

I went to open the door, "Hey Sullivan, I was just on my way out."

"That's ok. I was hoping to meet this cousin you've told me about."

"That would be me," Jamie said stepping up beside me, "I'm Jamie."

"Yes, Jamie, this is Sullivan."

The two of them exchanged a few words then Sullivan suggested we should get going. I promised Jamie I would call her later and then Sullivan and I left.

"So, where are we going?" I asked about four miles into the trip.

"Are you interested in dinner at a nice country restaurant?"

"Oh that sounds nice, I'm pretty hungry." I said, as I realized that I had not eaten since breakfast.

"I wanted to take you to Cedar Falls Inn, but that is at least an hour's drive. If you're very hungry we could find somewhere in town, maybe Pauly's?"

I was glad that Sullivan was driving and could not focus his attention on me because I know every ounce of color faded from my face. I started to speak, but no sound came from my mouth. Why would he even suggest Pauly's? Did he know something? Had he discovered my connection to Pauly's? What in the world did I think I was trying to do acting like I was worthy of a guy like Sullivan?

"Andrea, are you ok?"

I finally snapped back to the moment, angry at myself for listening to the voices in my head yet again. There was no way Sullivan new about my time at Pauly's or the frat parties. "Cedar Falls, wow, I've only been there once. I would love to go to the Inn, I've never eaten there. Am I dressed correctly for that setting?"

"You're absolutely perfect…I mean, your clothes are just right. I also really like the changes in your hair, the cut looks nice, and it is lighter too, isn't it?"

I blushed at his compliment. It was nice to be able to blush at such an innocent exchange. "Yes, Jamie did it. She is really good at that sort of thing."

"I agree. You look beautiful."

I could not have stopped the smile covering my face even if I wanted to, mostly because I knew that Sullivan truly meant everything he said. There was no ulterior motive of trying to get me into bed later. That was such a new concept for me, but I liked it very much.

During the remainder of our trip we talked a lot about our classes as well as the progress Sullivan and his team were making toward getting a ministry started at Stockwell. I was excited for them, but I didn't want to talk about SU too much because I was afraid Andrew's name might come up. I was already having anxiety about transferring there the next fall. But if I wanted to finish my course of study the most economical way Stockwell was my only choice. Besides if I let Andrew's presence deter me from moving forward in life then he would have succeeded in destroying me. I did not want to let that happen.

It was almost 6pm when we drove into Cedar Falls. There was still just enough light from the setting sun to illuminate the waterfall the place was named for. It was a lovely sight, and not too common to find a waterfall in the middle of the city limits. Someone in the history of Cedar Falls had decided that building a town around a waterfall would be a good idea.

Sullivan parked the truck in the back parking lot of the Cedar Falls Inn. Quickly he climbed out his door and hurried around to open mine before I even realized what he was doing. It was silly, but that simple act made my hear t beat a little faster. "We have just enough light to get a quick picture with the falls behind us if we can find a nice passerby." He said as he took my hand and whisked me around the corner of the building to the sidewalk that lead up to the bridge where the viewing deck was situated.

There were several people already on the observation deck, and before we even asked, a nice older man offered to take a picture for us. Sullivan put his arm around me and pulled me close to his side as the man tried to center us perfectly in the small lens of Sullivan's camera phone. After a few seconds he said, "Now give the little lady a kiss on the cheek!"

I'm pretty sure Sullivan felt as awkward as I did at the man's suggestion. But it was only a kiss on the cheek. I was actually shocked at my ability to feel shy over something as innocent as a kiss on the cheek. I never expected to feel that again.

I didn't even realize that I had lowered my chin toward my chest until Sullivan's warm fingers touched my china he gently lifted my face toward his. The breath caught in my throat, almost turning into a sob. He and Cam were the only two people I could remember touching me so tenderly. How could it be that such a tender moment could almost hurt in its intensity?

I swallowed the air in my throat on a gulp as my eyes met Sullivan's, their deep brown color twinkled, even in the waning light. "Would it be so bad?" Sullivan whispered.

I felt my lips curve into a tiny grin as I moved my head slowly from side to side.

"Hurry kids, we're losing the light!" Our new found friend exclaimed.

Sullivan's eyes kept contact with mine until they couldn't any longer as he leaned toward me and kissed my cheek. I felt the warmth of his breath and the soft moistness of his lips and for a second I thought my heart would explode. It was only a moment in time, but like a few moments I had shared with Cam, I felt like this one mattered beyond itself.

"What a great shot!" Our photographer hurried over and passed Sullivan the phone.

Sullivan showed me the picture. It was a perfect shot of us in almost complete silhouette as the sun was just sliding behind the mountain. We thanked our friend, then Sullivan grabbed my hand and propelled me back the way we had come, "Let's go get some food, I'm starving!"

Neither of us mentioned that moment when he kissed me on the cheek, but he did not let go of my hand as we walked toward the front entrance of the Cedar Falls Inn. I felt so comforted to have my hand in his hand.

We were treated like VIP's at the Inn. Everyone in the place seemed to know Sullivan by name, by nickname actually, as "Sully" rang out several times. I was looking over the menu, but Sullivan didn't even open his, which made me wonder how many times he had made the drive over to eat here. "The food must be out the world amazing here. Obviously you have been here before."

"As a matter of fact, the food here is just like my mama used to cook.... well, just like my mama still cooks."

As if on cue as Sullivan finished that statement a middle aged man and woman suddenly appeared in the small alcove where we were sitting.

"Sully!" The woman's clear voice spoke of more familiarity.

Sullivan was on his feet immediately enveloping the lovely woman in a hug. Given the dark hair and familiar look of the man, it was not hard for me to deduce that these were Sullivan's parents.

"Hey mom and dad," after hugging them both, Sullivan looked at me, "This is Andrea Sanders."

I know I blushed, and I'm sure my body language read awkward as I stood and extended my hand, first to the woman. "Oh, I'm a hugger!" She gushed as she took the few steps between us and wrapped her arms around me. For a moment I actually felt claustrophobic in that embrace, but I steadied myself the best I could. I heard her speaking near my ear, "I'm Sondra, and I'm so happy to meet you."

Thankfully Sullivan's dad did not attempt a hug, which was a relief to me since I was not sure how I would react to that. Instead he shook my hand as he said, "Hello Andrea, my name is Sean. I am pleased to meet you."

"I don't suppose Sullivan told you that we would be joining you for dinner?" Sondra asked.

I glanced at Sullivan as his face shone an angry red, "I'm sorry, I was afraid you wouldn't come if told you. And there really is no better place to eat for miles and miles."

I smiled tentatively, "I wondered why we had such a large table."

"By the way, son, Sadie and Suzanna are joining us as well. I hope that is ok." Sean interjected.

Suddenly my head was spinning, Sadie and Suzanna, who could they be, and why had this date turned into a party of six?"

A few minutes later two beautiful girls joined us in the alcove. They had hair as dark as Sullivan's and the same brown eyes. I learned that they were Sullivan's seventeen year old twin sisters. They proved to be every bit as kind and genuine as their big brother.

Another surprise was the Jeffries' owned the Cedar Falls Inn, and the only immediate family member I was not meeting that night was the oldest son whose name was Silas. He was a pastor at the Church of The Cedars, a nondenominational church. He was married to Joanna and they were expecting their first child around Christmas.

Dinner with Sullivan and his family turned out to be quite pleasant, and he was right about the food, it was delicious. We lingered over our dishes for almost two hours, during which time I came to feel like I was always going to be welcomed in this place. I could see that Sullivan had not fallen far from the tree. His family obviously all loved God and tried to show it with their lives.

Our drive back to Oakdale was not filled with a lot of conversation, mostly comfortable silence, which could be a good thing, yet as the minutes passed I found myself stressing a little about how this date would end. I had never experienced sweet dates that ended with an innocent kiss goodnight. Quite honestly, being a Christian did not diminish the fact that I was very attracted to Sullivan. I really did not want to mess this up. So I pieced together the best prayer I could think of as the miles passed, and hoped for the best.

Sullivan had never been to my house before so I gave him directions but he asked if I wanted to stop for ice cream or coffee before he took me home. I sensed that the silence was over and that he really wanted to talk. I wasn't overly excited about that, but if this relationship was going to develop we would have to talk.

We stopped at Two Scoops Ice Cream Shoppe and ordered two cups of chocolate ice cream. We sat at a corner booth, Sullivan on one side and me on the other. We both took a few bites of ice cream before he finally broke the silence that had become awkward somewhere along the way, "I really am sorry that I sprung my family on you like that. Well, my parents anyway. I didn't know the girls would be there."

"It's ok. I like them all very much. I can see why you are such a great guy, your parents are amazing."

Sullivan dropped his spoon into the ice cream bowl and reached to grab my free hand, which was just resting on the table. "I like you very much, Andrea. I want to get to know you more than just on the surface. Right now I hang on to every morsel of information I learn about you, which isn't much. I can see in your eyes a lot of pain sometimes and I want to be a part of your healing, but I can't if I don't know what the source of your pain is."

So here it was. The conversation I had been dreading. I did not want to be a disappointment in Sullivan's eyes when I told him who I really was. Honestly, I could not take his pity either. My biggest concern at this moment was how much I was willing to divulge. I could at least tell him about Cam. That was the safest place to begin. So I spent the next hour telling him about the time I had shared with Cam. Tears had been burning the back of my eyes so that by the time I related the story of Cam's accident I could not contain them any longer. They rolled, unheeded down my face, some of them met at my chin and then dripped onto the table. Sullivan tried to wipe them away with his fingers, but I resisted his attempt. "No, I need these tears Sullivan. I have needed them since that cold December day when they put Cam in the ground while I was throwing up beside a tree. These tears are different than the ones I shed that day, because now I have hope."

Silence crowded into our space after I stopped talking. I realized that was the first time I had shared mine and Cam's story with anyone. After a few moments Sullivan spoke, "I'm so sorry that you had to endure such a devastating loss, especially without hope. It just makes me more grateful that now you have Christ to comfort you, even if you don't want me to."

I turned my hand, which was still lying under his on the table; I laced my fingers with his and said, "Please don't think that I don't want you to comfort me Sullivan. It's just that there is a lot more to my story in the aftermath of Cam. I just don't think I'm strong enough to tell you those things yet. We might want to see where this thing with you and me is going before I dump all my issues all over you."

Sullivan's thumb caressed mine tenderly. The look in his eyes was so raw that I could not even look at him. I turned my head away as I reached up with my other hand to swipe at the tears still on my face.

"I'm not going to rush you Andrea. I have been praying since I was twelve years old for God to put the very best girl for me in my life. I think you are the one I have been praying for. But I'm not the only one who has to think so. I can wait, and I will never stop praying for you either way."

I didn't know how to respond to his confession. The thing ringing in my ears was how he had prayed for the "very best girl", if only he knew how much baggage I was carrying around. I was sure he would not think I was the "one" anymore.

"Thank you, Sullivan." That was the only response I could muster at the moment. A few minutes later we tossed our bowls in the waste basket and walked out.

It was not a long drive to my house. We were going up the drive way when Sullivan spoke again, "Do you mind if I walk you to the door?"

"That would be nice, but you don't have to."

"I want to." He had stopped by then and shifted the truck into park. He turned off the engine and opened his door. I had my door open and was out of the truck before he could get there. He reached for my hand as we started up the narrow path to the porch. I enjoyed the feel of my hand in his. But somehow my joy in the evening had waned since our talk.

Suddenly I was feeling less than worthy of him all over again. I did not know if I would ever get past the shame and guilt for all that I had done.

He walked me all the way to the door. I was not sure what to expect as I turned to face him. It was quite dark so I could not see his face to read his emotions, which left me feeling vulnerable. I was ready for a kiss if that was intention, but I had no idea what was on his mind. In a moment he lifted my hand to his lips and kissed the top of it. "I wish I could see your beautiful face right now." He whispered. "I want to kiss you and hold you, but I'm not going to do that, not right now anyway. I can wait."

I didn't know if I should feel good about that, and I had no verbal response. I just slipped my fingers out of his hand and said, "Goodnight, Sullivan." Then I opened the door and hurried inside before he could respond. I pressed my back against the door as I covered my mouth with my hand. A silent sob shook my body. I wanted to forget everything and just be in these moments with Sullivan. If I could somehow undo all that had happened since I was nine years old, surely then everything would be perfect. I should have thought to pray my way through the rest of the night, but old habits die hard. I spent an anxious night with my mind telling me that Sullivan was going to realize that I was not that great of a girl and by the morning he would be ready to move on.

26

The Wednesday after my date with Sullivan I got an email from Stockwell University. I was anxious and nervous about opening it. I had applied for several scholarships for the fall semester and I wasn't even sure if I qualified for some of them. One of the cool things about my job at the campus print shop was the freedom to do homework or whatever if the work was caught up, since I had nothing in the inbox that needed immediate attention I decided to go ahead and read the email.

I was halfway through the first sentence before I actually grasped that this message, though sent from his work account, had nothing to do with scholarships. It was a personal note from Andrew Harrison. I was amazed at how quickly I was transported back in time. I was thrilled and disgusted at the same time to think that he had written to me. I suddenly felt the need to read this particular message in privacy, so I stepped back to the office and told my work buddy that I was going outside for a short break. I took my laptop outside to a bench beside a tree near our office. I was glad no one was there as I sank down and reopened the email. I recalled the first words I had read just a few moments ago:

Dear Andrea,

I was surprised to see your name come across my desk...

There was not much there to make me think the message was

personal, but something inside me sensed that it was. Or maybe some warped part of me wanted it to be.

Finally I let my eyes scan the rest of the message:

Dear Andrea,

I was surprised to see your name come across my desk, pleasantly surprised, I might add. I cannot tell you how many times I have thought about you in the past two years. Honestly I miss you. I was also glad to learn that you had indeed finished high school and are embarking on a college education. We, at Stockwell look forward to having you here on campus as a student. I personally look forward to seeing you again. I regret the way things ended for us. I certainly hope there will be a time when we can talk at length.

There will be a special open house in the early summer, which I hope you will attend. The date and other details will be sent in the next few months.

Until we meet again,

Andrew Harrison, Student Recruiter

I clicked off as soon as I finished reading. I wasn't sure how to process what I had read. On the one hand there were professional tones to the message, but I thought I sensed more. Now I was left wondering if I should be angry, indifferent or terrified at the prospect of seeing Andrew again. Thankfully it was only mid-October, and the open house was a few months away. That would give me time to prepare myself. I went back to work after that.

I got off work at 5 o'clock, at 5:05 my phone rang. I saw that it was Sullivan calling. I had not heard from him since our date. I knew he had a lot going on with classes and ministry stuff, but I had thought he would at least call. I almost didn't answer because I was really confused now after reading that email. But I felt like I needed to hear Sullivan's voice so I swiped my finger across the screen and lifted the phone to my ear.

A few minutes later we ended our conversation after making plans to meet at the student services building where the worship team met to practice. I was flattered that Sullivan asked me to join them. He must really want to see me to ask me to sit through their practice so we could hang out together afterwards.

I picked up Chinese take-out to share with the group, which included Carter, Luke, Mason and Jenny, along with Sullivan. We all ate and shared small talk then they got ready to practice. Their instruments were already set up and ready. I started to gather up the trash as they moved toward the stage. But Sullivan grabbed my hand and said, "Come on, we want you to practice with us tonight."

I was caught off guard by his invitation, and not eager to accept. I had sung very little since the night Andrew spoke those harsh words. I might sing in the shower, and, of course, I sang in worship, but not loud enough to be heard.

"Yes, Andrea, please join us. I have noticed you during worship at Transform. You really put your entire heart out there. We need worship like that." Jenny said enthusiastically.

"I don't know...I don't really sing that much."

"You might as well say yes and get it over with. Mason and I were not on board for this at all when Sullivan first asked us to help him start this worship team." Carter interjected.

"Really, why not, you guys are great." I asked

"It wasn't in my plans," Mason joined the conversation. "But when Sullivan tells you that God encouraged him to include you in something you better believe God is in it. Then I was really thrown for a loop when God called me into ministry. Sometimes you just have to hold on tight and see where He is taking you."

"Honestly I didn't even realize I had the ability to lead others in worship until I met Sullivan and started attending small group with him. My heart almost jumped out of my chest when we learned about the great importance of pure praise. I was overwhelmed to think that God would use me in that way." Luke said.

"I'm not sure about this....but I will try." I finally said almost in a whisper.

"That's my girl!" Sullivan exclaimed.

Jenny shared lead vocal duties with Luke and they encouraged me to join in with harmonies if it felt right.

After we finished practicing I was feeling amazing because joining in felt so natural to me. It was strange but I almost felt like I was born to be on that stage. And just like that I was invited to join the Transform Worship Team.

27

The next few weeks were uneventful. School was going great and I was seeing Sullivan at least four times a week. Things at home were good, with the exception of conflicts with daddy. I was much better at holding my tongue, but that almost seemed to anger him more at times. I was praying a lot, which was very good. And there were glimpses of light at the end of the tunnel.

I loved being a part of the worship team. It was amazing to spend time alone with God in His word and study, but to be in that group dynamic with voices raised together to praise God was the most amazing thing. I could tell that God was transforming me. I rarely had thoughts of the past me anymore, though Cam was often on my mind. I was glad for that though, I never wanted to forget him.

A month after I began singing with the worship team Sullivan came into our practice session as excited as I had ever seen him.

"Guess what guys? Oh never mind, I'll just tell you! We got the green light for a ministry presence on campus at Stockwell!"

"Awesome! That's great! When do we start?" All this rang out from the others in the group.

Personally, I felt like I needed to digest the information for a minute. I had been excited to see this happen, but now that it was becoming reality

I was scared to death to think of going to the one place where I might run into Andrew. It was awkward to think, but my first thought was that I would. Was I really ready to take that chance?

I didn't say much during practice. I had been working on a song for a few days, which I was going to share that night. Instead I wadded up the paper it was written on and shoved it into my backpack, even as I pushed it to the back of my mind.

Sullivan and I usually hung out for a while after practice. Everyone else had already left as we locked up the building and walked to where we were both parked. "You don't seem too excited about Stockwell." Sullivan spoke into the darkness.

My eyes dropped to the dark ground below. I was glad the November evening had already darkened so he could not see my face. I know I blushed, and I'm sure my face was telling a story that I would not want to have to explain right then.

"Of course I'm excited. I know how much prayer has gone into this. I'm just not feeling well this evening." I lied, well not completely, I was physically fine, but I was having a crisis in my mind.

"I'm sorry. I didn't notice you were not feeling well. I was too preoccupied with the news."

"It's ok Sullivan. You should be preoccupied and very excited. I just need to go home now I think. I don't want to dampen your enthusiasm."
"Okay." He simply agreed.

We had been walking as we talked and had arrived at our vehicles. Sullivan opened the door and slid his guitar into the truck then turned toward me. In the purplish light streaming from the street lamp I could see his arms extended out inviting me into his embrace. Encircled in those arms was my favorite place to be, so I eagerly stepped into that hug. I pressed my body against his, just enough to make me feel secure as his arms wrapped around me. I laid my head on his chest and felt his heart beating against my ear. There was no place on earth I would rather be.

For a few moments neither of us spoke. We just enjoyed the closeness of the most innocently intimate way possible.

Finally Sullivan broke the silence, "Are you sure you're ok? You seem distracted or something that I can't put my finger on."

I snuggled my face closer to his chest and tightened the hold of my arms around his torso for a brief instant, then a pulled away from him, missing his warmth right away. "I'm fine, really, I promise. Tomorrow I will be as good as new."

Even in the faint light I was able to see the curve of his lips as he smiled at me, "Okay, let me pray for you."

He pulled me close again and bowed his head until his chin rested on top of my head. I closed my eyes and listened to his strong voice, and felt it vibrate in his chest at the same time. "Father God, thank you for Andrea Sanders, who means so much to me. Thank you for protecting her, for transforming her day by day, and for bringing her into my life. I pray you will make me a man who is worthy to call this daughter of Yours, mine, and mine alone someday, if it is Your will. Take care of her tonight, Father, help her feel better, and drive out any presence or power that might be trying to come against her, In Jesus name I ask these things. Amen."

When he finished the prayer, Sullivan pressed his lips against my forehead and held them there a few seconds. The best kind of shiver ran through my body, the kind of shiver that lets you know you have been touched by something that is pure.

"Someday I want to kiss you properly, but I can wait until the time is right." He whispered huskily.

A shiver ran through me as I realized in that moment that I loved this man. I would not say those words now though. I was still afraid that this thing we were building was like a house of cards that might topple if we rushed it.

We said our good nights after that and went our separate ways home.

The following Saturday our first worship service was scheduled at Stockwell. Sullivan's roommate, Justin had been a manager for the worship team, and he had made flyers and sent out invitations to dorms, and every group on campus he could think of. We had no idea how many people might show up. The leadership on campus actually seemed overly willing to help us succeed. They had given us free use of the main auditorium, which would hold a large number.

We arrived at 5 o'clock that afternoon to set up and do sound check. There was actually an entire team of people from Transform Church who came to help us. We had decided to call this evening's gathering "Visible". Mason would be sharing a message which we were all eager to hear. The hope was that we could actually call this endeavor a "church plant" and that Visible Church could meet here every week and partner with Transform to minister in the community.

We were scheduled to begin at 7pm. It was 6pm when people started to arrive. Actually a lot of people were arriving. We had been nervous that few would be there. But there was either a hunger already for God, or just massive curiosity about what we were doing. I was still struggling with the fear that Andrew might show up here.

At 6:30 Mason asked us all to join together to pray one more time. We gathered backstage in a large circle and were just preparing to begin when the back entrance opened and a group of people filed in. Sullivan immediately stepped forward, extending his hand to one of the men in the group. "Dr. Timmins, thank you for coming."

There was a flurry of activity as a lot of hand shaking went on, then I saw him. Andrew Harrison was among the group that had joined us. I thought I was going to be sick on the spot. My heart rate suddenly doubled and my vision literally closed in until I could barely see. I shrank back as far as I could. I mingled with the folks on either side of me. I hoped the muted light was enough to disguise me, or that perhaps I had changed enough in all this time that Andrew would not recognize me. I was frantic in my mind as I was realizing my worst fear coming to life. How was I ever going to step out onto that stage and sing into a microphone with Andrew here, and his former words hanging in the air? Why God? Why did You allow him to come here? I didn't say it out loud, but inwardly I was screaming.

I tried really hard to focus on Mason's words as he prayed, but I couldn't. The voices of insecurity and low self-worth were beating me up. The funny thing was I never really understood that those were prominent voices in my head until I after I prayed in the butterfly garden. Sullivan had actually been teaching in our small group that the enemy only bothers you on a conscious level when you surrender to the Lord. He knows that he has lost your soul for eternity, but he wants to keep you busy in your mind so that you are not effective for God. Somehow the memories of those teaching sessions started to penetrate until I felt the presence of God in the form of a calming peace in my mind. It seemed like a lot of time had passed, but my internal battle was over by the time Mason finished praying.

When I opened my eyes I did not dare look in the direction where I had last seen Andrew. To see him might send me back into chaos. It was almost 7 by now anyway and the worship team had to get on stage. I fell into step behind Jenny as we moved toward the stage. I felt my trepidation dissipate as the first strains of music began. The presence of the Lord was here and He deserved all of my attention.

We sang the three songs we had been practicing, following the response of the people gathered to decide when to move from one song to the next. The atmosphere was electric. Many of these people were not strangers to worshipping.

After the last notes were played, Mason moved away from the keyboard as Carter carried a small stool to the front of the stage where he laid Mason's bible.

After extended greetings and announcements about the future of Visible Church Mason began his message:

"Hey everybody, thank you for being here tonight as we launch this thing we call "Visible". My name is Mason Collins, on behalf of myself and the Visible team, welcome. We hope that tonight is just the beginning of something huge here. I'm going to dive right into our verses for tonight. If you have a bible that's great, if you don't that's fine too. We'll put the verses on the screen behind me. I've chosen just two verses out of the thousands and thousands to choose from, these two hooked me when I read them. There is a book in the back part of the bible, which is known as The New Testament. It is called Ephesians, it is actually a letter. A man named Paul, a great man of God, wrote the letter to a church in a city called Ephesus. In the first few chapters Paul reminds the Ephesians of all that God has done for them, all that He has given them of Himself, and then he counsels them on the things they still lack, just in case they begin to think they have it all going on. In the book of Ephesians chapter 5, verses 13-14(NKJV) it says: *But all things that are exposed are made manifest by the light, for whatever makes manifest is light. Therefore He says: 'Awake, you who sleep, arise from the dead, and Christ will give you light.'*

I suppose you could call these the theme verses of Visible Church. It can be a scary thing to be exposed to the light. Think of a dark night when your eyes have grown accustomed to being without light. The very moment light is introduced your eyes will blink, not really in pain, but certainly discomfort. That reflex action of your eyelid was a design choice God created in us to protect our eyes from injury. The light is not meant to hurt your eyes but your eyelids will take a stand against it. So often we do the same thing with God on a spiritual level. We imagine all these rules and laws that seem impossible to keep, and even feel imprisoning in their intensity, when in all actuality it's not rules that God wants to give. There are things we are warned against in His word, as well as things we are encouraged to do. The warnings are for the things that have the potential to hurt us in some way. The encouragement is for the things that will make us stronger, more loving, joyful people. God did make us uniquely compared to other sources of life, in that He gave us the intelligence factor that will allow us to choose, or reject Him and His ways. I've heard it said that God is a gentleman, who will knock on the door of your spirit through His own Spirit, but He will not open the door and enter unless He is invited. One verse that Paul wrote to a different church is 1 Corinthians 10:23, pretty much says a lot of things are permissible, but many of them are of no benefit. . In other words, God says go ahead and do whatever you want to do, but you better be aware that some things will bring death and destruction, eventually. This is why we need exposing by the Light of Christ Jesus that will make visible the things that will destroy us. No offense to anyone, but none of us are smart enough to "get it" without the wisdom of God to guide us. The sad thing about not surrendering to the Light is that we will not be investing anything into our eternity. If we fail to grasp even a tiny mustard seed of faith to believe and accept Jesus sacrifice, eternity will be a long time to think about what might have been. If we have a "faith" that says it's every man for himself we might make it into heaven by the skin of our teeth, but very little reward will be waiting. It is in our surrender and obedience that we are made alive in Christ. If you look a little further at this church in Ephesus you will find that Jesus had something to say to them in Revelation. To paraphrase, He also told them all the things they were doing right, but then He said, 'however'. When you throw a however in there it means something important will follow. In this case the however Jesus told them was that they were basically doing everything right for all the wrong reasons. There is only one reason that should motivate our actions. That is the love we have for God, the Father, the Son and the Holy Spirit. Those Ephesian believers had lost their first love. The very things they thought they were doing for God needed to be exposed to the truth that it had become about them and what they were doing, as opposed to just being about Him. The danger in losing our first love is that we may become weary in doing the right thing. It's not about how we begin as much as it is about how we finish. When we get tired we will let our guard down and a little ungodliness will creep in, which, if left unchecked will only increase to more ungodliness. The next thing you know we are basically dead. I heard a story some time ago about a young boy and cow. The cow belonged to the boy's neighbor, and unfortunately it had died. It was during the winter and the farmer who owned the cow seemed in no hurry to remove it. The boy had ridden by that dead cow with his mom several times when one day he said to no one in particular 'dead cows don't moo'. This struck the mom as a funny thing to say, but the more she thought about it the more she equated his statement with the church. It seemed to her that the church as a whole did not seem to be exhibiting the power of God, thus she concluded 'dead Christians don't praise.' She searched her bible and found this verse Psalm 115:17(NKJV) *The dead do not praise the Lord, nor do any who go down into silence.*

This is the truth, if we are still dead in our trespasses, having not been forgiven and raised to life in Christ, then we are missing opportunities to introduce others to the life-giving power of Jesus Christ. If we have received our forgiveness, yet remain unengaged in our culture with love in action among people, we are also missing opportunities. What things need to be made visible in your life? What is keeping you from knowing full freedom in Christ? What is hindering you from being the receptacle which God can use to shine His light? Those are important questions. Please do not leave this place without answering them. Psalm 22:3(NKJV) *But you are holy, enthroned in the praises of Israel (God's people).* What if your praise here in this moment and this place were the only praise He had to inhabit? What if the eternity of the other people in this room rested on your true worship? Would it make you want to be a living Christian instead of a dead, or sleeping one? Think about that as the worship team leads us."

There was quite a response to Mason's message as several people crowded to the front of the stage. He led them in a prayer then offered the option to meet with prayer counselors who were members of Transform Church. It was amazing to see it unfold as we sang a song Sullivan and Luke had written called 'Pour Out Your Glory.' It was plain to see that His glory was there.

When the place finally cleared out we began packing up our equipment. We were just finishing up when the group of leaders from the college joined us on the stage. Dr. Timmins made the rounds shaking hands and congratulating us on the evening. The others in his group also fell in line behind to shake our hands. I was afraid to look to see if Andrew was among them. I actually kept my eyes lowered as much as possible.

The fourth person to reach for my hand was Andrew. As hard as I tried to pretend that he was someone else, I could not, as the truth was standing right in front of me. The very moment my eyes met his I knew he recognized me. He knew exactly who I was. I wasn't sure if he would acknowledge me with familiarity, but I decided it would be up to him. I would be glad to pretend we had never met.

I could tell he was surprised as he held my hand a little longer than necessary. The tilt of his lips was not exactly a smile, as he spoke in a muted voice, for my ears only, "Hello Andrea. I didn't expect to see you here…in this setting."

I smiled a fake smile and replied, "Well, here I am just the same."

He finally let go of my hand and moved on. Soon the goodbyes were spoken, with the plan in place for the next meeting of Visible Church. It was an exciting time, especially for Mason. Of course, he would eventually build a worship team from among the students at Stockwell to free the rest of us up to continue at Transform. We would be looking for a new keyboard player as well. God would send all of the right people in His timing.

I had ridden with Sullivan so I joined him as we walked to where we had parked. I was silently hoping that he was still so hyped about the night that he did not notice how Andrew had lingered by me. I was deciding what to tell him, just in case, as he opened my door and waited for me to climb in.

"What an amazing time! God was surely in this place this evening.

There are several new believers and a lot of rededications. I can't wait to see where God will take Visible." Sullivan's voice almost vibrated with excitement.

"It is a little overwhelming just to be a tiny part of something like that. Sometimes I still can't believe that God wants me in this place with all of you who are such tremendous examples of Jesus."

"You don't give yourself enough credit Andrea. You are an example of Jesus just as much as any of us."

I nibbled at the inside of my lip, a habit I had picked up in an effort to stop biting my nails. I was feeling some kind of way again, and I was not sure where it would lead me. I knew that some truths from my past were going to have to rise to the surface if I wanted this to go on with Sullivan.

"You got awfully quiet. What's wrong?" Sullivan said with concern.

I was glad that darkness had settled because I really did not want him to see my face at that moment. It was ironic considering we had just heard that timely message about becoming visible.

"Sullivan, there are some things I need to tell you about me."

Even in the darkened cab of his truck I could see that he took his eyes off the road to glance at me. "There is nothing you can tell me that will change the way my heart feels."

He looked back at the road, and silence settled for a moment. I knew that my heart was already fully invested in him. But I could not continue to let this relationship grow without telling him the hard, ugly truth. I wanted to believe that he meant what he said about nothing changing the way his heart was feeling, but I felt like there were a lot of things that would keep coming back to knock me down if I did not expose them.

By this time Sullivan was pulling into my driveway. After getting out of the main road he stopped and turned off the engine. "This is as good a time as any to tell me what is on your mind. But I have something to tell you first. I really wanted a different setting for this, but the setting will not diminish nor strengthen what I have to say."

I was suddenly more nervous about what he had to say than what I needed to say. "I'm going to turn on the interior light." Sullivan informed me just before dim light flooded the cab of the truck.

I blinked a couple of times to get my eyes adjusted. When I was able to focus on his face the breath caught a little in my throat. I had never had anyone look at me like that before, not even Cam. It was like being swaddled in the warmest, softest blanket when you were cold.

He slid as close to me as he could get in the confining space, and turned his body toward mine. I followed the movement as he reached to grasp my hand in his intertwining his long fingers with mine. He lifted my hand to his lips and grazed my knuckles with a sweet tender kiss. I watched him kiss my hand then he lifted his eyes to my face. I saw his throat move as he swallowed, maybe he was nervous too. "Andrea I don't want to say this lightly. If I could take you on a journey into my heart and let you see how deeply you have been rooted there it would perhaps be the only way to make you understand that I love you beyond any words I can think of. I think I started falling for you the day I literally knocked you down. It was like God shined a great light down that made everything and everyone pale against you. In that light I found the answer to every prayer I had prayed since I was twelve years old. You are the one God made for me. I love you second only to Him, because He is love and has made it possible for me to love you with this intensity."

Silence hung between us for a short time, but not an awkward silence, just silence. I wanted to respond with everything I was feeling. I wanted to forget the past and start from today, which is what I had done with God in the butterfly garden. But Cam's words from long ago came crashing into my mind…'don't let the scars consume you….' Maybe it was God giving me wisdom, or just self-preservation, but one way or another, I knew that some scars would continue to be thin, tender layers until I confronted them, and spoke them out loud; exposed them. That was the only way to truly have scars that were about healing instead of hurting.

"Sullivan I am not eloquent enough to put into words what my heart is screaming right now. I just love you, like I've never loved anyone else in my life. Frankly, it scares me because the closest I ever came to loving another like this was Cam. If I lost you like I lost him I'm not sure I would survive. I don't want this night to be about anything other than love. The love of God that brought life tonight at Visible, and the love you and I have confessed. I will tell you the things you need to know another time."

"We can do whatever you want. Maybe we can talk Thursday. My mom is over the moon with excitement to meet your family, and to share a meal. That woman loves to cook. Thanksgiving is her favorite holiday."

"I wouldn't miss it for the world. I am a little nervous about my dad. You've met him so you know how withdrawn he can be. I think you've even seen his quick, dark mood changes a couple of times. I don't want that to happen with your family."

"Since we know worrying will not help at all why don't we pray right now, then we need to get some rest so we can lead worship at Transform tomorrow morning?"

We clasped hands and bowed our heads as Sullivan's strong voice filled the truck. "God, we are in awe of who You are: the very essence of love. And You created us with that same essence as we are in Your image. Thank You for sowing love in our hearts for one another. And God help us to trust our future to You. By Your power, may those things that Andrea struggles with have no more dominion in her life. God, if telling me is how her healing is to come, then prepare my heart to have the capacity it needs to respond as Jesus would. We continue to ask that You save Mr. Sanders. Free him from the demons that haunt him. And let us do all that we can to help the process, in Jesus' name. Amen.

I would never tire of hearing Sullivan pray for me. That was something I wanted to hear for the rest of my life.

28

The first part of the week went by quickly, and before I knew it Wednesday night was upon us. I had helped my mom make pumpkin and pecan pies, which were our small contribution to Thanksgiving dinner. David had already agreed to join Madison's family so he would not be going with us to the Jeffries. But daddy still seemed to be in a mood to go. I remembered a verse from a recent sermon that said we should pray continually, I thought that was a difficult thing to do. I mean who has time to stay on their knees all the time? But this dinner invitation was teaching me that praying continually was more about attitude than anything else. I had been constantly praying all week that daddy would not only go to dinner, but that he would be in a good mood.

The day turned out to be as great as Sullivan had always thought it would, and it just gave strength to my faith in God to answer prayers. Daddy was so relaxed and so personable it was like watching a different person than the one I had known all my life.

We had opted to eat at one, but had spent a big part of the morning together. Sadie and Suzanna adored Casey. They brought out the dollhouse their dad had built for them, which was a perfect replica of the Cedar Falls Inn. The three of them giggled as they played. Sean and the men, including daddy and Mason, had gone fishing for a couple of hours.

That left me and mama to help Sondra with food prep, while Silas's wife, Joanna rested. She was only a few weeks away from her due date and had been having some difficulties.

A few hours later Thanksgiving dinner was a wrap and the dishes all done. Mama and Daddy took the little kids and went home around four o'clock. Sullivan and I decided to take a walk in the Cedar Falls Park. It was unseasonably warm so there were quite a few people out and about. But we managed to find a fairly secluded spot where we spread the flannel blanket we had brought.

Neither of us spoke right away as we took a seat on the blanket. I was too busy looking around the park at the beauty still evident even though most of the foliage was gone for the season. Really I was trying to avoid the conversation that I knew I needed to have with Sullivan.

I finally decided the silence had stretched enough. I slid away from Sullivan because I was sure I could not say what I needed to say if he was too close to me.

"I can't put this off any longer, Sullivan. I have some things I need to tell you about my past. But before I do I have to ask you to just listen, and promise me that you won't automatically say that the things I tell you don't matter. I want you to listen to every detail and imagine them even worse. If you hear me and can still say you love me then I will know that nothing can ever tear us apart."

"No matter what you say I will love you still."

"Sullivan, please hear me out, and you have to promise that you will take some time to think about what I say. It's a lot of ugly stuff. I'm not proud of any of it, but it is what it is. I just need to know that when it is all said and done you can still say you love me with the same pure love. That is the only way the scars I carry can become signs of healing rather than perpetual broken places."

Sullivan nodded slightly and inhaled heavily, as if sucking in the words I had said, finally he replied, "I do promise to hear you with my ears, and to keep my heart open. You know I'm going into this more than ready to say none of it matters. But, I promise I will take time to think and pray before I give any reply."

I was satisfied that he meant it, so I began to talk. I went all the way back to when I was nine, beginning with the things I had told Cam before he died. By the time I finished talking I was hoarse and dry from breaking down in tears a few times. The light was beginning to fade from the early evening sky.

I don't know what Sullivan had expected to hear, but I could tell from his silence. And the look on his face that I would not have had to squeeze that promise out of him anyway. He had a lot to think about and I was not sure what the outcome would be.

We spoke little as we collected the blanket and started the hike back to the car. My heart was heavy as we descended the trail. The silence was killing me, but I had asked him not to reply right away. I wondered what was going through his mind. I had painted the ugliest picture possible. I even told him about Andrew, though I never gave his name. I knew that the integrity Sullivan lived by would cause him to want to confront Andrew. I was not sure that would turn out well. With Visible Church just getting established at Stockwell I did not want to chance interfering.

After a quick thank you and good bye to all of Sullivan's family, he drove me home. The silence between us had never been so loud. But it was exactly what I had asked for, so I was sure he was thinking and praying, just like he said he would.

I didn't see Sullivan until Saturday. We did not talk on the phone or have any communication. I was really working myself into a bad way in my mind. I don't know how long I expected him to think things through before he talked to me, but I was almost afraid he would never speak to me again. I was already planning to drop off the praise team, and probably look for another church if Sullivan did not want to see me anymore. Because if I had learned anything it was that I needed God. No Davider what people were in my life there was always the chance that they would no longer be for one reason or another, but God was my constant. In fact, if it weren't for praying since I talked to Sullivan that Thursday I would have lost my mind by now.

It was almost 4pm on Saturday when Sullivan showed up at my house. Daddy was gone hunting, and I was helping mama and the kids make ornaments for the Christmas tree when I heard the knock.

"See who is at the door." Mama said.

I was rubbing glue between my fingers and softly singing We Three

Kings along with the CD we were listening to. The words died on my tongue when I opened the door and saw Sullivan standing there.

"Who is it Andi? Can you hurry and shut the door please? We don't want to heat the entire block." She wasn't mad, but that sounded just like something daddy would say.

I snapped to attention then and invited Sullivan to come in.

"I hope it is ok that I just dropped by." Sullivan said walking into the room. "Hello Mrs. Sanders, hey guys."

Casey squealed when she saw him and dashed across the room with Mason a couple of steps ahead of her. They both slammed into Sullivan so hard they almost knocked him over. "Hey Sully!" Derrick exclaimed, using the nickname Sullivan had told him about.

"Looks like you guys are having a great time." Sullivan said as he dropped to his knees and hugged them, one in each arm.

"Yes, we are!" Casey confirmed. "Come on, you can help us."

"Thank you Casey, but I need to borrow your big sister for a few minutes first, if that is ok with your mom?" He said questioningly as he glanced at my mom.

"Of course, we are in a "hurry up and wait" position anyway. We can't proceed with these ornaments until the glue dries. Why don't you two go into the living room? I'll set these two up with a movie in my room."

"Thanks mama," I smiled nervously.

Sullivan and I proceeded into the living room with me feeling as awkward as I could ever remember. I literally had no idea how the next few minutes going were to affect the rest of my life.

"I've missed you." Sullivan said as he sat down in the rocking chair, effectively letting me know that he did not want me to sit beside him.

I sank down onto the couch, "It seems like more than two days since I've seen you for sure." I whispered.

Sullivan ran his fingers through his hair and sighed, I had never seen him do that before. "I don't know where to start, Andrea. I have spent the past 48 hours thinking, praying, and crying and I found that it was not an easy process. But I know where I stand and I am certain, so here I am. I spoke to your dad on the phone early this morning before he left. I also spoke to your mom. They both knew I was planning to be here at this very moment."

I'm sure my face showed my confusion. I didn't know how to respond. Actually I was holding my breath in fear of what he might say.

"I want you to know that I have considered everything you told me and none of it makes a difference to me. It matters to me because I hate the hurt you have endured, and forgiving your dad may be the hardest part of the process. But most of all it matters to me because it matters to you. And you matter to me. The bottom line is I love all of you and I don't see that ever changing. I just hope you can accept all of God's restoration and all of my love and that it will be enough."

Tears were snaking their way down my cheeks by the time he finished speaking, then he was out of the rocking chair and across the room. I stood just as he stepped in front of me and leaned into his arms. "I love you so much Sullivan." I said against his chest. "Thank you for still loving me. I don't begin to understand why God brought us together, but I am so thankful He did."

I was so relieved after that conversation. My life was back on track, actually more on track than ever before.

29

Life happened like clockwork the weeks slipped by. Sullivan and I spent as much time together as we could between work and classes. Being a part of the praise team was a plus with practices adding to our together time. We alternated time between his house and mine, and I even helped out at the Cedar Falls Inn sometimes. I was thrilled to be invited to be at the hospital when Joanna gave birth to baby Maxwell Anderson Jeffries. He was born on December 21, exactly four years after Cam died. He was a beautiful reminder that life goes on.

As January passed I kept working hard to maintain good grades and was applying for scholarships in earnest.

It was the beginning of February when Beverly called me. I had not heard from her at all since I walked out of Pauly's for the last time. Sometimes I felt guilty for not checking on her, and I had no good excuses for why I hadn't. She wanted to meet me at the old Holy Grounds Coffee Shop, which was no longer owned by a church, It was now called the Java Bean Café. I was not overwhelmingly excited to be in that building again, but I was looking forward to seeing Beverly.

We met on Tuesday afternoon after I got out of class. I was off work that day and had told Sullivan about the meeting. I had told him about

Beverly when I told him about my days at the frat house. He assured me he would be praying as I went to meet with her.

I walked into the café a few minutes before our 2pm appointment. It was totally different than it had been before. The old couches and mismatched tables had given away to new armless couches and tall, elegant café tables with tall chairs. The floor was all wood and the bar in the back was now a food counter. It was not an unpleasant place to be. In fact, the delicious aroma wafting through the air reminded me that I had missed lunch that day.

I asked the hostess to seat me near the front so that I could keep an eye out for Beverly. She led me to a small corner table. I had only been there a few minutes when I saw her. She came in the door as if in a hurry. I could tell she was winded. The hostess welcomed her and exchanged a few words then I watched as she proceeded to lead her to where I sat waiting.

I stood as she approached, not really sure how I should greet her. I felt compelled to meet her with a hug. I moved around the table and opened my arms, she willingly stepped into my embrace, I felt healing in that moment. I hoped she did too.

We took our seats and ordered a coffee. As the waitress walked away I said, "Beverly, it is truly a joy to see you."

She smiled, "I didn't know what to expect since the last time I saw you was the day you marched into Yana's office and quit Pauly's. I can see that you are doing well. I hope you don't mind that I called you. But I needed to make sure you were ok."

I was so touched by her concern for me, and felt even guiltier that I had not shown the same for her. "I am so glad you called. I have thought about you a lot. I have wondered many times how things turned out for you."

I quit Pauly's about two weeks after you did. When Yana hired another girl and took her to the frat house the first Saturday night she worked I saw that it was a pattern I didn't want to follow any longer. I told my parents what had been going on and my dad talked to law enforcement about it."

"Oh my goodness, I didn't know that. What came of it all? I never heard anything on the news."

"To be honest I'm pretty sure Yana did have some friends in law enforcement because she quickly sold Pauly's and moved out of town. I don't even know where she ended up."

"What about the parties at the frat house?" I asked because Sullivan had been on a quest to do something about the goings on there since I told him what had happened there.

"I'm sure there are the normal frat parties, but I know all social activity was shut down for a while. Apparently Yana was just beginning to build her own little empire of call girls. I still can't believe how you and I got caught up in that mess."

"Me either. That was a terrible time. I'm glad we both survived it. But, let's discuss the present, how are you doing now?" I reached across the table and covered her hand with mine.

The waitress returned with the sandwiches we had ordered. There was a momentary awkwardness as I paused, ready to bless my food, but not sure what Beverly would say. "Do you mind if I bless the food before we eat?"

If Beverly was surprised I didn't pause to see. I just bowed my head and spoke a quick blessing.

We ate our lunch and spent time catching up. I found out that Beverly had gone to cosmetology school and already had a job at a salon in town. I also found out that Beverly had already been a Christian when we worked at Pauly's. She had carried around a different kind of guilt than I had. It was courageous of her to confess everything to God and her parents. She said the forgiveness she felt then was much sweeter than what she felt when she had first prayed as a little kid. I guess because she felt like she was dirty and needed cleansing. That reminded me of another teaching from our small group about a woman who had been forgiven of many sins. She loved Jesus so much that she washed his feet with her tears and dried them with her hair. I thought about all those tears of mine in the butterfly garden, and every tear I had cried since then. I wondered if maybe God would accept those as my way of "washing Jesus' feet." I really hoped He would.

Beverly and I parted ways after a two hour lunch. We had plans to get together weekly to support one another and to develop a friendship since our previous time together had not really given us that chance.

30

The next few months went by quickly. I had introduced Natalie to Beverly, and the three of us decided to start a small group to work with high school girls. We met twice a month, once in Cedar Falls so Sadie and Suzanna could come and bring friends. The other week we met in Oakdale, so that Natalie's younger sister, Natasha could bring her friends. During the past six months we had spent time mentoring 17 girls.

Mason had assembled a praise team for Visible Church pretty quickly, which freed the rest of us up to more time into Transform. We got a new keyboard player named Freddie, well, Fredericka, after her grandfather. "Freddie" suited her much better. She was almost as talented as Mason and added a great spark to the praise team.

I finished up my associate's degree in general studies in May and was registered to begin class as a junior at Stockwell in August. Things were great with Sullivan and me. His family felt like my family and for the most part he felt the same about mine. Daddy seemed to be changing one day and going back to his old ways the next. I tried on occasion to talk to him about God, but he would have no part of those conversations. So I decided to just keep praying instead.

Casey and Derrick had been invited to go to the beach with Uncle Paul's family the first week in August. Since mama couldn't get off work, they would be going without her. David had moved into his own place a couple of months before, and with Sullivan away for two weeks at a ministry leadership conference, it looked like it was going to be just me and my parents for at least a week. I wish I could have been more excited about that prospect, but I was actually dreading it in a way.

Our time together began on Friday afternoon. I had offered to take my parents out to eat, in fact, I was planning on driving to Cedar Falls. They had not seen the Jeffries since Thanksgiving and I thought it would be a nice outing. Unfortunately daddy came home from work in a bad way. It was the worst I had seen him in months. He was like a dark cloud that threatened to spill out a storm any moment. The words that came out of his mouth were as vile as anything I had ever heard. Unlike every other time, this time daddy's anger seemed to be directed at mama instead of me. I didn't like that at all. There would come a time in the near future when I would be moving out and I didn't even want to think about leaving if daddy started taking out his bad moods on mama. Someone had to be the buffer.

The difference between me and mama was that she would not fight back with her words, or actions. I knew now that she was retreating into a shell of prayer, but old habits die hard when old adversaries raise their heads. I was determined not to be intimidated by daddy. I suppose I thought I could fight this battle by myself.

"What happened at work today to set you off?" I raised my voice in response to the string of profanity that still hung in the air.

"Don't you get sassy with me, girl, you might be all grown up. But you still live in my house. I can let off a little steam if I want to!"

"Is that why you have that beer?" I asked in a more moderate tone.

In response he slammed the case of beer down so hard I thought it could have broken the table where it landed. Visions of a younger me frantically reaching for my car keys flooded my mind. I actually flinched as I remembered that night right here in this spot where he had slammed my head into that same table. I felt a little sick to my stomach remembering that horrible night. *"You could have died!"* Those words sounded in my mind in a sneering tone. At the same time another thought was vying for attention…*"Don't let that scar get a hold on you again."*

Daddy almost pushed me over as he moved past. Grabbing a chair he jerked it out and sat down by the table, in one quick motion he reached into the box, pulling out a can. After popping the top he lifted the beer to his lips and tipped his head back, swallowing compulsively at least four times before pulling the can back down.

"Please don't do this." Mama pleaded. "You know how you get when you are drunk."

Daddy turned his eyes on mama and for the briefest of moments I saw the softest, most vulnerable expression on his face. Quickly he hardened his features, erasing any tenderness that might have been displayed.

The next few minutes passed quickly, but seemed agonizingly slow. As the situation escalated and I realized that I was powerless to protect mama, I did what I should have done many times before. I got my phone and dialed 9-1-1.

I told the operator what was going on. Then I laid down the phone, but did not break the connection. I would do whatever I could to keep daddy from hurting mama too badly until the police came.

It was a terrible scene that two officers burst in on a short time later. Thankfully the officers were able to get control of the situation quickly.

The next few hours were difficult to get through, as daddy was manhandled and finally dragged away in handcuffs, while mama and I were taken to the hospital. Mama had to get stitches on her hand. We were not even sure where the cut came from. Neither of us had to have stitches on our face, but we were beaten up badly, and emotionally wrecked.

Daddy would be spending the night in jail. When we finished at the hospital I called to ask Natalie if she could come to the hospital and give us a ride home. She insisted on coming in to help clean up the mess we had left in our wake. Together we settled mama into bed. A nurse had given her something to relax her so she was barely lucid when we got home anyway. I was glad for that. If we could clean up while she was asleep it would help.

After we had gotten the furniture righted and cleaned up everything Natalie said, "Can we sit down and talk for a minute before I leave?"

I was exhausted, but so grateful for her friendship that I couldn't say no. We took a seat in the living room. Natalie did not beat around the bush, "Andrea, I don't know why God allowed this to happen to you while Sullivan is away. I know he is the one who usually prays for you, but I would be so happy if you would allow me to in his place just this one time."

I had to admit that the thought had run through my mind several times…why now? Didn't God know how much I needed Sullivan? But the deeper thought knocking me down was, why did God let it happen at all? We had come so far, and daddy had been doing so much better for months. Why a setback now?

"I can see by the look on your face that you have been questioning God. Maybe that is why I am here." Natalie said.

"Do you remember the message from Pastor Colin from last weekend? Just in case you don't, let me remind you. He read from 2 Corinthians chapter 12 about God's strength and our weakness. Andi, you are weak, but Christ in you is strong. God even says His strength is made perfect in your weakness. Perhaps it is in our admitting that we are weak and need His strength that His strength is perfected in us. Do you think God let this happen while Sullivan is away so that you would learn to lean more on Him than any person…even Sullivan?"

I digested that for a moment, and I had to come to the conclusion that it made sense. But knowing it and applying it don't always happen on cue. I was sure I would have to think more about it before I accepted it. I had to reply in some way as Natalie was not moving until I did. "It makes sense, but will I be a horrible Christian if I say that it may take a while for it to settle into my heart?"

Natalie patted my knee and said, "Absolutely not." Then she bowed her head and began to pray, as I began to cry silent tears, wondering why God would love me enough to give me such good friends.

After she prayed, Natalie said, "Will you call Sullivan tonight? Or will you wait until tomorrow?"

I had already mulled this over in my mind so I was ready with a reply, "I'm not going to call him at all, and I don't want you to either."

"You have to tell him Andrea." Natalie advised. "Imagine when he finds out if you don't call him. He will be hurt and angry. You would be too if the shoe was on the other foot."

"I don't want to bother him at the conference. That would be such a distraction. He might even withdraw early and come home. I can't do that to him."

"I understand where you are coming from, but you can't start protecting him from hard things in your life. Total honesty is the only way to have a healthy relationship. It is best to live a life uncovered. That way the enemy of your soul cannot use anything against you."

I was silent for a minute as I thought about what Natalie had said. I knew she was right. Whether I wanted to tell Sullivan or keep it from him, telling him would be the better option. "I don't know how you got so wise at such a young age, but I know you are right. I will call him tomorrow morning."

I walked Natalie to the door after that, hugging her and thanking her for all her help and advice, and mostly her friendship.

I went straight to bed, sleeping only a couple of hours at a time, as I was worrying about mama and wanted to check on her. By the time the morning came I was more than ready to just get up and stay up for a while. I had decided to call Sullivan early before his day got started. It was 7:45 when I dialed his number.

"Good morning beautiful," he answered on the first ring. "I wasn't expecting to hear from you so early, but I'm glad I did."

I told myself I would not cry, but the sound of his voice was soothing, and knowing he was so far away made me want to melt into his arms even more. So despite my best intentions my voice cracked on a sob as I replied, "I...Sullivan, I have something to tell you."

"What is it Baby? You're scaring me now." He was suddenly alarmed.

"I'm sorry," I said through my tears, "I didn't want to cry, but I guess it was bound to happen."

I proceeded to tell him about the horrible scene with daddy the evening before and how he had turned his wrath on mama. He listened in silence, allowing me to finish before he responded.

"Baby, I'm so sorry I wasn't there. I'll see if I can bow out of the conference early and reschedule since we just got started. I can be home in about six hours."

"Please don't do that. I only told you because I would not have wanted you to keep something like that from me. There is nothing you can do at this point anyway. Mama and I will go to the police department at 10 this morning to see what happens next. If you can pray, Sullivan, I don't know if I have the capacity to forgive daddy anymore." I said honestly.

I heard Sullivan suck in his breath and hold it for a minute. I imagined him sliding his long fingers through his hair. "I promise to pray, but I have to be honest and tell you that I don't know if I can forgive him this time either."

His admission took me by surprise. I could not remember a single time since I had known him that he had said something like that. Maybe this time I would have to dig deeper for forgiveness so that I could help him do the same.

Sullivan prayed for me after that and we ended the call shortly after so he could get to his session on time. I had a lot on my mind a few hours later when mama and I left the police department with a plan in place. We had decided not to press charges against daddy if he would get counseling to try to figure out what set him off so quickly. I had called Sonia Rutherford who was a Christian counselor I knew from Transform Church. She had agreed to meet with daddy beginning that very day, even though it was Saturday. She felt like it was imperative to start therapy while he was willing. She also told me and mama we should not come with him to the session. There would be a time for group therapy once she got to know daddy individually.

The two weeks while Sullivan was away were long. I missed him terribly, but it was time for me to work through my emotions where daddy was concerned. I had decided that to withhold forgiveness from him would only hurt me, and somehow slow down his healing process. He had been to six counseling sessions already, and I thought I could detect glimmers of hope. He had at least apologized to me and mama. That was something he had never done before. It felt like a small victory.

In mid-August I became a student at Stockwell. I was a junior and Sullivan was a senior. It was good to get to see Mason as we joined a small group with some people from Visible Church. The only thing that cast a shadow over me was the fear of running into Andrew. I had told Sullivan all of the details about my history with him, except I had never given him Andrews name.

It was three weeks into the semester when I got the first email from Andrew. It was fairly benign, just a welcome to campus and well wishes for my time at Stockwell. When I got a second email the very next day I knew it wasn't a bulk message for all new students. I was shaken when I read his words asking if we could meet. Why would he even think I would want to talk to him? The more I thought about it I was able to convince myself that he probably wanted to apologize and settle the past. It was late into the night when I emailed him back agreeing to meet him somewhere on campus the next day. I figured it would be morning before he replied, so I was surprised when the mail icon lit up almost immediately. I guess he was more anxious than I was to iron out the past so that we both could move into our future with no baggage.

I knew Sullivan would be working after class the next day, so I arranged to meet Andrew at the university coffee shop at 2.

I had a nagging thought that I should tell Sullivan, but I needed to do this on my own.

I entered the coffee shop at 1:55 the next day. I saw him immediately. I was glad that he had chosen a small booth near the front of the room. I smiled at the hostess and told her I was joining someone, then moved past her and made my way to the table where Andrew was sitting. He was on his feet by the time I got to the booth. There was an awkward moment as neither of us knew how to greet the other. Finally I just said, "Hello Andrew, why don't we just sit down?"

He seemed relieved to settle back into the seat. I sat down across from him and waited for him to say something. When uncomfortable silence began to stretch out I decided I would have to take the lead. "How have you been Andrew?"

I saw the muscles in his throat as he swallowed before he replied. "I'm doing well. I love my job here at the university. I suppose you heard about how things went down with Yana?"

I hated that he mentioned Yana. I had done a good job of leaving her in the past where she couldn't hurt me anymore. But I was glad Beverly had filled me on those details.

"Yes, I heard. I hope the activity at that frat house does not go in that direction anymore. It was not a good environment for the female population here, especially the inexperienced, naïve ones."

"I can't really speak to that. I try to distance myself from some of the things that go on here."

"I suppose you think that gives you an excuse not to do anything about any inappropriate things if you keep your head buried in the sand." I regretted saying those that as soon as it came out of my mouth. "I'm sorry I should not have said that."

"Let's forget about the frat house and talk about us." He changed the subject.

"Us?" I said questioningly. "Andrew there is no "us", apparently there never was to begin with."

In a quick movement he reached across the table and laid his hand on top of mine. Immediately I noticed the indention on his ring finger, an indication that he had been wearing a ring for some time.

I yanked my hand away and whispered angrily, "Andrew, are you married? Even if you're not, what makes you think you have a right to hold my hand?"

He blushed, an angry red as he glanced around to make sure no one was listening to us. Finally he answered, "I did get married two years ago..."

He left that admission hanging in the air. I was not sure what he was expecting of me. "You're more disgusting than ever then. If you have a wife and removed your ring to meet up with the girl who used to be your lover, you obviously have questionable motives."

I could tell that he was uncomfortable, but he quickly composed himself and gave me a smug reply. "Well, you were sitting on ready waiting to meet me apparently, because here you are."

A quick retort tried to surface, but I swallowed the words. I figured the better response would be to get up and walk away, Of course, I knew there were a few things I needed to say first. I didn't want to leave him with any impression that he could contact me again. After gaining control of my thoughts I trusted myself to speak,

"I came here because I thought you might have regrets about the way things ended for us. I was sadly mistaken to think that you might actually want to apologize. But I have moved on with my life and I am in a good place. I will not let you jeopardize the happiness I have found. I'm pretty sure I could cause trouble for you, or at least make your life uncomfortable for a while. You need to go home to your wife and be a man....be a husband."

"You've changed so much Andrea. Why couldn't you have been this accomplished woman I see right now back when we first met? I could have brought you to church and introduced you to my family. Maybe you would have been the bride who walked down the aisle and became my wife."

I actually thought he was going to cry as those words poured out of him. For an instant I wanted to feel compassion for him, but I decided pity would be safer. I remembered the last night I was at his house. When his friends left he had told me about the nice girl his mother had introduced him to. Instinctively I knew that she was the one he had married, and just like I had thought back then, he was in more of a prison of scars than I was.

"You made your choices Andrew. I can't change any of that. I had to dig my way out of the hole that I had allowed myself to get sucked into back then. I am not the same girl I was then, you are right about that. I left her, really am still leaving her, little by little as God transforms me day by day into a new creation. I don't know if you even understand that, but He is the best thing that has ever happened to me."

"When I saw you at the launch meeting for Visible Church I was surprised, well, shocked would be a better word. Then to hear you singing…it nearly tore my heart out."

"I don't know exactly what you were thinking when you asked to see me. If you thought you would find a desperate girl ready to sneak off and have an affair with a married man, you can see the futility in that. Not only do I have a relationship with God, I also have a relationship with the most wonderful man, the best one for me. I would die before I hurt him."

Andrew looked as if he would be sick, as every ounce of color drained from his face. "I…don't know what to say. I suppose I really don't have a second chance with you."

"I'm leaving now Andrew. I really do hope you will go home and fix things with your wife." I didn't give him time to reply before I was on my feet and moving toward the door. The thing that was running through my mind was that I should have told Sullivan I was coming to meet Andrew. And I was worried that he would think I was longing for my old life.

I left the coffee shop after that, content that I had laid to rest a skeleton from my past. All that was left was to tell Sullivan, which turned out to be harder than I had thought it would be. A month passed before I finally found the nerve to confess everything about Andrew. It was a Sunday afternoon. We had enjoyed a great worship time at Transform, and were on our way to Cedar Falls for lunch with his family.

Sullivan was quiet for a few minutes after I told him about the meeting with Andrew. I was still reluctant to give him Andrew's name. I was afraid he might want to confront him.

"Andrea, you have to tell me who this guy is. He seems to be the only obstacle to our chance at a real future together. I trust you beyond words, but I don't trust him, and I don't even know who he is. How can I protect you from someone I don't even know?"

"I want to tell you Sullivan, but I just don't know if it is the wisest thing to do."

"Don't you trust me Andrea? Do you think that I would go out of control and fight him or something? I should hope that you would know me better than that by now. It is often hard for me to turn the other cheek with your dad, but I've done pretty well, haven't I?"

I was devastated by his questions, because I knew he had every reason to feel hurt. I meant it when I told Andrew that I would die before I hurt Sullivan. And now hurt him is exactly what I was doing.

"I'm so sorry Sullivan, of course I trust you. I can't believe I let my fears overshadow all that I know you to be. You have so much integrity and character, and even though you will be angry, I trust that you will do the right thing." I paused, looking out the window at the scenery passing by as we drove. "His name is Andrew Harrison, he works in the....."

"Student Recruiters office." Sullivan finished my sentence.

"You know him? I guess he knows a lot of people on campus."

"Yes, I know him," Sullivan's voice took on a different tone. "I can tell you that I am so angry, I want to turn this car around and go find him right now, but the Holy Spirit in me tells me it is a good thing that you told me here and now. I have an entire weekend to process and pray about what I should do, if anything."

"I feel so much better now that I told you. This has been hanging over my head far too long."

Two weeks passed before Sullivan said anything else about Andrew. He told me then that he would not approach him as long as he did not go out of his way to contact me again. And since the activities at the frat house were settled down now we could leave that scar in the past.

31

Time passed and life happened. Before we knew it another year had gone. The ministry at Visible Church and Transform Church was growing as we partnered together. Sullivan and I stayed busy with school, work and praise team duties. We also had to make time to spend with our families. It was no wonder the days were going by so quickly.

My dad was doing well. I wanted to be able to say great, but honestly he had a lot of his own scars that I knew nothing about. Only his scars were really more like open wounds, but counseling with Sonia Rutherford, and a lot of prayer was helping. It was just a process that had no shortcuts. We had all gone for group therapy a couple of times, which was hard. It was difficult to see daddy vulnerable because that was not normal for him. We continued to pray that he would surrender himself to God to find his real healing. We had faith that one day he would.

Sullivan graduated from Stockwell in June with an Accounting degree. He was already registered to begin seminary classes at Bingham City Bible College. Bingham City was a little over three hours away from Oakdale. I was not looking forward to August when he was scheduled to leave. He had been fortunate enough to find a job as a CPA in the city, and would be living in a small apartment off campus. I had never even been to Bingham City before and could not imagine how things were going to be for us while he was there.

A few days before my 21st birthday Sullivan informed me that he had a special outing planned as a way to celebrate. My birthday was on Monday, but his plan was to take place the weekend before.

"I spoke to your parents and mine about the surprise I have for your birthday because it will involve an over- night stay." Sullivan almost sounded nervous when he told me.

I didn't really know how to feel, or I should feel any way at all. He and I had never even shared a kiss beyond brushes on the cheek or forehead. I was wondering if he was thinking of putting aside convictions and taking the physical part of our relationship to a different level. We had talked about it many times, and the attraction was most definitely there. How would I react if he was going in that direction?

There must have been an entire conversation taking place in my facial expressions, as Sullivan said, "I guess I could have announced that differently. Umm, I would like for you to come to Bingham City with me tomorrow. We will have a nice dinner and if you're interested there is play at the Bingham City Playhouse Theater. I know you like music and artsy things, so I thought you would enjoy a show. Saturday we may find some other adventure before we come home."

I loved this man so much already, but just to think that he planned such an outing to make me happy made my heart beat a little faster. "Thank you Sullivan, you are the most thoughtful person I know. I would love a trip like that for my birthday. I'm sure we are mature enough to keep our boundaries for one night."

"Oh, I guess I should have mentioned that my dad's college roommate owns a hotel in Bingham City, and he has offered to let us have two rooms for the price of one. He wasn't going to charge us at all, but I insisted on paying something. Your honor and reputation mean a lot to me, Andrea. I would never put either of us in a situation so filled with temptation that we could not overcome it."

I blushed when he spoke of my honor and reputation, after all, he knew every sordid detail of my past, yet I almost felt innocent with him. With God's help I had gotten better at redirecting my thoughts when old memories tried to crowd my mind. I suppose that was a battle I would fight for the rest of my life. Kind of like the 'thorn in the flesh' thing that Pastor Colin spoke about recently.

"I can't wait! I am especially excited to get dressed up a little. What should I wear on Saturday?"

"Since you like to get dressed up every now and then, why don't you wear a pretty dress Friday and Saturday?"

"Sounds good, I'll go by Natalie's mom's boutique and see if I can find something special."

The next day went by so slowly. I was beyond excited now that I knew where we were going. I had told my parents goodbye Thursday night. David had taken Friday off and was taking Derrick and Casey to the zoo. I was standing on the porch waving to them as they went down the driveway when I saw Sullivan's truck. I grabbed my bag and hurried to meet him. He had told me we would go by the hotel before dinner so I packed my dress and would change when we got there.

It was a beautiful day, which made for a nice drive. We made good time and were pulling into the hotel parking lot at 5:15. After getting our room keys we made a plan to meet back at the truck at 6.

I decided to put my hair up, which was rare for me, but this was a night of new experiences so a fresh look was called for. I had found two cute dresses at the boutique, a pale pink one, which I had chosen for Friday night, and a white one for Saturday.

Sullivan was waiting by the truck when I came out. He looked more handsome than usual. The blue shirt he was wearing made his brown eyes seem a little browner. His dark wavy hair always had just enough body to never lay flat on his head just the way I liked it. I could tell by the look on his face that he was pleased with my appearance as well.

Dinner was at a very nice restaurant called Chelsea's Kitchen. The food was delicious and there was live music for out entertainment. A few couples twirled around a small dance floor. I was thrilled when Sullivan asked me to dance. I was not a great dancer, but just the feel of his arms holding me made it alright.

After dinner we strolled through Bingham City Park, which was adjacent to the theater where the play would begin at 9pm. I was very excited to see the production of Cinderella in musical form. Sullivan must have thought I was like a silly school girl when we were seated and waiting for the first act to begin. He never seemed to be uncomfortable or embarrassed by my enthusiasm, which only proved to endear him to my heart even more.

When the curtain came down on the final act I was a little disappointed that it was over. "Thank you so much for this evening Sullivan, I loved every moment."

We had already exited the theater and were walking in the warm evening to where we had parked the truck. Sullivan put his arm around me and pulled me close to his side. We slowed our step for a moment and he dipped his head until his lips found my cheek. I closed my eyes and enjoyed the tenderness of that moment.

"I'm so glad you had a good time, Andrea. I enjoyed it because of you."

It was almost midnight when we got back to the hotel. "Let's say goodnight now, Baby, I know you must be tired. I have an idea for another little adventure before we head home tomorrow. How about we meet back outside our rooms at 9:30 in the morning?"

"That's sounds good to me." I answered as we entered the hotel and headed for the elevator.

Neither of us spoke as we ascended to the third floor, nor as we walked along the corridor to our rooms. His room was just before mine. We paused outside his door, and stood facing each other. Barely a moment passed before I threw my arms around Sullivan, burying my face against his chest, "I love you so much Sullivan."

He rested his head on top of my head and held me close. "I love you too Andrea."

We met as planned the next morning and decided to have breakfast at the restaurant in the hotel. After putting our bags in the truck we went into the restaurant. The owner was there and we asked him to join us. It was a good opportunity to thank him for the generous discount on the rooms.

It was almost 11am when we stepped outside and headed to the truck. I was wondering what sort of plans Sullivan had for the day, but I didn't ask. Anticipation could be a good thing.

Sullivan maneuvered through the traffic like a man on a mission. He obviously knew where he was going. A few minutes later we were parked outside the Bingham City Museum of Art.

"Oh, are we going to see an exhibit!" I exclaimed.

"Yes, I thought this would be a good finale to your birthday celebration."

"I don't know how you will ever top this for future celebrations."

"Before we go inside I need to tell you something." His tone was suddenly serious.

"Okay." I said feeling somewhat uneasy.

"I checked out this gallery a few weeks ago to see what the exhibit would be this weekend. I learned that they cater to several local artists, keeping a rotation of their works constantly on display. But there is one section of the building that houses traveling exhibits. They are usually here for a couple of weeks at a time. As it turns out the traveling exhibit here this weekend is titled 'Our Hands', the artist is from London, her name is Angela Cornwell."

"That is very exciting to see the work of an international artist!" I interrupted.

"Yes, it is exciting, but the truth is Mrs. Cornwell was an abuse victim during her childhood. The collection has some pieces that depict that. I just wanted you to know. If you think it will be too difficult to view we just won't go inside."

I digested the information, trying to imagine what an art piece might look like that would depict abuse. I realized that Mrs. Cornwell must have found healing in the process of doing it, or she most likely would not have included it in her exhibit. I decided that this was not 'happenstance', I was sure God wanted me to see it.

"I need to see it. I believe God orchestrated this for this time." I whispered.

He smiled as he reached to caress my cheek with his thumb, "I could kiss you right now."

I would not have minded at all if he did just that. But there was a purpose in our choice so we would wait. "Let's go see what Mrs. Cornwell has created." I suggested.

The interior of the museum was about what I would have imagined. It was clean and very open with many windows to allow natural light in to enhance the art. It was also quieter than the library. There was something that felt sacred being there. Perhaps art was a sacred thing, considering that God created people in His image and we are never closer to the Creator than when we are creating things. I had never thought about it that way before. But I liked the thought that someday when I finished college I could find a way to create something that could be like an act of worship; I had to smile at that.

We thoroughly enjoyed every exhibit, as we softly discussed the personality we imagined for each artist based on their work. When we had finished the first part of the tour we started toward the back part of the building to the traveling exhibit. I was feeling a little nervous about what we might see.

"Mr. Jeffries." An attractively dressed woman appeared seemingly from nowhere.

"Hello Mrs. Jergens, so nice to see you again." Sullivan extended his hand to shake hers.

"This is Andrea Sanders, the young woman I was telling you about when we spoke before."

"Hello Miss Sanders, I am happy to meet you. We are so glad you came to visit our little gallery."

I was a little embarrassed as I shook her hand. I was at a disadvantage because she knew of me, but I had not known that Sullivan had previously been here and discussed me with her, "I'm pleased to meet you, and the gallery is beautiful."

"I wanted to extend an invitation to you both before you view the 'Our Hands' exhibit. This particular work is only on display for a week at a time, and the artist travels with her work. Normally she does not make an appearance at the gallery unless there is a showcase event, but when I told her about you two she insisted that she would like to meet you. She is waiting in my office as we speak."

I could tell by the look on Sullivan's face that he was surprised to receive such an invitation.

"We were not expecting such an honor, but we would be delighted." Sullivan answered for both of us. He could read me so well. He knew I would like nothing more than to meet Mrs. Cornwell.

We followed Mrs. Jergens to her office. Upon entering we were met by a petite woman who seemed fragile and strong at the same time. She wore a veiled hat, which I thought was odd. I extended my hand as I introduced myself. The hand she held out was really just a thumb and forefinger. The rest of her hand was not there. It was just a stub covered with scar tissue. I tried not to seem awkward, but honestly, it was hard not to have some reaction. I barely saw her smile a gentle smile through the veil she wore. Once the introductions were completed Mrs. Jergens excused herself and left us. When we had taken a seat Mrs. Cornwell spoke.

"I am honored to meet you both. I hope my appearance is not too much of a shock. I am going to remove my veil now."

Slowly she removed the veil to reveal a face that was more scar tissue than smooth flesh. Again I tried not to react, but my sharp intake of breath was like thunder in my own ears. I was uncomfortable and embarrassed.

"It's okay Dear," she patted my hand with her mangled one. "You could not know what you would see as you are not familiar with my story. I wanted to see you before you view my work so that I can explain. I understand that you have been a victim of parental abuse?"

I glanced at Sullivan, not sure if I should be angry at him, or grateful to him for telling strangers about my life. "Yes, ma'am, my father has a heavy hand at times." I admitted through the lump in my throat.

"I understand your struggle in some way, as I too, was hurt at the hands of my father. His anger was ferocious and overflowed in the worst way when I was 17 years old. He became so enraged that he doused me with kerosene and threw a lit match on me. I used my hands to shield my face so the bulk of the kerosene was on them, thus the worst damage was done there. But, let me tell you, there is healing after the scars come. The scars cannot keep you from having a full life with love, laughter and joy, unless you let them. I married a wonderful man named George Cornwell III. We were married for 55 years before he passed away. I have three children, all girls, triplets in fact. They have families of their own now. They have given me 9 grandchildren. Life has really been good to me. God has been good to me. Without Him I would most likely have died that day when my father set me on fire. It was God's gift of hope that kept me going."

I didn't realize I was crying until tears slid under my chin and dropped onto my hands as they lay on my lap. I felt ashamed to feel like such a victim compared to Angela. She was very wise, and read my expression.

"Do not imagine that you are any less a victim than I. Any amount of abuse of any kind is too much. Freedom, real, true freedom, lies in forgiveness, and not wearing "victim" like a badge of courage. Real courage is to allow God to use the hurt to propel you to places in life where you would not be without the scars, the internal ones, more than the external."

"Somehow echoed in her words I heard Cam practically begging me not to let my scars consume me.

"I'm sorry that your father did such a horrible thing to you." I whispered.

"Though he went to his grave angry, and never asked, I forgave him a long time ago. It was the only way for me to find peace and healing. Honestly it had little to do with his actions, and much to do with my own reactions."

"You are very wise Mrs. Cornwell." Sullivan's voice was husky. With a glance I saw that he too was wiping tears.

Angela chuckled, perhaps to lighten the mood, "I certainly am old enough to be wise!"

"Thank you for sharing your story. It gives me a lot to think about concerning my father."

"The power of a story lies within the telling of it, my Dear." Angela moved forward in her seat, and Sullivan was instantly on his feet to help her as she stood. I also stood and took the few steps separating us. I would have shaken her hand again. Instead I leaned into the embrace she offered. I was short, but she almost made me look tall, so I had to bend forward a to fit into her arms. "We have a kinship, young one, I'm so glad to have met you," she whispered in my ear.

As we pulled apart Angela continued to speak, "One day the two of you will visit me in London. My tour with the exhibit will continue until next May. Any time after that I will be back home and ready for visitors. Now go, enjoy the pieces, the creating of them was a big part of my healing process."

Sullivan and I both thanked her again then we exited Mrs. Jergen's office and returned to the exhibit. I took a deep breath as we walked through the marble archway that was the entrance to Angela's display. Sullivan's hand found mine, and it seemed appropriate as we began the viewing of "Our Hands."

32

The exhibit was larger than I had expected. A glance around the room revealed more pieces than I could have imagined. Who would think of that many ways to depict hands with art? The first section was titled "Innocent Hands", it was child hands. One display, a Plaster of Paris casting, was two chubby hands clinging to each other, the label underneath read "My First Friend". That one progressed to a portrait of two slightly larger hands poised over the keys of a piano. The placard read "Learning Hands". Still another display was a watercolor painting of two children turning a jump rope, as a third prepared to jump in. The emphasis was on their hands holding the rope. This one was called "Together Hands".

The exhibit went on and on, with every depiction of a testament to Angela's life, but also to her incredible artistic ability. Each piece incorporated one or more forms of artistry. With Angela's extensive hand injuries it was amazing to see all that she had created.

"Imagine how these pieces would have looked if Angela were not working with scarred hands." Sullivan whispered as we stood looking at the clay sculpture of a wrinkled old hand grasping the tiny fingers of a childish chubby hand, the title, "Great-Granddaughter".

I mulled over Sullivan's words then replied, "Honestly I don't know if Mrs. Cornwell would have created any of this without her story and her scars."

He smiled and nodded. We moved on because a few other patrons had begun entering the exhibit.

The next section was titled "Dark Days". I knew without a doubt that the hard pieces of the collection would be in this grouping. The layout in this section began with dark images depicted in various media, finally ending with a charcoal painting all in black of a teenage Angela with her hands in front of her face. A dark splash of color, representing kerosene seemed to flow across the page. I flinched as I stood there by Sullivan's side. His fingers tightened around mine. If only she could have avoided the kerosene and the fire….If only daddy would love me enough to defeat his own scars. But he was making an effort, and I knew that God would break through the darkness that consumed him. I knew in that moment that my story would end differently than Angela's. My father would find his redemption with God, and in the end our relationship would be restored as well.

Tears were covering my face as we moved away from that display. There was a bench near the wall, Sullivan propelled me toward it and pressed me to sit down. He knelt in front of me and grasped my hands in his, "Baby, I'm so sorry. I didn't know it would be this hard for you."

I managed a smile through my tears and whispered as passionately as I could, "Oh Sullivan, you don't understand. These are happy tears. I just had the most wonderful peace wash over me. I know Daddy will be okay, and all the enemy has stolen will be given back. It will be even sweeter than it would have been if all the ugliness had never happened."

Sullivan leaned in and wrapped his arms around my waist. "That is our amazing God."

I hugged him for a moment, "Let's finish the exhibit. I don't want to end on the "Dark Days."

It seemed as if the flow of patrons to the exhibit had increased in the few moments that Sullivan and I had sat down. They seemed to part like the Red Sea when we moved to the last part of Angela's art. It was titled "New Beginnings". In that section there were portraits, drawings and sculptures of life events ranging from graduations to getting a job. Sullivan steered me in the direction of one piece that was titled "The

Proposal". It was a plaster cast of what had to be Angela's actual left hand, and the right hand of a male. His hand was holding a ring, as her scarred finger eagerly awaited the union of the two. Sullivan moved so close to the piece that I was afraid he would knock the suspended hands to the floor. When he reached to touch it, I whispered frantically, "Sullivan, don't! You might dislodge it."

"Look Andrea, that's an actual ring!" Sullivan exclaimed in a whisper.

"That's probably one of the reasons Angela travels with the exhibit. It is most likely her actual engagement ring." I surmised.

To my horror Sullivan reached toward the sculpture and slipped the ring off, "What are you doing Sullivan! Mrs. Cornwell was so gracious to us, we can't deface her art!"

"This ring looks like it might fit you, Andrea."

My horror turned to complete shock when suddenly Sullivan dropped to one knee in front of me and held the ring up. "How about it Margaret McClain Sanders... Andrea, will you marry me?"

I could only imagine the display of emotions across my face. Was he serious, or was this a joke?

"Sullivan, this is no time to be silly."

"I'm not trying to be silly. I have thought about this for a long time. And I have decided that it is about time that we just go ahead and follow through on what our hearts have wanted for a long time. I've told you before that I knew I loved you the moment I saw you on the ground when I literally knocked you down. It wasn't exactly sweeping you off your feet, but I'm sure God whispered to my spirit "she is the one you have been praying for". If I doubted it at all, that night in butterfly garden where you chose Christ was the cementing moment. I love you, and I always will. I cherish you, and I always will. I want to take care of you, and I always will. So, Andrea, will you marry me?"

Looking at Sullivan as he knelt there in front of me I knew that I had loved him from the same moment in front of the English building. Things changed for me in the butterfly garden too, when I began the journey to feeling like I deserved to be loved. Sullivan was a big part of the reason that I could feel worthy. How could I not marry him?

"Yes, Sullivan, I would marry you right here and now."

My hand was shaking as I extended it so he could slide the ring on. It fit perfectly. I wondered how long he had been planning this. He stood then and melted against him as his arms wrapped around me. He kissed my forehead and my cheeks repeatedly and whispered against my ear, "I will kiss you properly on our wedding day."

I had been so wrapped up in the moment with Sullivan that I had not noticed the other patrons in the art gallery forming somewhat of a circle around us. I looked around then and noticed that every one of them was holding a red rose. One by one they came and presented the roses to me, each one offering well wishes. When the final rose was in my hand I had counted 44 of them. It was a beautiful bouquet.

To say I was overwhelmed would have been the biggest understatement ever. I had no doubt that Sullivan would be surprising me for the rest of our lives.

EPILOGUE

We decided to get married the following year, after I graduated, and Sullivan had several seminary classes under his belt. His job was going well and the apartment he had would be a great place for us to begin our lives together.

It was the most beautiful wedding I could have imagined. My gown barely brushed the top of my bare feet, and yes, it was white. Was I virgin, no, not in the physical sense of the word? But the healing and realization of how my heavenly Father saw me made me feel as if I were something deeper. And the unconditional love Sullivan Jeffries had extended to me had helped me with the transformation process. Part of me really wished that Cam could somehow know that I had found a way to believe in Jesus and everything He did for me. And that I had gotten to a place where my scars were no longer reminders of brokenness as much as they were about my healing. Of course, someday he would know, because I would see him in heaven when my time on earth ended.

My bridesmaids wore pale yellow, spaghetti-strap sundresses and carried simple bouquets of daisies with yellow ribbon tied around them. They had baby's breath woven into their hair, which was swept up in loose, lush curls. They also were barefoot. My sweet little sister, who was only 7 years old, was at the place of honor as the maid who would stand right beside me. I had hugged her just before she started down the path to the makeshift altar. She triumphantly opened her hand to show me the ring she clutched. The ring, a circle that had no beginning and no end that would be a visual symbol of the pledge I would make to love Sullivan for the rest of forever.

After Casey had stepped away my dad appeared out of the shadows where he had remained, giving me time to share a moment with all of my girls, which included Beverly, who had been just as scarred by our time at the frat house as I had. Jamie was there, as beautiful as ever, the one who had literally saved my life in recent years. Then there were Sullivan's sisters. Sadie and Suzanna, both of whom had become so dear to me. And, of course, Natalie was there, my friend, who had opened her heart and her home to me at a time when I needed it the most.

There were tears in daddy's eyes, which almost made me lose my composure. It was a miracle that he had even agreed to be here to give me away. He was still reluctant to embrace Christ and the salvation He offered, but he had taken some steps. He had admitted that he had some unhealthy addictions, and he continued weekly meetings with Sonia Rutherford. Someday the real demons would be uncovered so that daddy could find his healing. I had to believe that it would happen that way. My faith was sure. Then we would have eternity to reclaim all that the enemy had stolen from us. I had a unique perspective from which to pray for daddy, because I knew what it meant to reject God's grace because it just doesn't feel natural to be loved and forgiven when the only feelings you have for yourself are shame and a sense of dirtiness. Daddy would get there in time.

"Thank you, daddy, I would not want to do my wedding day without you." I whispered as I moved to link my arm with his. The love that surged up in me for him was a novelty because of where we had come from, but little girls, and grown women alike, always want to love their daddy.

I saw his throat move as he swallowed. I'm sure he was trying to swallow those tears that were threatening to spill out. He never cried, but just the fact that I had seen the glistening in his eyes was enough to let me know that he did have a capacity for love. Awkwardly he slipped his arms around me in a tentative hug. He had no idea how many times I had needed those arms to protect me in the past.

"I'm glad you let me be here, I know I don't deserve it."

"None of that talk, daddy, we have plenty of time to hash out things that need hashing after the honeymoon." I stood on tiptoe then and pressed my lips to his rough cheek. "Let's do this." I said as I linked my arm through the crook of his elbow.

I had chosen a worship song we often sang at Transform as my wedding march, as the notes filled the sunroom at the Cedar Falls Inn daddy and I began our walk. I tried to make eye contact with as many of our guests as possible. I saw so many who had become so important to me. My heart was happy. I turned my attention to the front of the room where Sullivan waited. Beside him his dad was smiling broadly, along with Justin, Carter, Mason and Luke. All of them were like brothers and extra protectors to me. My girls were lined up opposite them, all smiling. Every eye in the place was on me, even Silas, who anchored the wedding party as the minister who would perform the ceremony. It could not have been any better if we were in the pages of a book.

In a short time the vows were repeated, the rings exchanged, and Silas gave Sullivan permission to kiss his bride. We had kept this for this moment, some would think that silly or old-fashioned, but the journey that brought us together, and the depth of love and respect we shared deserved a first ever real kiss after the vows. I lifted my face eagerly toward Sullivan as he first cupped my face in both hands then dipped his head until his lips found mine. If I had any doubts about our future they were swallowed up in that kiss. No words could really explain a heart overflowing with pure love for another.

We had a simple reception at the inn after a few pictures were taken. Sondra outdid herself with every tasty dish. Soon we were ready to leave for London for our honeymoon. Angela had not been in good health to be at the wedding, but she was eager to show us around her part of the world. I think I pinched myself at least 20 times that day to make sure I was still living my real life.

I had no idea what the future held for Sullivan and Andrea Jeffries. Maybe there would be scars, but I was learning every day that God gives us scars as physical evidence of the fact that we can heal. A thought ran through my mind that somehow real life begins with a scar anyway; the scars in Jesus' hands truly make forever life and forever love possible. In that moment I knew that I would be Sullivan's forever and he would be mine, bound together for eternity by a nail-scarred hand.

THE END

Printed in the United States
by Baker & Taylor Publisher Services